WRETCHED WOOL

A COZY CORGI MYSTERY

MILDRED ABBOTT

WRETCHED WOOL

Mildred Abbott

for
Alastair Tyler
&
Winifred Hera

Copyright © 2020 by Mildred Abbott

All rights reserved.

No part of this book may be reproduced in any form or by any electronic or mechanical means, including information storage and retrieval systems, without written permission from the author, except for the use of brief quotations in a book review.

Cover, Logo, Chapter Heading Designer: A.J. Corza - SeeingStatic.com

Main Editor: Desi Chapman

2nd Editors: Ann Attwood & Anita Ford

3rd Editor: Corrine Harris

Recipe provided by: Cloudy Kitchen - CloudyKitchen.com

Visit Mildred's Webpage: MildredAbbott.com

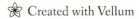 Created with Vellum

My twin stepsisters screamed and covered their mouths in unison, looking like mirror images of each other, save for Verona's long hair being blonde while Zelda's was brunette. In synchronization, they leaned forward to see each other past my mother nestled between them and screamed again.

Watson, my napping corgi who'd been snoring away on the hearth, shot up with an annoyed grumble, then headed off toward the bedroom. He made it halfway before experiencing a change of heart, and turned to scurry off into the kitchen. A second later, the dog door flap sounded. Apparently, he decided he needed a little time in his "corgi-cave" dog run and that girls' night was too much for him.

For their third scream, Zelda and Verona lifted their hands in the air, twinkling their fingers together —despite being nearly five years older than me, which placed them a few years from their fifties, they pulled off the chittering squealing of high school cheerleaders that I wouldn't be able to fake on my best day.

Mom giggled and looked half a mind to join them.

From her spot beside me on the floor, Katie winced and darted a quick gaze my way as a blush rose to her cheeks. "I said I *think* Joe is *thinking* about proposing. Not that he did, or even will."

They screamed again.

That time, Mom gave a little chirp and clapped her hands.

I leaned around, trying to peer into the kitchen, wondering if a miracle might occur and I could squeeze through the doggy door and join Watson. I caught myself quickly enough and focused on the importance of the moment, *not* the squealing, and turned back to Katie. "Propose? Katie! That's..." Showing that at the ripe old age of forty-one I was finally learning to stop and think before shoving my foot down my throat, I tried to predict my best friend's reaction. Would she be excited, terrified, ready to run for the hills? All of the above? I decided not to guess. "How do you feel about that? Excited?" Well, maybe a prompt?

She started to nod, but stopped abruptly, though

her brown spirals continued to dance around her plump cheeks. "I..." Her mouth continued moving, though wordlessly for a few moments before her tongue caught back up. "It might make me crazy, especially so soon, but I think I'd say yes."

Zelda and Verona screamed again and launched up from their seated positions to do a dance that was part jog, part convulsion.

"Good Lord, you two!" I shot them a glare but couldn't help feeling some of their excitement course its way into me.

Mom giggled again and leaned forward, reaching her thin hand across the coffee table and clutching Katie's. "I'm happy for you, dear. He's a good man. A kind one. You both deserve every happiness."

Katie's blush increased. "Thank you, but... like I said, Joe hasn't proposed. He merely mentioned something about getting married the other night. I think it shocked even him. He rushed ahead before I had a chance to quite catch what he was saying, but..." She paused, then finished with a shrug, refocusing on me once more. "It's too soon, right? We've only been dating a few months. Not even a year." She swallowed. "Barely more than half."

My heart began to palpate. "Well... that is pretty quick."

"Oh, come on." Verona waved me off. "Nothing is too quick in love. When you know, you know."

"Exactly." Zelda shot me a scowl as if I was threatening to murder Cupid. "Not everyone moves as slowly as you and Leo, Fred. There are icebergs that move quicker."

"Zelda!" Mom gasped and used the tone as if the twins were her daughters from birth, before addressing me, then Katie. "That is the thing about love. It has its own timetable, not dependent on anyone else's. Take Charles and me. The minute I met him, I knew. And Barry..." She shrugged with a quiet smile. "Well, decades were spread out between our love story."

Taking a bite of one of the chocolate chip cookies —which sported a luscious pool of salted chocolate on top—that she'd brought for our girls' night, Katie let out a long, shaky breath. "When I think about it, at least when I'm able to get my nerves calmed down around it, it just feels right... You know?" Her smile toward me was calmer, more at peace. "Like you and Leo. Married or not, things just fit... like those puzzle pieces you always talk about."

"Yes, I do know." Like my mother had done before, I reached out and gave Katie's hand a squeeze. "I'm thrilled for you. *Whenever* it happens.

As long as you're happy, that's all that matters to me. And I agree. You couldn't ask for a better man than Joe."

Thankfully, the twins didn't make any more comments about Leo and me, but began speculating on all the ways Joe might propose to Katie, and, really took off when my mother suggested *Katie* might propose to Joe. While I let them carry on, doing my best to smile and nod and be a good best friend, I couldn't deny I was slightly self-conscious about Leo and me. Both things were true. Katie and Joe's romance had been a whirlwind, though not one of blazing fire, or out of a steamy romance novel, from what I could tell. More like two soulmates finding each other and coming together softly and quietly. The romance might've happened quickly, but they'd known each other for years.

That was true for Leo and me as well. Friendship had blossomed into more. I couldn't boast that I knew the moment I saw Leo Lopez that I would spend my life with him—anything but. Cupid practically had to shoot a two by four into my heart instead of one of his dainty little arrows, for me to take the leap.

But... marriage? A wedding?

Try as I might, that didn't make me feel excited.

Definitely nothing akin to what I was witnessing with the other women in my living room.

It was different for Katie. She'd never been married. Different from my mom as well. Her marriage to my dad had been almost Hallmark worthy. And that was what I'd thought I was embarking on when I'd married Garrett. And *that* was the difference for me—I'd seen the ugly result of marriage, the pain and betrayal that lay on the other side of lace and wedding cake, at least for some people.

Though I didn't fear that kind of relationship with Leo. Not at all. I might not have known instantly, but I knew now who held my heart. But marriage, a wedding?

What if it messed everything up?

Warmth nudged my elbow, and I looked down in time to see Watson shove his head into the crook of my arm, his fox-like ears angling to attention as he forced his way through—I'd not heard the flap of the dog door when he'd reentered. My heart warmed and my soul calmed as chocolate eyes looked up at mine. He always knew when he was needed… somehow.

"Well, that's enough about me—at least enough about proposals and weddings and such. As far as I know, it could be a year or more away before Joe actually asks." Katie stood to begin gathering dishes. "Plus, it's starting to shoot up my anxiety. Let's clear the space and get on with the festivities, shall we?"

Katie and Zelda transferred all the dishes to the kitchen, while I put on a pot of hot chocolate. Mom and Verona stayed behind, opening up the boxes of crystals and gemstones. Watson darted back-and-forth, searching for crumbs, many of which came from Katie and Verona "accidentally" spilling a little bit here and there.

By the time the dishes were finished and the hot chocolate was poured into mugs, each with a stupidly large mound of marshmallows, the living room of my small cabin looked like the inside of a mining cave. I had to admit, it was rather beautiful with the firelight glistening off the endless rainbow-hued stones.

I carried the tray with the remaining hot chocolate to Mom, who was standing at the fireplace, inspecting the knickknacks and photos on the mantle. "I love this one Delilah took of you and Watson all dressed up in roaring twenties garb. Completely charming." She held the chocolate with one hand and with the other, ran a finger over the wood carving Duncan Diamond had made of

Watson with the tip of her finger, then stroked the knitted version of Watson that Angus Witt had given me. "Watson is quite the beloved celebrity, isn't he?" She grinned down at him. "For good reason, I might add."

Watson peered up at her, grinning, his tongue hanging happily. He sniffed expectantly for a few seconds, and then his expression changed when it was clear no morsels were coming from his grandmother. Once that had been determined, Watson ignored the compliment, turned around, and trotted away to beg elsewhere.

Mom chuckled, then tucked the remaining auburn strand in her long silver hair behind her ear and narrowed her gaze on the newest addition to the mantle. "I do wish you would get rid of that, Fred. You're going to drive yourself crazy."

"I know." There was no point in arguing; she was right. Though I had the image memorized, I followed her gaze to the photo. Actually, it wasn't a photo, but a color copy. A little more than a week earlier, I'd gotten the original photograph in the mail from a woman who'd been murdered a couple of days before. The image showed my mom and dad—so young, just a few years before I was born. They were visiting my great-grandmother, Evelyn, in the nursing home. They stood on one side of Evelyn, and Beulah Gerber and her husband, Tony, stood on the other. Beulah and Tony were the grandparents of Ebony, the murdered woman who'd sent me the photograph. She had written one word on the back— *Curious?*

I glanced to Katie, who was giving in to Watson's pleading, and the twins, who were arranging gemstones on the coffee table, before turning back to Mom, keeping my voice low. "It means *something*. It doesn't match all the other things Ebony sent out before she was murdered." I tapped the cameo my great-grandmother wore in the photo. "We can't find any proof that this is missing, so we can't be sure Ebony was trying to expose the kleptomania when she sent this to me."

"We haven't found it at all, Fred." Mom's voice lowered as well and was unusually firm. "Not being able to have anyone in the family locate it is hardly proof it wasn't stolen."

In truth, her logic made more sense than mine. Stubbornly, maybe willfully so, I shook my head. "No. Ebony wasn't trying to do me any favors, but I don't think her sending the photo had anything to do with that brooch. I think she was trying to tell me her grandmother is... or was part of the Irons family."

The hand that had been touching all the mementos on the mantle clasped mine and trembled. "Fred. You've *got* to let it go. You've got to. Ebony is gone. There's no way to know what she intended by—"

"The Irons family isn't gone." Even though I whispered, I couldn't deny a slightly unhinged quality to my voice. Nor could I deny I'd spent way too much time staring at that photo. "That's got to be—"

"Your dad *is* gone." Mom's grip tightened. "They killed Charles. I've asked you before, but I'll do it again. Please, don't let them take you from me as well. Nothing you can do will bring him back."

"But Dad would—"

"Your dad would be the first one to tell you to live your life." Her grip hurt now. "The last thing he would want is your search for his murderer to get you killed. And you know if you ever got too close, that's exactly the course of action they would take, just like they did with your dad."

Watson pressed against my leg, pulling my attention downward. There he was again, knowing I needed support, grounding.

"Come on, my love." Mom released me, smiling gently. "Let's live. Right here, right now."

I couldn't deny her. Besides, I could stand there for the next five hours and argue with circular logic around that picture. Around the Irons family. I'd done it for what seemed like years. With a final glance toward my great-grandmother and the young version of Beulah Gerber, I let the past stay where it was and gave in to enjoying both my family of blood and heart around the coffee table.

Zelda was midcomplaint. "You'd think that Britney would have the decency to show up to help us tonight. Even if it wasn't enough to be with family, but considering we're making jewelry for *her* cheerleading fundraiser. But no. She couldn't be bothered. Fred *just* got her order of mystery novels, and we know she'd much rather be arranging the mystery room than stringing crystals."

"Well..." Verona sniffed, saving me from having to answer that claim. "I did try to tell you allowing her to do such capitalistic and misogynistic pastimes wouldn't lead anywhere good."

Zelda narrowed her blue eyes at her twin. "While I can't completely disagree with you on the misogynistic aspect of some of those cheerleading outfits and dance routines, I hardly see how cheerleading is a symbol of capitalism."

Katie chuckled as she strung an icy-blue stone

over a reddish orange one. "I'm not one to put down capitalism, as I make my living in retail at the bakery, but I must point out that we are making jewelry to *sell* for a cheerleading fundraiser."

"Exactly." Verona brightened in triumph as she strung beads of quartz together. "Exactly my point."

Mom shot me a humorous glance as she brought yet another plastic container of gemstones out of the large cardboard box, but she didn't offer any commentary.

"Did you forget, *Verona*, that both of our husbands own a shop downtown, as do *we*? It's not like Chakras operates on the barter system." Zelda flipped a foot-long lock of brunette hair over her shoulder. "Not to mention your brand of designer foot—"

"Fine!" Verona held up her hands in surrender. "I admit. I'm being a touch hypocritical. But I wish I lived my life more along the ways that I preach."

Chuckling again, Mom patted Verona's shoulder. "Now if everyone who preached could admit that sentiment, the world would be a better place." She turned to Zelda. "And give Britney time. The teenage years can be hard. I know she's been going through a rough patch these last few months."

"Rough patch?" Zelda's voice shot up, and then

she seemed to collapse. "I thought the mood swings would be getting easier when she turned sixteen, not worse." She glanced toward me, then back at Mom. "Did Fred give you fits when she was a teenager?"

Mom started to shake her head, then paused before sending me an undercover wink. "You have no idea, dear. Well... you've seen how stubborn Winifred can be."

I merely chuckled, though I thought the last bit might've been a reprise of what had just been said at the fireplace. Truth be told, I remembered Mom fearing many times over my teenage years that I *hadn't* rebelled. Even going so far as to encourage me to sneak out in the middle of the night or stay out past curfew. Dad had pointed out that once Mom had instructed me to do so, it would hardly qualify as rebelling if I followed those directives.

"Here." I snagged my cell, opened the camera app, and flipped it to selfie mode. "Gather up. We'll take a picture of all of us and send it to Britney. Who knows? Maybe it will make her jealous or guilty. Win-win, right?"

"She'll probably just comment about how Verona's crow's-feet are getting deeper." Zelda threw her arm around her twin, and Mom pulled me in closer. Katie did the same with Watson, who squirmed at the embrace, and I snapped the photo.

I didn't even have a second to inspect it before Verona turned on Zelda. "And as far as my *crow's-feet*, need I remind you that we are identical?"

Katie and I both chuckled, while Watson fled—lest we pull him into another photo shoot—and curled up on the warm hearth once more.

Mom reached into the cardboard box and pulled out yet another container of crystals. "Here we go. These amethysts match perfectly with the school colors. I bet they'll be popular."

"Oh!" Katie snagged one. "Purple. Yes, please." She began to thread it onto the blue-and-red necklace she'd been making.

As one, Zelda and Verona both sucked in gasps and reached toward Katie in horror. Though it was Zelda who spoke. "What are you doing?"

Katie flinched, and the amethyst fell down the string and clicked against one of the blue stones. "Uhm... making jewelry?"

"Oh, Katie. You've got to start all over again." Verona took the necklace from Katie and began plucking off the crystals and gemstones. "I'm sorry I didn't notice when you started."

Zelda tsked. "You *never* use carnelian with blue lace agate."

"Carnelian?" Katie's brows furrowed, then smoothed almost instantly. "Oh. The stones. I take it that's the orangey-brown-reddish one?"

The twins sighed, and Verona explained, "Yes. Carnelian *boosts* energy while blue lace agate *calms* energy. They totally cancel each other out."

"Oh, well, as long as it doesn't cause the world to implode, I say take the risk."

Zelda scowled at Katie's teasing tone, then nodded emphatically, having achieved unison with Verona once more. "You jest, but this is a very serious matter. Granted, neither stone is as picky as emeralds. But unless they're properly cleansed and charged, I don't know if you want to take the risk."

Katie shot me a glance. "And people think baking is complicated."

"Actually—" Mom piped up before the twins could launch into another diatribe, "—somewhere I have a whole container of lapis lazuli, which helps foster clear communication. Let me just see…" She dug through the box, then moved to the next one down, pulled out four Tupperware containers, and placed them on the coffee table. "I think it's one of these." She opened the first one and then shut and put it aside. "No. Obsidian. That's definitely not it. Though it does help guard against negativity." She shoved the second one aside as well when it was nothing more than a tangle of old necklaces and earrings. "Here." She opened up the third, revealing a collection of deep-blue stones. "Here we are."

"Oh, this is lovely." Katie pulled at a long, tarnished golden necklace from the jumbled box. "It looks old."

Mom barely spared a glance. "Oh yes. I should probably take that whole container to Percival and Gary. Most of it's costume jewelry, if I recall, but some of it might be actual antique."

Katie attempted to untangle the necklace, but only succeeded in revealing a mass of knotted jewelry at the other end with a twisted silver chain, caught on what appeared to be a long string of rosary beads.

I gaped at the space that was revealed underneath the mass of necklaces, thinking I was seeing things, that my recently heightened obsession was causing illusions. It wasn't until I reached out and plucked the brooch from the tangle that I actually believed it was real. After running my thumb over the coral-colored ivory carving of a Victorian woman's profile, I turned toward my mom. "Look, Mom. It's your grandmother's cameo."

Mom paled and with trembling fingers took it from me. Her thumb made the exact same motion as mine as it passed over the woman's face. Then she glanced up at the framed photocopy on the mantle. "Yes. It is."

Fairy lights stretching over the patio from the roof to the line of aspens by the river competed with the birth of stars overhead while Leo and I placed our order of green chili pizza at Rocky Mountain Pie.

"And a grilled chicken breast with no seasoning for Watson?" Ruby twinkled her fingers toward Watson who propped his forepaws on Leo's thigh and peered over the arm of his chair.

"That would be perfect, thank you." I gave the old woman—whose beehive of dyed hair matched her name—a quick smile before she turned and walked away. Then I glanced over my shoulder toward the adjoining patio of the restaurant next door. "If we've spent so much time here recently that our waitress knows Watson's order, we're in danger of hurting Marcus's feelings."

"Nah." Leo waved off my concern as he ruffled Watson's head. "Joe, Paulie, Carl, and I ate at

Habanero's while you had girls' night, remember? And trust me, Carl drank enough margaritas that Marcus isn't hurting for business."

I snorted out a laugh. "I don't know if I'm jealous you got to see whatever show Carl put on, but I think I'm glad I missed it." Indulgently, I offered a tortilla chip to Watson, who snagged it and then dipped below Leo's chair to crunch away. Instead of drawing my hand back I grabbed Leo's. "I forgot you and Joe decided to extend the invitation to your buddy date." Leo and I hadn't seen each other since before I'd had dinner with Mom, the twins, and Katie. I'd known it was going to be a late night, and with Leo being one of the supervisors at the national park and spearheading the updating of Chipmunk Mountain, he had to get up at the crack of dawn, so he'd slept at his apartment. "It was sweet of you."

He shrugged and repeated his earlier sentiment. "Nah, I love Paulie. Though it was interesting to hang out with him without you, Katie, or Athena. Poor guy is so self-conscious he was nearly vibrating." Leo chuckled. "Though half a margarita helped him as well. As for Carl..." He bugged his eyes. "With Anna going from one extreme to the other in her control of him, you'd think the old guy was a bachelor and two seconds away from a kegger at a frat house."

I chuckled along, thinking of Carl and Anna, owners of the high-end log furniture shop across the street from the Cozy Corgi. "He'd better be careful. I know Anna's determined to be more loving to him, and rightly so, but it's new to her. She might have a relapse."

The night before, Leo and I had spoken briefly over the phone about the discovery of my great-grandmother's brooch, and I'd wanted to dive into that the moment we sat down, but at the mention of Joe... especially if the margaritas had been flowing, I couldn't hold back my curiosity. "Anybody talk about proposals last night?"

Leo had just taken a swig of his water and choked. "Propo—" He jumped again, cutting off his word.

Watson popped up beside the chair, cocking his head toward Leo and whimpering in concern.

Leo patted Watson's back as if he were the one choking and then finally managed to suck in a breath. "Um... no?"

For being fairly intelligent, sometimes I could be downright daft, which was proven by how long it took me to realize what Leo was thinking. And my reaction to that realization proved I probably wasn't as nice as I should be. "Wow. Good to know the thought of marriage makes you try to drown yourself."

"No!" Leo reached for me with both hands, forgetting Watson for the moment. "Fred, you know that..." His eyes narrowed, either catching the humor in my tone or remembering he knew me. He opened his mouth to continue, and then, almost resembling Watson, cocked his head. "Don't tempt me, woman. I'll pull out my ukulele and sing you a proposal song right here and right now. The only catch is that since they'll only play John Denver here, you'll just need to tell me which song you want."

Despite the teasing, from both of us, my heart leaped. As did my anxiety. "Let's... keep the ukulele where it is." When I noticed a flicker of disappointment in his yellow-brown eyes, I pretended to look over his shoulder. "You don't actually have the ukulele with you, do you? Have you been practicing?"

"You bet I have, all over the mountainside." Leo kept pace with me. "Why do you think tourist season comes to an end tomorrow?"

I chuckled. "Oh... It's not that school is starting back up?"

Instead of answering, he squeezed my hand and refocused on Watson, giving him his second and final tortilla chip. "I'm all right, still breathing. At ease."

At that moment, Kesha Denver, who owned the pizza place with her husband, stepped up to the table. "Good to see you guys tonight. We're slammed, and Ruby asked me to deliver your drinks." She placed a cherry Coke in front of Leo and iced tea in front of me, the lights glinting off the tattoos covering her brown arms. "Are you guys going to stay after you eat? You should. Since it's the last night of the season, we're adding a second John Denver karaoke session this month. The prizes are even better than normal."

"You know, Kesha..." Leo's expression went evilly playful again. "I was just telling Fred there's a song I'd like to sing to her. Is there a particular John Denver number that you think would be best for—"

Laughing, I lifted partway and reached across the table to cover Leo's mouth. "We won't be long. Though we'll hate to miss it." I looked up at Kesha. "Leo is helping me unbox a rush shipment of books tonight that came in yesterday."

Realizing she wasn't in on whatever the joke might be, Kesha shot a smirking glance between the two of us. "Okay then, one of these times." After a quick wink at Watson under the table, she left us.

Before things got serious, I clarified, "Don't pass this on to Joe—" It was a silly disclaimer; Leo wasn't the gossipy type. "—but Katie feels he's thinking about proposing."

Leo flinched. "So soon?" Before I could react, he shook his head, "Actually, I guess it's not that soon, is it? They've known each other for a while. And... they're great together. Why wait?"

Once more I could see the thought behind his eyes, and once more we were saved as Ruby, freshly splattered pizza sauce covering the top of her tie-dyed apron, showed up and placed the large green chili pizza between us. "And here we go!" She glanced at the drinks we hadn't had a chance to touch and nodded in satisfaction. "Right. Holler if you need anything. Gotta go."

I did want to spend my life with Leo Lopez. Not only *wanted* to—I *knew* that was going to happen. But for whatever reason, for maybe a million reasons, I didn't want to think about the marriage part, proposal or otherwise, at the moment. "So what are your thoughts on the cameo?"

A solitary blink was all Leo required to get on the same page and make a seamless transition. If his feelings were hurt, he didn't show it. "It confirms your belief that it wasn't connected to the other photos Ebony sent out before she was killed. That she wasn't trying to tell you about your grandmother's brooch being stolen."

"Exactly." I nodded and felt myself ease into my chair as Leo served a slice of pizza onto my plate. It probably said absolutely horrible things about me that talk of murder and crime syndicates was more relaxing than the idea of proposals, but... whatever. "Ebony was tattling..." I considered for a second. "Yes. That is what it feels like. She was tattling on her grandmother."

"Which means you think it's a definite that Beulah is part of the Irons—" Leo was cut off as Watson used his nose to nudge Leo's elbow, nearly causing him to drop his own slice of pizza. "Hey now, little man. Focus on your own... oh." Leo looked back up at me. "I forgot. Watson hasn't gotten his—"

"Here we go." Ruby chimed in again as she made a run-by delivery. "Sorry, I missed it the first go 'round. Chicken breast for the cute hairy one." She was gone again nearly before the plate touched the table.

A few seconds later, Watson's chicken breast was cut up, and he feasted away at our feet as I continued where we'd left off. "I think so. Beulah is somehow connected to my father's death."

Leo had taken a bite of pizza and chewed for a couple of seconds before responding. "I think that has to be considered, but there's a lot of other possibilities too. It could be some connection with your great-grandmother. Ebony liked to hurt people."

Though I'd never met my great-grandmother, Beulah had made it clear to me that Evelyn Oswald wouldn't have approved of the woman her great-granddaughter had become. However, as my mom and uncle had assured me, Evelyn also didn't approve of *them*, or their mother, for that matter. "I don't think so. It's more than that. And if she was merely trying to rub it in my face that a woman I'd never even met wouldn't have cared for me, her writing *Curious* on the back doesn't quite flow."

"Yeah. I agree." Leo lifted the slice halfway, but paused. "Still, despite it being hard to picture ancient, scrapbooking Beulah Gerber being part of the Irons family, it makes the most sense, where Ebony is concerned. She knew you were looking into the Irons family, everyone does. Though if it's true, and Ebony knew of her grandmother's part in the Irons family, then providing you that hint was a little more than tattling. Given the severity, that would be more along the lines of snitching."

"True." I took a bite of my own slice of pizza, considering. "And Ebony wasn't murdered by anyone connected to the Irons family. So she didn't pay for that act of snitching, as you say, with her life. Though she was killed *before* the photo was delivered, so who can say what the fallout might have been? Maybe there's some other connection between Beulah and my father?"

Once more Leo opened his mouth like he was going to speak, then hesitated. After a moment he pressed on with caution. "What if... and this is accepting the assumption the photo *is* about the Irons family, but from everything we understand, it sounds like your great-grandmother wasn't exactly the warm and cuddly type. Beulah says herself they were close. So..."

"So, what if my great-grandmother was involved with the Irons family too?" That thought had been playing through my mind as I helped customers at the Cozy Corgi that day. "Maybe." My anxiety shot up again, in a fashion that didn't have any of the pleasant buzz associated with the idea of a proposal. "Which means, that she would have some connection as well to my father's death. Even though she died decades before he was murdered."

Leo winced. "Hadn't quite made that leap yet. But..." I could practically see him rolling over facts in his mind. "I know there's tons more we *don't* know about the Irons family than we *do*, but are we clear on when it was formed? How long it's been around? That picture was in 1976. We've been so focused on current events, with everything that happened with Branson and his connection, I'm not sure."

I flinched at the name of my traitorous, dirty-cop ex but cast the thought of him aside. "I agree. And I haven't gone much further back than when my father was murdered. So... I don't know." I made up my mind right then and there. "I'll talk to Simone tomorrow." I glanced around, not wanting to be overheard as I didn't want to blow the potter's undercover FBI status. "She'll know the history more than me."

Leo didn't look convinced. "I don't think she'll take you seriously."

He raised a good point. "You're probably right. But honestly, who will? I'm like the boy who cried wolf. I've seen the Irons family too many places that they weren't to be believed, now I'm actually certain."

He sat a little straighter. "So... you *are*? Absolutely certain Beulah is part of the Irons family?"

"I don't have proof, obviously, but... yes." The feeling that had been growing and then exploded with the discovery of the cameo the night before, solidified. "Yes, absolutely."

Leo almost seemed to relax. "Your gut?"

I didn't have to ask for clarification. There were times my gut instinct was wrong or misled. Not often. This time wasn't one of those. "Yeah. I'm certain. Without a doubt. I don't know how, but I'll prove it. Ebony gave me the first real clue I've had, and I'll use it to connect the dots from the Irons family, to her grandmother, to the murder of my father."

At that declaration, a little bit of peace that had evaded me since I'd lost my dad, and then been chipped away even more by Branson's betrayal and the revelations that the Irons family was all around us in Estes Park, slid back into place. Like I'd said, I didn't know how, nor did I know when or how long it would take, but I was going to get answers. Guaranteed.

With the stars and fairy lights twinkling above us, John Denver crooning over the tie-dyed tabletops, Leo and I polished off the entire pizza as we whispered plans, possibilities, and theories. All the while, with his chicken devoured, Watson snored away beneath us.

"Leo?" A handsome older man seated at the bar caught Leo's arm as we walked through the interior of Rocky Mountain Pie toward the front door. "Didn't know you were here. Want to join me for a beer?" His gaze flicked to me and down to Watson, noticing us for the first time. "Oh, you're with your girl."

I didn't mind being referred to as Leo's girl, in some cases. But the way he said the words—not cruelly, not even all that dismissively—though I wasn't sure why, it rankled. I stuck out my hand. "I'm Winifred Page."

"Oh, I know who you are." He took my hand and gave a firm shake. If there was a flash of derision in his tone, it was gone in an instant. "How could I not? You're all this man talks about. You've got him wrapped around you little finger. And so does the dog."

"Fred,"—Leo motioned between the two of us—"this is Steve Masters. He's a Parks law enforcement officer. He's been taking the lead investigating the uptick of poaching lately." I didn't catch any dislike in Leo's tone, but neither was there an abundance of warmth as he refocused on the man. "Fred and I actually just finished dinner. Thanks for the invitation, though. I'm helping her at the bookshop tonight. Maybe... another time."

A loud popping burst of flames pulled our focus. John Denver, Kesha's husband, withdrew his freshly baked creation from the glowing pizza oven, which was positioned in front of the wall with the tie-dyed mural of the actual John Denver with his mouth open wide in song. Feeling our attention, he looked our way, and after sliding the pizza onto a tray, winked and twirled the large wood and flat-metal shovel in the air as he sang along to "Take Me Home, Country Roads."

Steve looked back at me, either not impressed with the show or not bothering with commentary. "See... helping you in *your* job late at night after a long day on the mountain. Wrapped around your finger."

Watson growled.

"Bud, I'm wrapped around a lot more than just *one* of her fingers." Leo punched Steve's shoulder playfully. "Might see you tomorrow."

Steve rubbed his shoulder, making me think the punch hadn't been as playful as I'd assumed.

Leo took my hand and started to walk away.

"Nice to meet you." I held Steve's gaze for just a second, then followed, Watson trotting along behind.

We'd just stepped out the door onto the sidewalk running along Elkhorn Avenue when Watson growled again at the colossal man who was heading into Rocky Mountain Pie.

The ash-blond giant turned his pale-green eyes on me, ignoring Leo and Watson entirely, no pretense of social niceties to be found. "Always in the way, aren't you?"

Leo made a noise and started to step forward, but I squeezed his hand, stopping him. "I'll be more in your way tomorrow, I'm afraid, Dean." As I spoke, I wound Watson's leash tighter around my hand, taking away any slack lest he decided to attack. "I plan on coming down to talk to Beulah again about the photo your sister sent me."

For the first time since I'd met him, Dean Gerber smiled at me, and the slightly cool mid-August breeze turned frigid. "Oh good. I'll look forward to that." Without another word, and without looking at Leo, as most other men would've, he pivoted around us and stepped inside the pizza place, the songs of John Denver spiking in volume as the door opened once more.

Leo's hand trembled in mine, and his voice

followed suit in apparent rage, though not directed at me. "I swear, Fred. I love your fire and your bravery. But... could you try *not* to taunt someone you think is connected to murdering your father?"

Shocking myself, I laughed. "I could say yes to that, but we both know I'd be lying."

"You're hoping this will take days, aren't you?" Ben Pacheco came to a stop beside where I stood with my arms crossed in the middle of the Cozy Corgi's mystery room. My assistant knew me well.

Before I could respond, Watson—who'd been napping in a ray of morning sunshine pouring from the front windows—sprang up, his nails clattering over the hardwood floor of the bookshop. Though it had been a literal matter of ten minutes or less since he'd fallen asleep, he greeted one of his three beloved heroes with fresh abandon, nearly knocking over Ben in his explosion of adoration.

Demonstrating the feeling was mutual, after steadying himself, Ben knelt on one knee and lavished all the love imaginable on Watson, covering the recently mopped floor around them with a layer of corgi hair. After a few seconds, he glanced up and grinned, "This never gets old."

"I wouldn't know." I chuckled, knowing Watson loved me more than anyone in the world, yet he rarely displayed such frantic affection, unless he was jealous of another dog. I refocused on the bookshelves. "And you're not wrong. Leo helped me unbox all of them last night as we just needed to get the shelves refilled, but I haven't sorted them to my heart's content." I shot him a wink. "It's like Christmas came early. Not to mention how many titles I ordered that I haven't read yet."

He gestured toward a couple of the bottom shelves. "And it looks like you need to reorder more soon. The last rush of tourists over the past week really did clear you out."

"True. But now with school back in session, things will be a little more manageable. Plus, I'm considering saving some space for Christmas theme mysteries, since it's coming in a few months." Despite telling Leo the night before that I couldn't promise not to antagonize certain individuals, I'd forced myself to move slowly that morning. Watson and I had taken our leisurely morning stroll through the woods outside my cabin, then spent a few minutes with Katie in the bakery, chatting as I had my first two dirty chais of the morning. Since then, I'd gotten lost in the enjoyment of mentally rearranging the shelves of the mystery room as the flames crackled in the river rock fireplace. I had a huge list of people I wanted to speak to that day, after finding my great-grandmother's cameo and coming to the firm belief that Ebony was pointing me in the direction of the Irons family. But who first? The undercover FBI agent, the local detective, or Ebony's family?

In truth, I already knew. As I'd said to Leo, I'd cried wolf a few too many times. Neither Simone nor Susan would see the cameo discovery with as much certainty of Irons family connections as I did. But... maybe I could get some clue from Beulah and Dean that would help solidify my case when I spoke to Simone and Susan later. Even so, I was glad I'd taken a part of the morning to get centered. I needed to be on-game and as unemotional as possible.

"You know..." I addressed Ben again as he gave a final ruffle to Watson's fur and stood. "I think I've hit a wall for the moment. Mind manning the bookshop while I do a couple of errands downtown?"

It was merely a question of polite formality, and we both knew it. The times I'd left Ben to go around snooping on Elkhorn Avenue during the height of tourist season were countless. He was able to handle each of those without a glitch. Now things had slowed considerably, Ben probably wouldn't notice if I didn't come in for weeks at a time, save for the lack of a middle-aged woman sitting on the antique sofa by the fire reading mystery book after mystery book while drinking endless dirty chais. However, he was kind enough not to say so. "Absolutely. The only rush going on right now is the end of breakfast in the bakery. If you don't mind, I might spend some time between customers formatting my query letter to different agents and publishers."

"Of course not. You know I don't mind. I more than—" I jolted, the meaning behind Ben's words taking me out of my own plans for a bit. I grabbed his arm excitedly. "You're ready to try to get your novel published? For real this time?"

He blushed and nodded. "I still won't know if it's perfect. But I've reworked it and reworked it and..." He finished with a shrug.

"Ben!" I couldn't help myself and wrapped him in a tight hug. He'd nearly taken this step before, but he sounded more certain.

Joining in, Watson squeezed between our legs and let out a happy bark. Or... maybe was just telling me to back off his man.

I leaned back just enough to meet his gaze. "I still have some ties in the publishing world. I can make some calls. They won't publish it if they don't love your manuscript, so don't worry about special undeserved treatment. But it might get your book in front of their eyes quicker."

Ben shook his head, like I knew he would. "Thank you. But I need to know I did it all by myself."

I wanted to argue, but I remembered that logic, feeling I was supposed to fight single-handedly against the world, especially in my early twenties like him. "Okay, well... if you need anything, I'm here." I hugged him once more. I just couldn't help it. He'd worked so long, and I knew how scary it could be. Having owned my own publishing company at one time, I also knew that writing the book was only one small portion of the road that lay ahead of him.

I forced myself into a meandering pace as I walked up Elkhorn Avenue. The few tourists that remained seemed in the same mode, stopping here and there to gaze into the windows of the 1960s style mountain shops, watching the salt-water taffy machine twist the light blue candy, then stare at candied apples displays, touristy T-shirts, and Estes Park knickknacks. Even the air seemed changed, as if on the same schedule. Though Halloween was still over two months away, the crispness in the breeze hinted at changing leaves, spiced cider, and long nights.

Every once in a while, Watson trotted along beside me when he was on his leash, or more frequently, he lagged behind, wanting to sniff here and there, or simply protested unrequested exercise. However, on this occasion, he pulled ahead at his leash, frustrated I was so intentionally slow. I wasn't sure where he thought we were going, as he never enjoyed visiting Beulah Gerber in Mountain Memories. Maybe it didn't matter. He probably just wanted to get whatever errand we were on completed so he could return to Ben and enjoy the perfectly nappable morning ray of sunshine turning to the perfectly nappable afternoon ray of sunshine.

Absentmindedly weaving through the few tourists, I repeated a mantra of calm as we neared the scrapbook shop. I needed to keep my temper. I needed to catch more flies with honey, as they say. I needed to be smart, calculated, intentional. And above all, aware. If Beulah and Dean were part of the Irons family, which I was willing to bet they were, it wasn't like they'd announce it or offer a written confession. But maybe some unintentional flinch, narrowing of eyes, slight grimace at a particular word, phrase, or question might help me know which direction to go.

Nearly there, I paused at the shop next door to Beulah's, Knit Witt. Though not decorated for any occasion, the beautiful gradated skeins of yarn pulled my attention, but only for a heartbeat. I stopped dead in my tracks as I saw the new display Angus had erected in front of that rainbow-hued array, and stood dumbfounded.

Watson yanked on his leash, but I barely felt it.

Angus stepped into view, smiled, and waved me inside.

Spell broken, I turned toward Watson, then toward Mountain Memories. Angus hadn't been on the list of people to speak to. But I'd been all over the map with the old man. One moment, Angus was nothing more than a kind grandfatherly type figure, then the next he might be the linchpin to the whole Irons family. Chances were, he was somewhere in the middle. Maybe.

Giving in to the impulse and his invitation, I stepped inside Knit Witt.

Watson glared from a seated position on the sidewalk refusing to budge, and then his head cocked, clearly seeing what I'd noticed through the window. On high alert, he stood, sniffing with his nose in the air, then padded inside. Soon as the door shut behind us, he led the way—right past Angus and his greeting—then slowed to a cougar crouch at the knitted masterpiece that filled the back corner of the store.

Angus chuckled and looked from Watson to me, and though pride filled his green eyes, there was no arrogance when he spoke. "You like Samson?"

Captivated as much as Watson, I stepped forward and lifted my hand, only to hesitate. Still, I couldn't tear my gaze from the massive elk to look at Angus. "May I?"

Another chuckle, warm and pleased. "Of course."

I touched the elk's nose, much like I would a horse in a stable. I almost expected it to feel warm and fleshy. To feel its breath. But the lifelike illusion ended there. The tightly knitted wool, though smooth, was slightly scratchy to the touch. Unable to stop myself, I stroked my hand up its snout. "He's... he's..." Words failed and I finally looked over at the knitter of this masterpiece. "Angus, I didn't think you could do anything better than what you've done, or that anyone could. But he is..."

Angus beamed. "Thank you, Fred." He glanced down at Watson, who was sniffing the knitted hooves and issuing a warning growl. "And you too, Mr. Watson. If you're finding him so lifelike."

I looked back at Samson, captivated once more. I wouldn't have needed Angus to tell me his name to know which specific elk it was. The majestic, beloved animal had been poached and killed in the mid-'90s. Even now, the town both grieved and remembered him through legend, statues, and now... knitting, it seemed. The creation towered over me, a full-size replica of a real bull elk. And though the texture made clear it was all knitted, just a few feet away, with the perfect gradient and texture over the body, it truly looked like Samson was back to life and had decided to go shopping in Knit Witt. My gaze traveled up to the one aspect that wasn't hand-crafted. To a crown of truly spectacular antlers, their spikes jutting upward to the ceiling.

"Don't worry, you can assure Leo no elk was harmed for those." Angus moved beside me, smoothing his hand over the other side of the elk's face. "Some majestic beast shed those a couple of years ago. I found them during a hike. I've been working on him ever since."

It didn't surprise me that Samson had taken years to create. Though I addressed Angus, I continued to inspect the elk. "What will you do with him? Is he for sale?"

The loud burst of a cackle was completely unlike the casually stylish Angus. "Hardly. Samson will stay here for the holiday season. Then there's a knitting exhibition the Louvre is launching in the spring. So he'll be traveling internationally for a while. After that..." He shrugged. "I'm not really sure where he'll end up. Although maybe at that point someone really will be willing to fulfill that particular price tag."

"I didn't know this level of craft was even possible."

"Neither did I, to be honest." His laughter returned to his typical easy elegance. "I am pleased you like it, Fred. As you know, I hold your approval in high regard." He smiled toward Watson, then lowered slightly to offer his hand. "As I do yours, good sir."

Watson spared Angus's hand a glance, but neither licked nor sniffed and returned to inspecting the elk.

Angus always did this to me. There were moments like these, where I liked him intensely—his easy charm and gentle nature. But there'd been flashes where he'd shown a core of steel that sometimes listed toward vengeance and threats, though never toward me. I knew he might look like a kindly grandfather, but there were fangs under that cultured smile. Once more I did a mental dance, trying to decide where he fell on things. My trusted gut seemed to flip-flop on him just as much as my mind.

I'd planned out various conversations with Beulah and Dean, depending on how things went, but hadn't given much thought toward Angus. With him in front of me, I dove in, not willing to waste the opportunity. "Angus, were you friends with my great-grandmother?"

"Evelyn Oswald? Lord, she was a force." As was typical, Angus neither looked caught off guard nor surprised. However, he laughed—just once, hardy and deeply genuine. After a second, he patted my arm. "Ah... the young. Thinking all of us old fogies were always old."

"I don't know if I'd qualify forty-one as young—"

"It is." He cut me off with another pat and then lowered his hand. "And I was probably around that age when Evelyn died, give or take. I was closer to Marion's age; however, she was a bit younger. The two were nothing alike, though both were strong. Like you." He considered. "That seemed to skip a generation with Phyllis. Still... she's just as loving and kind as her mother."

People often made that mistake with my mom. She was gentle, loving, and kind. Also, at times, a little flighty and scatterbrained. She had a core of strength, though, as strong as anyone I'd ever met. She'd survived heartbreaking tragedy and was resilient and good enough to still see every single day as beautiful and a gift. However, the rest matched what I'd heard. It sounded like my grandmother, Marion, had made certain her children, Mom and Percival, were protected from some of her own mother's harsh critiques and expectations. Instead of correcting Angus's view of Mom, I pulled the framed photocopy I'd been keeping on my mantle from my purse. "Has Beulah shown you this?"

He took it, his head cocking curiously as he studied the image. From his intensity, it was clear he was seeing it for the first time. Before long, his green gaze flicked up to me. "What do you make of this? Beulah, your great-grandmother, *and* your parents. You think it has to do with your father's murder?"

I started to comment how he'd left off Beulah's husband from that list but forgot that little detail as he finished his question. Unlike Angus, I was thrown off. "Why did you go *there*?"

"*You* did, didn't you?" He cocked his head again, though this time the curiosity was with me. "I know you, Fred. You're thinking Irons family."

My breath caught as if he'd just confirmed everything. "So, it's true."

When Angus chuckled that time, I couldn't catch the emotion behind the sound. "Darling Fred. Haven't you thought the same about me?"

Why lie? "You know I have." And why hold back? "Are you... part of the Irons family?"

Dark shadows seemed to pass behind his eyes, but they were fleeting at best. "No." His nostrils flared. "I'm not."

He'd denied it before or shrugged it off, or simply played aloof, depending on his mood. But he'd never answered in quite that same way. And for the first time, I heard the genuine ring of truth. "You're not?"

He met my gaze and held it. "No."

There it was again—unflinching, unquestionable truth. But... I *did* question it. Angus had fangs. I'd seen them. He always knew a little more than he should, more than came along with silver-haired wisdom. And his reaction to the photo...

Before I could determine which path to go down, Angus decided for me by handing the image back.

"You were taking this to Mountain Memories, I assume?"

I nodded.

"Ebony sent you this before she died, when she laid all of Martha's secrets bare." It wasn't a question. Though his knowledge threw me off, it wasn't exactly like it was a well-kept secret. I'd asked several people around town about the photo, and the scrapbooks that Ebony had mailed out had been the stuff of gossip fodder throughout the town. "Evelyn's brooch wasn't stolen after all, not like the rest."

Again, it wasn't a question. And while the matter-of-factness shocked, it didn't necessarily surprise me. I wasn't the only one good at putting puzzle pieces together.

"Winifred." Once more, Angus spoke before I could reply. "If you go down the path you believe this photo is leading you, it's not just your murdered father in the photo alongside Beulah. You have other members of your family there."

It'd been a horrible thought, but not one I'd been too afraid to look at. "Evelyn?"

He barely offered a shrug of one shoulder by way of response.

"I always want the truth, Angus. You know that." I took the tiniest step forward and felt Watson leave where he'd continued to sniff at the elk and move toward me. "It's also clear you know more than you've said."

He studied me for a second, his gaze feeling hard and calculating, then it softened. "Here's *one* thing I know, Fred." Genuine concern and warmth filled his voice. "Dean Gerber won't send you little hints or teases like his foolish sister. I don't want you to get hurt. And don't you think, even for a moment, Beulah will call off her dog."

I'd felt that from Dean. The man was deadly. Clearly. It didn't take much insight or survival instinct to notice that. So it didn't surprise me that Angus was aware, but his dig at Beulah did. "I thought you and Beulah were friends."

"Let my life be a lesson to you, Winifred. You have surrounded yourself with friends and family, as others do gold." There was no warmth in his smile. "You may want to reconsider. I've discovered that gold, at least—or wool, actually—will not betray you. But even those you count as family not only can but *will*. It's just a matter of time."

It didn't matter how many possible variations of my conversation with Beulah and Dean I'd practiced in my mind, after my interaction with Angus, they were all swept away. I recognized that as I stepped out of Knit Witt, turned to the right, and moved directly in front of Mountain Memories' door. That realization should have been enough to prompt me to return to the Cozy Corgi and gather myself for later. If not, the fact that Watson instantly started to growl as I reached for the handle should've provided a wake-up clue.

It did. I couldn't pretend I wasn't aware I should head back to the Cozy Corgi and try again another time. Nor was I unaware stubbornness had more to do with me entering the scrapbook shop than any amount of intelligence.

Mountain Memories was as empty as the knitting shop had been, proving the height of tourist season was officially over. Further proof was demonstrated by Beulah and her grandson unboxing a new shipment of scrapbooking supplies—clearly compensating for the final rush, just as I had in the mystery room.

The old woman had always looked small and frail, but never more so than as she stood near Dean, who seemed to fill the entire room, both with his large muscular frame and the unadulterated hate that poured from his eyes as he glared down at my growling corgi.

"I've made it perfectly clear, Winifred, that I'm not fond of animals in my establishment. Especially ones that display such aggressive tendencies." Beulah's voice was calm, matter of fact.

"I'd suggest leaving." Dean's nearly colorless green gaze lifted from Watson to me as he spoke. "It wouldn't be my first time taking down a dog in self-defense."

I flinched at the threat against Watson, even as Angus's reference to Dean being Beulah's dog himself rang in the back of my mind. I pulled Watson's leash closer and stepped over him, giving him shelter under my broomstick skirt, before lifting my chin toward Dean in a defiant act of bravery that was more bluster than reality. "I'm surprised such a large, muscular man as yourself has such a powerful inferiority complex that he would feel the need to threaten the life of a dog that doesn't even come up halfway to your knees."

Dean flinched, surprising me that he allowed the sting of my insult to show, however briefly. He didn't take the bait, though.

Mountain Memories was similar to Knit Witt, with the scrapbook paper arranged against the far wall. Both were a kaleidoscope of beautiful colors. The similarity with the elderly owners didn't stop at their commitment to crafting. Albeit a recent discovery, Beulah Gerber had fangs as well. Though I hadn't determined if she had a bite of her own, or if that was why Dean had taken Ebony's place.

Trying to get back on track, I dug in my purse once more. I didn't bother with the framed photocopy; Beulah had taken the original photo right out of my hands the last time I'd been in. Instead I pulled out the brooch and held it toward her, though far enough away she couldn't snatch it.

Beulah didn't feign ignorance. "Evelyn's brooch." A soft, genuine smile played on her withered lips. "She loved her cameos, but I do believe that one was her favorite. The way the woman's hair falls down in ringlets, such a lovely, delicate detail."

"It was the one she was wearing in the photograph with you and my parents." I curled my fingers around it, just in case Dean decided to try to take it.

"I'm aware." Her cloudy eyes met mine. "I have the original photograph, which was mine to begin with, if you recall."

It looked like she was going to be a little coy after all. "Since I had it, actually since *Mom* has had the cameo this entire time, Ebony didn't send me that photograph as a hint my great-grandmother had been a victim of compulsive stealing."

"No. I suppose not." Her chin jutted slightly.

Dean shifted his weight but remained silent, clearly awaiting commands.

Though Watson still rumbled beneath my skirt, he didn't attempt to leave his shelter.

"Then why did Ebony write '*curious*' on the back of it?" I dropped the cameo into my purse, though I never looked away from Beulah.

She sighed. "I attempted for many years to try to understand my granddaughter, to predict what she would do, and help form her path." The edge of sorrow that laced her words didn't appear to be for show. "I failed her. Just as she failed me. So I'm afraid I can't tell you Ebony's motive. Though I'm willing to bet, Winifred, you can snoop all you'd like, but you won't find the answers." She started to turn away and paused. "On the off chance you do, I wonder if you'd like what you uncover." She instantly looked like she'd regretted the impulse and glanced at Dean.

I jumped in before she could give him any directive. Her words were too similar to what I'd just heard. "Angus hinted that very thing when he saw the photo. What do the two of you think you know about my family?" I pressed on, pulling from a conversation Beulah and I had engaged in before. "Angus wasn't friends with Evelyn, he was in a different generation. However, you and Angus are about the same age, and you said you were very fond of my great-grandmother. So what do you and Angus know?"

"I wouldn't trust Mr. Witt's ravings. I'm afraid he's recently gone a touch senile." She shot a glare to the wall shared between Mountain Memories and Knit Witt. She and Angus had always seemed like dear friends, however, judging from both of their reactions, something had shifted.

"Was..." I let out a shaky breath. This question shouldn't be so hard. It shouldn't wrap cold fingers around my heart. I'd never met the woman. She'd died before I was born, but yet... "Was Evelyn part of the Irons family with you?"

That got no response, not from either of them. No flinch from Dean, no flash of anger from Beulah.

I couldn't tell what the nonreaction meant. Whether confirmation I was on the right track, or had I truly gone off the deep end?

I hadn't. Ebony was telling me something. I didn't know why she would betray her grandmother like that, but that's what she'd been doing. I was sure of it now that we'd found the cameo. There was no other explanation. So in true Winfred Page fashion, I pushed on. "Is that why he's here?" I flicked a hand toward Dean. "You lost Branson doing your dirty work when he was exposed, and Ebony didn't measure up, so you brought in your grandson as the new recruit?"

Dean took a step forward.

Somehow sensing the shift, Watson shoved his head from under my skirt, his growl growing clearer.

I tightened my grip.

Beulah only chuckled softly. "I said it before, but it truly is heartbreaking. I had such respect for you at first. But..." Another sigh accompanied by a shake of her tired-looking head. "Evelyn would be so horribly disappointed in you. She couldn't abide baseless conspiracy theories, nor did she suffer fools."

As they had before, her words struck home, despite my intention to ignore them. How many times had I seen the Irons family where they weren't? And yet again, there was that word on the back of the photo... *Curious?*

I *wasn't* wrong.

"You said it yourself, Beulah." I took a step forward as well, both covering Watson with my skirt once again and refusing to allow Dean to get the upper hand or know I was intimidated. "Maybe it was a slip on your part, or perhaps you're starting to flaunt it. You told me you'd hoped to pass on your empire to Ebony, but that she'd been a disappointment. And that Dean will not only manage it but will help your empire grow. You honestly expect me to believe a scrapbook store is the *empire*?"

She'd shoved that accusation away the last time, but now she didn't as fire seemed to burn in her eyes, and her withered body shook in apparent rage. "Have you researched where Dean moved from?" She tilted her head slightly. "Surely you have. You are the nosiest of busybodies I've ever seen."

Dean shifted his gaze to his grandmother, surprise breaking through his stone features. He gathered himself quickly enough and drew up even taller.

Beulah continued. "How about my children? Have you researched them? Maybe you assigned that menial task to your Google-loving, baking best friend? To some other member of your ragtag Scooby Gang, as you call yourselves?"

However intimidated I might be of Dean, he completely vanished in the room as far as I was concerned as Beulah caused my blood to turn to ice.

She smiled. "I have five children. Three boys, two girls. Two of them moved to different parts of the country. Three of them each relocated to different continents."

When she paused, I waited, completely lost on where she was going and having no idea what to ask next.

Still she smiled. After a moment she looked up at her grandson. "Dean, would you care to tell Fred where your father moved? Where you and Ebony are from?"

His nearly invisible blond brows furrowed as he looked down at Beulah. "Grandma, are you sure—"

"Dean!" She barked his name.

Beneath my skirt, Watson's growl faded to a whimper.

Dean hardened instantly and turned back to me with the rigidity of a soldier, and spoke two words. "Kansas City."

I couldn't help it. I gasped, and then felt my eyes sting.

Kansas City. Where I'd grown up. Where my detective father was murdered in the middle of his case to bring down the Irons family.

I refocused on Beulah, shocked. "You admit it?"

Her trembling faded along with her rage as Beulah feigned confusion. "Admit what, dear? It's hardly like I shared a secret. Dean moved from Kansas City. That's public knowledge, on record." Beulah gave another shrug. "Goodness, you *do* leap to conclusions, girl."

A million things flashed through my mind, quite literally a million—questions, accusations, visions of vengeance, but survival instinct grew stronger than all of them, and it didn't take long to add up the equation she was spelling out. "Come on, Watson." I looked down at my feet, refusing to take the risk that Beulah or Dean might see the fear in my eyes. "We need to go."

Turning my back on the two of them was one of the most terrifying things I'd ever done, and when Watson attempted to stay behind, growling, I practically had to drag him along with me, refusing to look back.

The gentle warmth of the late-morning August sun didn't register as I sucked in the deep breath of fresh air on Elkhorn Avenue. It felt as dark as midnight and just as cold.

Beulah could pretend all she wanted, but it was a confession. Not only was she part of the Irons family, but she was directly connected to my father's death. And if she was willing to let me know that... It wasn't a hint, it wasn't even a threat. It was just a fact—Dean, sooner rather than later, would come knocking—at the bookshop, at the door of my Mini Cooper one night, or at my home—and I would meet the same fate as my father.

Watson and I traveled at the exact same pace as we rushed back down Elkhorn Avenue. Without the overabundance of tourists, we didn't even have to weave all that much. He paused momentarily when we were in front of Cabin and Hearth and stared across the street to the Cozy Corgi, clearly thinking his mama had lost her mind and couldn't find her bookshop.

"Not yet, buddy. Come on." I patted my thigh, encouraging him to follow, and hoped I could get out of view before Anna or Carl Hanson noticed us outside their shop window and came to see what was going on, probably expecting I'd stumbled on a dead body.

In an atypical act of unstubborn corginess, Watson offered a whimper toward the bookshop, probably a murmur of longing for the sunbeam-filled napping spot, and then scurried to catch up with me.

Luck was on our side as neither of the Hansons emerged, nor did Paulie as we ran past his pet shop. I tossed the notion of luck away—I wanted to save that for something that mattered, preferably where *I* wouldn't be the dead body stumbled across.

"Simone, I need to—" At the end of the block, I halted inside the Koffee Kiln at the sight of a woman with whom I typically required a lot of self-talk and preplanning before engaging in an interaction.

Ethel Beaker stood at the far side of the coffee-shop and pottery studio combo, in front of the espresso machine. She turned slowly our way, her expression suggesting we'd radiated a putrid aroma. She'd been lifting a small porcelain espresso cup to her lips and continued the motion, pinky finger lifted, took a sip, then sniffed, casting her haughty gaze down my body before narrowing to a glare when she reached Watson at my feet.

On the other side of the counter, the owner of the coffee shop, Carla, looked near tears. If I had to guess, chances were I'd interrupted another session of Ethel reminding her daughter-in-law how she didn't measure up to the Beaker name. Though not blood kin, the look in Carla's eyes shifted to match Ethel's perfectly as she saw me. However, I also thought I caught a flash of relief. I couldn't blame her. I'd want someone else to be the recipient of Ethel's scorn, too. There was no hint of relief or veiled tears as she began to lecture. "Fred, I don't have time to listen to you pontificate with faulty claims that your subpar baker makes better scones than what I serve here. Besides that, I thought we were beyond frequenting each other's establishments." She lifted her chin, causing the heavy weight of her blonde bob to fall back from her face. "Speaking of, I have a strict no-pet policy now."

I didn't have the time, energy, or... anything... to play this game, and strode farther into the space and stopped in the middle of the empty tables. "Is Simone here? I'd like to speak to her?"

"Didn't you just hear Carla?" Ethel took a step toward us, and only then did I notice she was wearing a full-length white fur coat. Even in the state I was in, I marveled at the woman. There was barely a chill in the breeze and she was going full force into winter glam. And I was willing to bet that unlike my uncle's boysenberry fur coat, there was nothing faux about hers.

I ignored Ethel, focusing on Carla. "Is Simone here?" Unwilling to wait, I continued on my way, heading toward the hallway that led to the pottery studio in the back.

"Well, I never," Ethel practically screeched. I didn't even look her way until I felt the leash grow taut. "Call off your rabid hound, Ms. Page."

Despite everything, I laughed when I turned and found Watson straining at the end of his leash, attempting to sniff Ethel's glossy black high heels. Though it had been long ago, at one point when Watson and I were sequestered on the front porch of Ethel's mansion, she'd tossed some fancy sausages off the tray in a fit of anger, which Watson had ravenously appreciated. And though no such miracle had happened in our dealings with her since, it seemed Watson's hope sprang eternal. "Sorry, Ethel. He associates you with sausages."

Her expression turned even more sour.

"And seriously? It's the middle of August, and not even noon." I couldn't stop myself. "You're dressed like you're going to the New York Symphony Orchestra in the middle of a blizzard. Who are you trying to impress?"

Carla's blue eyes went saucer wide, and she lifted a hand to cover her lips, as if on the verge of laughing.

Ethel's bony face went white in rage. "Considering I've seen homeless vagabonds with better fashion sense than you, forgive me it I don't put too much stock in your approval of my attire."

Perhaps I deserved that for lowering myself to judge someone's fashion, especially with my catty tone. Even if I did, I wasn't about to apologize. "Come on, Watson. I'll buy you a pound of sausages once we leave here."

Still he strained toward Ethel's feet.

"Treats, Watson. *Treats.*" I gave another tug, though at his favorite word, it wasn't needed. He whipped around, tongue lolling. "I'll buy you a pound of treats when we leave here."

He scampered toward me, chocolate eyes wide with joyous anticipation.

A sting of guilt bit through me, as I knew my tone had promised treats then and there. But there was no time to waste. I'd have to beg for his forgiveness later, probably with a *literal* pound of treats. I dug deeper into the lie by lilting my voice in a promising manner. "Come on. This way."

With Ethel and Carla screeching behind us, I hurried down the hall, past the restrooms, Watson leading the way like a bloodhound on the scent of a wild hare, and we burst into the back room.

At first, I thought it had all been for nothing. The

pottery wheels were empty and even the massive kiln emanated no heat.

Watson looked up at me expectantly, then seeing no treat coming, chuffed and began a sniffing search of his own.

"Carla, what in the world are you..." Simone emerged from behind the kiln, her cell phone to her ear and faltered when she saw Watson and me. Her tone lowered instantly. "I'll have to call you back." When she refocused on me, her voice was hard. "Fred, I don't have the time nor the energy."

I flinched, thrown off and confused. That sort of reaction was expected from Carla and Ethel, and for a while, from Simone herself, but we'd gotten past that.

It didn't matter. After a glance over my shoulder, I headed toward her again, keeping my volume low, and spoke so fast my words were probably slurred. "Beulah is part of the Irons family. She and her grandson. She all but threw it in my face that she's connected to my dad's murder."

"She confessed?" It was Simone's turn to flinch. "What do you mean she—"

"What's happening here, exactly, with you two?" Ethel spoke up from behind us, and I turned to see her enter the back room, Carla peering over her shoulder. Though she spared a glance at Simone, she narrowed in on me. "I know how you operate. This special kind of crazy only occurs when you're trying to solve a murder. But I've not heard of one, not at least in the past week." Without waiting for a response, she narrowed her glare at Simone, suspicion ripe. "I also know Fred enough to be certain she isn't begging for entrance into that trashy Pink Panthers sorority you're a part of. Something's been off with you from the beginning. Carla is too much of a daft imbecile to know it, but I do. What's going on?"

"I'm not a..." Carla shoved past her mother-in-law, making the taller, older woman teeter on her heels for a second. It seemed Carla's temper had finally gotten the better of her. "How dare you! I've had it up to—"

"Shut up!" Simone yelled, enough of a command that even Ethel straightened and didn't attempt to respond.

Watson darted beneath my skirt.

Simone strode past me, and with her long, coiled braids swaying musically behind her, she almost resembled an old-time goddess. She went straight to Ethel. "It's none of your business what Fred or anyone else has to say to me. And I'm tired of you snooping. You've done it from day one. You might be able to bully Carla... Lord knows I've tried to tell her to never let you darken the door here again, but I'm over it, Ethel Beaker. Turn yourself around and get out of my studio." Before Ethel could respond, Simone turned to Carla. "I'm sorry. I don't want to make things worse for you, but I've got my own things bubbling over right now. I need some space."

Carla mouthed wordlessly, her expression alternating between hurt and offense. She seemed to settle on hurt. "Fine." Without a look toward me or her mother-in-law, she turned and disappeared into the coffee shop.

Ethel wasn't so easily dissuaded, but she took her time replying, inspecting me for several moments as if she'd see the truth on my face, then whispering toward Simone in a hiss that promised vengeance. "Been advising my daughter-in-law to get rid of me, have you? Interestingly enough, I've been telling Carla to rid herself of *you*." She pointed a bony finger toward Simone. "I've held back because you're Carla's friend, but that ends now. I'm taking you out, mark my words. The likes of you shouldn't be in business with a Beaker. I won't stop there. I'll run you out of town and ruin your reputation so—"

Simone yawned, making a show of it, then

grinned. "The likes of me?" When Simone leaned closer and smiled, her expression held as deadly a promise as Ethel's hiss. "Your elitism and racism is beyond passé at this point, Ethel. When I choose to leave Estes, it won't be *my* reputation that's ruined."

For once, Ethel was speechless, though clearly more out of rage than concern. After a moment, not glancing my way again, she turned and left the room. In the silence that remained, the clomp of her high heels could be heard retreating, then the sound of the chime over the door as she left the Koffee Kiln.

I stood there, numbed shock at the scene. After the last fifteen minutes, it felt like there had been explosion after explosion after explosion. I wasn't sure if the bombs were all connected to one battle or merely conflicting ones merging.

That was too much of a coincidence, wasn't it?

Beulah's barely veiled threat toward me and for all intents and purposes flaunting of being part of the Irons family, then to witness Ethel, moments later, threaten the undercover FBI agent. It hadn't been the first time I'd wondered if Ethel Beaker was part of the Irons family—with her money, power, and ugly heart.

When Simone finally refocused on me, she looked exhausted. Though still beautiful, she seemed about two decades older than the last time I'd seen her. That sight helped pull me out of my own panic. "Sorry. I wasn't trying to start anything between you and Ethel."

She snorted with almost a hint of a smile. "You didn't. That's been brewing since the day I arrived." Simone's smile shifted, sad that time. "I'm one of the few areas Carla defies her. She's a good friend, Carla. I hate lying to her."

Watson peered out from underneath my skirt, checking to see if the coast was clear.

Simone's smile altered again, to something a little sweet as she watched Watson, though she didn't attempt to pet him. She knew Watson had never exactly warmed to her.

"Do you suspect Ethel is part of the Irons family, Simone?" I kept my voice low but moved closer, unable to hold off for anymore niceties. "Is that why you went into business here with Carla? To be closer to Ethel? The same reason you joined the Pink Panthers when you suspected Delilah."

Simone sighed and sounded as exhausted as she looked. "As ever, Fred, you see your obsession under every rock and pick a new target depending on which way the wind blows." She rolled her eyes and kept on before I could respond with either indignation or defense. "And you came here to what again? Tell me that Beulah Gerber is the big kahuna of the Irons family? Organized crime *does* sound like something a scrapbooking grandmother would get involved in. I guess you solved it—case closed. I can go home now."

I immediately jumped in with facts to defend myself. "Ebony sent me a picture of Beulah, my dad, and my great-grandmother from the '70s, the same time she sent all the scrapbooks. I didn't come to you about it then because I didn't want to bother you with more speculation when I wasn't certain it was connected to the Irons family. But I am certain now. I was before I went to speak to her, but even more so after. Not only that, but she was blatant about it, to the point I'm actually rather afraid that she'll sic her grandson on me."

Simone gave a second eye roll. "What is it, Fred? Another gut feeling, intuition?" Then *another* eye roll. "You are an embarrassment to the feminist movement, you know that? All your feelings and instincts, as opposed to hard work and facts." She rubbed her temples with one hand, partially covering her eyes. "Will you finally leave it to the professionals?" She lowered her hand and looked at me once more. "Trust me. Not only can I handle it, but things are very much in my control right now. The only thing you'll do is throw a wrench in the gears right at the end."

I stood wordlessly, truly stung. There was a time I'd thought Simone was part of the Irons family. A time when she thought *I* was part of the Irons family. But since then we'd helped each other, been respectful of each other. I would've called us friends. "Simone, how can you...?" Some of what she said, once I got past the insults, solidified, and I cocked my head at her. "What do you mean *right at the end*? Something is going down with the Irons family?"

Her lips thinned, barely noticeable, but enough to realize she hadn't meant to give that much away. And whether she found my intuition and gut instinct an insult to feminism or not, I knew what I saw.

Another realization hit. "You already knew that Beulah's involved." Simone had scoffed about an old scrapbooking grandmother being part of the crime syndicate, but it had rung hollow, and there hadn't been surprise, either, at the accusation or the revelation. Somehow Simone had been a step ahead of me.

She blinked then cleared her throat. "I'm sorry if I was harsh, Fred." She attempted a friendly smile, or at least I thought. "I'm just tired and stressed. What I meant to say is, *will you please* stay out of the way for a little bit. It will all be over soon. I promise."

"Fine, I'll..." I started to promise I would but couldn't make myself. Watson had taken a place beside me. Despite Simone's harsh tone, he hadn't responded like I'd been in any sort of danger or receiving a threat. But there was something else happening, though I couldn't place my finger on it. "What aren't you telling me, Simone?"

Anger flared at that. "You are an intelligent, good woman. But you are *not* an FBI agent, like me. You're not even a part of the police, like Susan." There was a flash of hesitation, and then she pushed on, going in for the kill. "You're definitely *not* the type of detective your father was. So yes, there's a host of things I'm not telling you, Fred. Nor do I need to." She started to push open the door into the hallway but paused. "Stay out of the way, please. If you don't, this won't end well for you."

I moved just out of view of the Koffee Kiln once we stepped back onto the sidewalk on Elkhorn Avenue, then leaned against the brick wall of the shop between the sets of windows, trying to make sense of all that had happened. I'd grown used to many things over the past couple of years, to the point I could nearly stumble across a dead body without flinching. But in the span of less than half an hour, not only had my father's murder been thrown in my face twice, but I'd been threatened that same number of times. And once by someone I considered a friend. Someone on the same side of justice as myself, or at least so I'd believed.

"You know, I only quit officially hating you about two seconds ago." Detective Susan Green looked up from a pile of files on her narrow desk through slitted blue eyes. "But if you're going to start casually popping into my office, unannounced, I'm reverting to my first estimation of you."

Her typical brusque manner gave me no pause and I stepped in, closing the door behind me. Apparently feeling the same, Watson practically made himself at home and darted under her desk the moment I released his leash. "We need to talk about the Irons family, quickly." I'd taken all of three minutes to get my bearings after leaving the Koffee Kiln, then drove straight to the police station.

"The Irons..." Susan sat straighter, then seemed to collapse upon herself just as quickly with an already exhausted exhale. "This is what I get for indulging you so often. You're like a weird cult or a religion." Susan's gaze flashed back to me. "No, like a *vampire*. An innocent person cracks open the door, just a bit, and the bloodsucking fiend mistakes it for an invitation, then clamps its fangs on their neck whenever it wants. If I could've predicted having to interact with you so frequently, I'd have driven you out of town the moment I—" Susan sat straighter again, pushed back her chair from the desk, and glared down at the footwell. "I beg your pardon, fleabag, your boundaries are just as bad as your mama's."

I angled to see underneath the desk where Watson was literally shoving Susan's booted feet out of the way with his nose.

"Good Lord, I'm going to be covered in dog hair for the next month." To my surprise, Susan complied and lifted her legs partially, giving Watson room.

With his nose now firmly planted on the floor, he zigzagged across the small space, snorted, and chuffed as if hunting for something just out of reach.

"I think he remembers the beef stick he found that your brother left here. He's had a fairly disappointing morning as far as trea—" I barely caught myself. "As far as snacks go. We just ran into Ethel, and he now equates her to gourmet sausages, of which he received none, so he's a little desperate."

She grunted and returned to Watson, lowering her bulky frame to peer closer under the desk. "There's no stale beef jerky, fatso. You ate it last time."

Watson spared her a hopeful glance, grinned as if he'd grown as fond of her as I knew she secretly was of him, and then continued his determined search.

"Fine!" Susan shoved backward off the desk, nearly causing the chair to crash into the wall behind her, then stood. "Have it your way." Still glowering, she gave him space, and perched on the corner of her desk, refocusing on me. "Before you open your mouth, Winifred Page, here are the rules." As she spoke, she numbered things off on her fingers. "Number one, I'm giving you five minutes, that's it. Actually no... three and a half. Number two, this is probably going to be the last time I ever allow you to utter the words *Irons family* in front of me ever again, unless you're bringing one of their heads to me on a platter. And number three—" Her tone softened a little— "thanks to Chief Dunmore's bright idea, the station is updating to a bright and shiny new computer system. Which means I was up at two-thirty in the morning, and I'd much rather be at home in bed than dealing with you and your overgrown warthog."

In what surprised me as much as it did Susan—judging from the horror that suddenly washed over her face—my eyes burned, and I felt a tear roll down my cheek. Her diatribe and overabundance of scorn-filled insults felt like a warm blanket being wrapped around me in a safe embrace. It took a second for my throat to unclench. "I do love you, Susan Green."

She reared back and probably would've completely fallen off the corner of her desk if she hadn't caught the edge of it. Susan was silent for several seconds, and maybe for the first time ever, no scathing retort arrived when she finally spoke after several blinks and clearing her throat. She stood once more, squeezed my shoulder with her large, strong hand, and then motioned to the chair across from her desk. "Have a seat. Tell me what's going on."

I nodded, completely surprised and thrown off by my wave of emotion.

As I sat, Watson belly crawled out from the other side of the desk, nearly getting stuck, and propped his head on my knee, looking up at me quizzically. While he was frequently attuned to my emotional needs, considering the betrayal around the promise of undelivered treats and the remembered scent of the previously eaten stale beef jerky, his concerned affection was even more meaningful.

Tears burning again, I smiled down at him, stroked his face. "I'm okay. Thanks for checking."

He nuzzled my hand for a moment, then with a quick lick to my wrist, ducked his head once more and then forced his way back under Susan's desk.

She either didn't notice or decided to not let on as she folded her hands on the desktop and met my gaze directly. "You said Irons family. You're clearly upset." She licked her lips. "Has Branson returned again?"

"No." I shook my head. "But while he's not exactly involved with the Irons family anymore, I know at least two who are. Beulah and Dean Gerber." I pushed on when Susan opened her mouth to argue. "Beulah pretty much told me as much less than an hour ago. Not so subtly threatened me while waving my father's murder in my face."

Susan blanched, proving how far we'd come since the days we truly had hated each other; she took me at my word. "Okay. Fill me in."

I did. Sharing every detail of my interaction with Beulah and Dean that morning, and then what had just gone down with Simone.

Through it all, her expression remained stone-cold placid. I couldn't tell where she fell on things—until I got to Simone. Susan's scoff accompanied an expression suggesting she'd tasted something rancid in the back of her throat. "That woman is insufferable. Which is to be expected in interactions between the FBI and *mere* law enforcement. Especially undercover FBI agents. Talk about a god complex." I'd only been witness to a couple of power struggles between Simone and Susan, but I definitely had gotten the impression a whole lot more had happened between the two of them that I'd not been made aware of. Susan started to lean forward, then grunted and shot a glare at her desk as if she could see through it. "Still no beef jerky, fleabag." Then she focused on me, all interest. "You're certain Simone implied the end of the Irons family is near?"

"To that effect. I don't know if she meant the entire Irons family or just Beulah and Dean..." I shrugged. "But yes. She said I was going to mess things up 'right at the end.'"

"As if *she's* done any better with the Irons family than you have." Susan considered this for a heartbeat, clearly unaware she'd paid me a compliment, and that the insult Simone had offered was exactly something Susan herself would say given the right moment. "I've not noticed something going on. If anything, since all that happened around Ebony's murder, things have been straight-up boring, save for the horrid new computer system. There's hardly been a spike in crime, let alone to the Irons family level."

"You've... not had any complaints about Dean?" It was hard to imagine he didn't have a similar effect on others than he did with me. Although... I'd witnessed him with customers at the scrapbook shop. He turned on so much charm he nearly sparkled.

"No." Susan acted as if that didn't bother her. "I'm not saying you're right about the Irons family, although what Beulah said is definitely concerning and strange. And I'm not convinced Dean is part of the Irons family either. But..." She lifted a finger. "I agree with you. While I can't find proof, that man has the eyes of a killer if I've ever seen them."

"I agree." I wasn't sure if I was impressed with Susan or embarrassed by my lack of thoroughness that she'd researched Dean when I hadn't. "You've looked him up. Is it true, him being from Kansas City?"

Susan shrugged. "Yes. But that doesn't mean he's part of the Irons family. Lots of people are from Kansas City, like you."

"Are you..." I ignored that, then considered if I

wanted to finish the question I'd started, afraid it would truly make me sound paranoid. But why stop? "Have you confirmed Simone is actually part of the FBI?"

"I have. Not that doing so pleased her." Susan chuckled, started to lean back, then grimaced as her feet collided with Watson again, but she paid him no insult. "But that doesn't mean much. Both Branson and Chief Briggs were official members of the Estes Park Police Department, and they were Irons family too."

It surprised me she hadn't scoffed at the possibility of Simone being dirty. I didn't think she was, but something wasn't adding up, *a lot* of things weren't adding up.

Susan kept going. "As far as Ebony sending you the photo of your great-grandmother, even if the cameo wasn't actually missing, I hardly think that's definitive proof that she knew her grandmother was part of the Irons family. If anything, I think it's the opposite." She raised her hand when I started to argue. "If Beulah *is* part of the Irons family, then the old bat is smarter than I ever gave her credit for. Ergo, she should have had a clear grasp on the kind of woman her granddaughter was, and from the disappointment you say Beulah has verbalized about

Ebony, then she was aware. *If* all that is true, then Beulah wouldn't have been foolish enough to involve Ebony in it."

I'd already crossed that bridge. "I think it's different when it's family, her own granddaughter. She would've had more faith that Ebony could change than she would've someone else. She wouldn't have thought Ebony would betray her." That time I lifted my hand in the air, stopping Susan. "But for argument's sake, let's say that's true. That Beulah didn't trust her or confide about her involvement in the Irons family. Ebony was a sneak—she loved nothing more than finding people's secrets and using them against them. Maybe she found out her grandmother's secrets on her own." But that didn't feel right to me. "However, I don't think so. Beulah had said too much about her hope that Ebony would take over the empire. And there's no way she means a scrapbook store. The thing I can't figure out is why she referenced her kids. Dean and his father being from Kansas City, sure. Why point out that her other four children are spread across the globe?"

"Oh for crying out..." Susan had barely been listening as she shoved herself away from her desk again and glared at Watson, at least I assumed, as I couldn't see him from where I was seated. "Fine, you little nuisance. You're just as stubborn as your mom." Susan twisted and started to reach toward her file cabinet, then paused to send a death stare my way. "Don't you say one word, and I don't just mean to anyone else. Don't even say one word to me. I don't want a comment, a smirk, a chuckle. Nothing."

I sat there, completely confused as to what was about to happen.

"I mean it, Fred." She shook her finger at me. "Not a word."

I lifted my hands in surrender. "Okay. Not a word."

She leveled her narrowed gaze on me for several more seconds, then twisted back around, mumbling to Watson, "I don't even know how you do this, or how your nose is so mutated you can smell an unopened package through a file cabinet, but it just proves you're some sort of freak." She continued muttering as she opened the bottom drawer and pulled out a red plastic-packaged pouch and tore it open. "And if you tell other dogs that I did this for you, I'll make a holiday where the whole town feeds corgis to bears, I swear I will, you fat fleabag."

Though the image on the package was clear enough, it wasn't until she pulled out the crinkly wavy-looking stick that my eyes accepted what they were seeing. I continued to stare, feeling like I'd tumbled into an alternate universe. I kept my promise to not say a word but couldn't keep from standing and leaning nearer to see over the desk to where Watson sat, beaming up at Susan as she pulled bacon-shaped treat after bacon-shaped treat out of the bag and gave them to him.

After five of them, she closed the bag and glared down at him. "There you go. There's enough cholesterol there for a heart attack... hopefully." The corner of her lips quirked but was smooth again before she looked back up at me. "All right, now that the fleabag rodeo is finished at my feet, we can get on with it. I..." She glared yet again. At me.

Realizing my mistake, I sat down, and once more tears stung my eyes as I battled with the laughter that threatened to spill forth. Not trusting myself to make any more of a sound, I merely cleared my throat.

Satisfied, Susan smoothed her hair, though it was pointless as it was pulled back so tightly in her trademark miniature ponytail that no strand would dare to be out of place, and then she continued. "Here's what I'm going to do. And it doesn't mean I'm convinced Beulah is part of the Irons family, but..." She jumped over the rest of the thought. "I'll have officers swing by your cabin at various intervals over the next couple of nights. Just to make sure. Dean is no good, and regardless of what Simone may or may not be up to—*which, trust me*, she'll be getting a call about you as soon as you leave my office—I want to make sure the people in my town are safe. And while you sometimes see the Irons family in places they aren't, I trust your instincts and your nerve. If you felt danger from Dean today and enough fear that you're coming to see me, then he's a threat, whatever his reason, and we'll treat him as such."

I couldn't bring myself to say anything, couldn't even bring myself to nod.

Watson broke the moment by popping up and propping his paws on Susan's thigh, twisting so his head craned over the lip of the desk, and he just managed to nudge the bag with his nose.

Susan smirked again.

When Katie abandoned the Cozy Corgi with me early that afternoon—leaving the Pacheco twins in charge, naturally—there was no talk of impending proposals as we settled on the sofa with our laptops in front of my fireplace. There were, however, an abundance of cookies with pools of salted chocolate and a few lemon bars that Katie grabbed on her way out. There was also a large thermos of dirty chai for me, and another filled with hot chocolate for Katie. And despite having had more than his share of treats at Susan's hand, I made good on my promise and brought home several of Katie's all-natural dog-bone treats. Having made swift work of them, Watson lay on the hearth, his hearty snores broken every so often by a hiccup or satisfied belch.

Watson's rudeness didn't harm Katie's appetite as she picked up a cookie and a lemon bar, debated between them, then with a shrug, placed the cookie on top of the lemon bar and took a bite. Despite the heaviness of the morning, I couldn't hold back a laugh at her shudder. Before it faded, however, she tilted her head, considered it again, then took another bite before speaking with her mouth full. "Actually, that's kind of an interesting combo. I may have to play around with a chocolate chip lemon bar or a chocolate chip cookie with a pool of lemon curd in the middle."

"I'll take your word for it." I had already chosen one of the cookies and followed the sweetness with the spicy swig of dirty chai. Now *there* was a combo. However, pondering upcoming treats from Katie's bakery was hardly the point of why we'd left work early and secluded ourselves in the privacy of my cabin. Sitting the cookie back on the plate, I dusted off my fingers, glared at the discarded Irons family tomes Katie and I had already searched and began typing away. "I can't believe Jake's books didn't have anything about Beulah or Dean. Nothing. But I feel utterly ridiculous that I didn't do *this* the minute I met Dean. A basic Google search on someone threatening should be a given."

"*I'm* the Google queen. If anyone should feel stupid it should be me. But lest you forget, we were kind of in the middle of things with figuring out

Ebony's murder and all the fallout of the town council elections. I'd say our slip was forgivable. Plus..." She gestured toward the large books. "—clearly Jake wasn't suspicious of them either, as he literally wrote theories about *everyone* else who's ever stepped foot in Estes Park." Then, as it had before, her gaze darted back and forth, this time between her computer and the pastries. Opting for efficiency, she plucked what remained of the stacked cookie-lemon bar combo and popped it in her mouth, then followed my example by dusting off her fingers, and began clacking away as well.

Proving that it truly had been an unforgivably simple oversight on my part, Dean Gerber came up on the very first search. It was only because Katie had taken a few more seconds of chewing that I beat her to it. Just as she started to crow in triumph, I shifted, angling the computer toward her. "Here he is."

Katie gave a glower but allowed me my win. "Kansas City?"

I nodded, barely having to do a scan. "Yes. Kansas City. Birth, graduation records, the whole thing." I clicked on another link. "And here we go. Family photo."

Katie leaned closer. "Ah... they take after their mom."

"They do." The photo showed Ebony in a high school graduation cap and gown, flanked on either side by her mother and father, Dean standing off to the side, right over their father's shoulder. The caption revealed the names: Oliver and Cynthia Gerber with Ebony and Dean. Even in the black-and-white photo, it was clear that Cynthia was as pale as her children, long, white-blonde hair nearly reaching her waist, and was just as beautiful as Ebony had been. While he'd gotten his mother's complexion, Dean had inherited his father's massive size. However, though it was only one photo, there seemed to be a coldness in Dean's eyes that wasn't present in Oliver's.

I stared at the family; though Ebony and Dean were much younger than me, the date confirmed they'd been raised and living in Kansas City the same time I'd lived there. We wandered the same city, going about our daily lives, maybe coming close to crossing paths. Who knew... maybe we'd crossed paths on multiple occasions. Had they known me? Had Oliver or Dean planned the murder of my father?

"You okay?" Katie snagged a cookie from the tray

and offered it to me as if it would solve the problems of the world. "I know that's a silly question, considering everything, but—"

"With the exception of Dean looking like a murderer, they're just a normal family." I couldn't bring myself to turn to Katie or take the cookie; just continued to stare at the picture. "Who would ever guess they're part of the Irons family or some crime syndicate. That's got to be insane."

"*You* didn't sound like you thought it was insane when you got back from Susan." Katie gestured toward the photo with her free hand, her finger coming just short of touching the screen. "I could tell from your expression, the sound in your voice, that this was different. You were scared. Of him. Of them."

For some stupid reason I started to protest. But this was Katie. I didn't need to pretend to be brave. Besides, if I was right, I would be a fool to not be afraid. Clearing my throat, I pressed on, opening a new tab in the window and began typing again. "Well, knowledge is power right? And whether Beulah told me about her family because she plans to off me in the next little bit or not, I'd rather know what I'm dealing with. I doubt there'll be any—" Again, it was so simple and so fast that it was nearly painful I was only now seeing it. Before I could even finish my statement, an old picture of the Gerber family filled the screen. It looked like it was probably in the '60s based on the clothing and hairstyles, though I couldn't be sure. Even if the photo hadn't accompanied an article in the *Chipmunk Chronicles*, I would've known it was in Estes Park from the rock formation in the distance behind the family of seven. The caption wasn't anything special, just a shot of them at the Fourth of July celebration—one of the biggest days of the year in Estes Park—but it provided all their names: Tony and Beulah, with their children, Oliver, Simon, Nicholas, Irene, and Rosalind. And again I just stared.

They were just a family—wholesome-looking as apple pie. They could've been that family gathered around the Thanksgiving table in the Norman Rockwell print. Had Beulah already been part of the Irons family when this photo was taken? Was it some little fantasy in the back of her mind waiting to come to fruition? The photo was taken at least a decade before the one at the nursing home with my great-grandmother and parents. Were she and Evelyn already friends then...? Was it my great-grandmother who ignited some flame in her? I narrowed in on the younger version of Beulah. There was no killer glint in her eyes. Her expression was sweet, motherly. And yet... "Somehow it's easier picturing Beulah as a young, vibrant woman being part of the Irons family than it is with her now as this old scrapbooking-grandmother type."

"Now, don't be ageist." Katie nudged me playfully with her elbow. "Why, back around 1940, there was this Italian grandma who killed three women."

Finally, I turned to look at Katie.

She gave me a knowing nod, misinterpreting my expression. "It's kind of a sad story. She was trying to protect her family, but she turned to the occult to do so and ended up sacrificing three women to that effort."

"She... sacrificed..." Despite myself, I was pulled down Katie's bunny trail.

"Yep." She nodded again, sagely that time. "Turned them into soap and tea cakes that she sold in her little shop."

"Tea cakes?"

Another nod. "She said the last one was the sweetest."

"Katie!" I swiped at her.

"What!" Katie swiped right back. "*I* didn't do it. Nor do I put people in *my* tea cakes." She scrunched her nose. "Not that I make tea cakes all that frequently."

"Thank goodness, considering the amount of things I've eaten from your bakery." I shuddered and laughed. "Maybe that lady is where the idea of *Sweeney Todd* came from."

"Nope." That time, Katie shook her head, curls bobbing. "*That* was inspired from a story called '*The String of Pearls: A Domestic Romance.*' That was back in the mid-1800s, so a good century before the Italian grandma and her teacakes."

"*Sweeney Todd* was inspired by a story that's called a *romance*?" I waved my hand, cutting her off. "Never mind. Not the point." I narrowed my eyes at her. "However, I'm ashamed that I owned a publishing house and you know more about the publication dates of literature, than I do. Even if it is questionable subject matter." I started to turn back to the computer then another thought hit me and I gave Katie an appraising glance. "I have to say, you never stop impressing me. There's no way you were bingeing killer-grandma trivia last night. You just pulled that out of the vast recesses of your mind."

"That I did." Katie beamed, pleased, and rewarded herself with another bite of lemon bar.

Beside the fire, Watson traded his hiccupping and belching in his sleep for a bit of flatulence.

"I think he's had a few too many treats today." I shot him an indulgent smile, which was wasted considering he was still lost to dreams.

With a little grimace, Katie returned the lemon bar to her plate. "Now... where were we?"

Nestled in my home, Watson asleep and Katie being Katie, made everything seem a little more manageable, a little less terrifying than a couple hours before. It did not, however, make the threat any less real. "If Beulah is involved in the Irons family, which I one hundred percent believe she is, *and* she was giving me a threat in the form of a clue, which I also one-hundred-percent believe she was, then there's some answer in this photo." I pointed to the child version of Dean's father, Oliver, my finger tapping the screen. "He grew up and went to Kansas City. Beulah made a point of bragging how her children went all over the world, two of them international. So—"

"On it!" Katie cried out, fingers already flying over the keys. "I call the girls. You find the other boys."

That took a little longer to locate all of them in present day, but five minutes at the most, not nearly long enough to satisfactorily feel like things had been hidden from me instead of laying out in plain sight. I stared at the notepad where Katie had written the location of Beulah's children: Oliver in Kansas City, Missouri; Simon in Manchester, England; Nicholas in Yokohama, Japan; Irene in Moscow, Russia, and Rosalind in Boston, Massachusetts.

Katie studied the list with me as she chewed on a cookie. "The Irons family is a worldwide organization. Beulah has kids spread out over the globe. At least in some limited capacity."

"Yeah. Maybe if we look at the next generation, Ebony and Dean's first cousins, we'll find out that they really are more global. Maybe some of them are in Africa, Australia, Brazil, or something." I started to turn away to research Beulah's grandchildren, but something about the list held me captive.

Katie started to toss it on the sofa, but I grabbed it from her.

"What?"

I didn't answer her, exactly, instead began talking things through out loud. "In our defense, we have been talking about the *Irons* family. Not the Gerber family, so maybe I need to quit beating myself up that we've not been searching for Beulah and all her children this whole time. I've never heard of a connection between the Irons family and the Gerbers."

"That's a valid point." I could hear the reprimand in Katie's tone. "Although I don't really feel either one of us should be beating ourselves up."

I ignored that. "I didn't really think the organization was based around a family with the last name of Irons, either. Honestly, I figured it was more like the mob is a 'family,' not an actual family, but..." My words trailed off as I read and reread the list of Beulah's children and where they were located. After a moment, I quit reading where they lived and just focused on their names, speaking them out loud. "Oliver, Simon, Nicholas, Irene, and Rosalind."

Oliver.

Simon.

Nicholas.

Irene.

Rosalind.

My jaw began to tingle as the realization hit. "Katie!" I turned to her. "The Irons family is based off of *one* family. Beulah is the matriarch, I have no doubt."

"Great!" She nodded and furrowed her brows. "What am I missing? Where's the proof... not that I don't trust your gut, I just—"

"Here." I pointed at the names. "It's an anagram. The Irons family is an anagram of her children's names. Start with Irene and end with Simon. *Irons*."

"Wow." Katie sighed out a breath of exclamation then nodded slowly before refocusing on me once more, her voice grave. "Okay then. Not that we really need more proof, but as Whoopie Goldberg said in *Ghost*, 'Fred, you in danger, girl.' " The statement could have been a joke, but there was no humor in her tone. "Beulah laid it all out there for you. Bragging, doubtlessly, but—"

"She wouldn't have done that if my days weren't numbered." Though it wasn't a new realization; it was just more confirmation. As a chill trickled down my spine, I glanced out the window toward the fading sunlight.

EIGHT

Leo draped his arm over my shoulder in the doorway of my cabin as we watched Officers Jackson and Lin drive away. They'd stopped by to say hello on their first pass through of the evening. At the edge of the clearing, one of them flashed the red and blue lights in a goodbye, illuminating the tall pines surrounding us.

I let out a sigh, leaning into Leo's side. "I may be overreacting about Dean, but it is so kind of Susan to have her officers checking in through the night." Though true enough after my time in Mountain Memories, after finding all the confirmation I needed with Katie a couple of hours ago, I could feel eyes watching me from every shadow, and none of it felt imaginary.

"It is. She's got a heart of gold that one, even if her exterior is a little crusty." Leo pulled me closer yet, as if he was feeling the same tension as me. "But

I hardly think you're overreacting. That's never been your way. If you feel like the Gerbers were threatening you, then they were, especially considering what you and Katie pieced together this afternoon. Although I wish you'd have texted. I'd have left the park earlier."

Before I could respond, approaching headlights lit up the retreating police cruiser and I stiffened.

Leo went rigid beside me.

Watson scurried from where he'd been napping by the fireplace and rushed to our feet.

A van and the police cruiser pulled up beside each other and paused for a few moments. Then Jackson and Lin continued on their way, and the shadowy vehicle headed toward us once more.

"I guess all is good, and we're about to have visitors." Leo relaxed.

Chuckling, I pointed down at Watson, who was bunny hopping over the threshold. "One guess who."

Leo glanced down and chuckled along with me.

A few seconds later, I could easily make out my stepfather's old Volkswagen van... or, as he'd say, his *classic* Volkswagen van. It showed how stressed Leo and I truly were that we hadn't recognized it instantly.

Watson made a break for it as they drew nearer,

but Leo moved lightning quick, scooping him up. "Sorry, little man. With the sounds that van is making, mountain lions shouldn't be anywhere near, but we're not taking any chances."

As he loved Leo as much as Barry, Watson only gave the smallest of protests at being held in the embrace.

Within moments, Mom and Barry were on the porch, and Leo transferred Watson to another set of arms. As with every time the two of them met—which was countless at this point—the greeting was the type of long-lost lovers reunited near the end of a Greek tragedy.

By the time they were inside, Watson was a quivering mass of joy, and Barry's jacket was hardly discernible underneath all the fur. He didn't notice as he slid it off, revealing his trademark tie-dyed tank top—red and orange on this occasion—despite the weather.

In a similar fashion, though we saw one another constantly, the four of us made the rounds of welcoming hugs. Barry's was as warm as ever, but my mom's, though she hung on tightly, felt a little cold. As we pulled apart, I looked down to find her glaring up at me. "You're in such a dangerous position that the police are swinging by to check up on you, and I had to hear it through the *rumor mill*? You didn't call me directly?"

Feeling like a reprimanded teenager, I cringed out an apology. "Sorry, Mom. But it's not really like..." I paused. "Rumor mill? Who in the world told you?" Susan wouldn't have gossiped, nor Katie.

"Who... I..." Mom swatted me. "Really? *That's* what you're going with?"

Chuckling, I pulled her in for another hug, equally as tight but less cold. Plus, she had a point. The order to put my cabin into the rotation for the next few nights would've gone through dispatch. It wasn't like it was a national secret; there were plenty of police who liked to gossip just like everyone else.

Within a few minutes we were together in the living room, this time with steaming mugs of hot chocolate and a tray of the remaining chocolate pool cookies Katie brought from the bakery. As they were prone to do, Barry and Leo sat on the floor, flanking Watson and making him the happiest soul in the world. His big chocolate eyes filled with the dreamy, contented expression as Barry scratched his left ear and Leo stroked his right side.

Mom and I took our places on the couch. "I don't know how she does it. Everything Katie makes is utter perfection. I wish I could shrink myself so I was small enough to stand on the edge of this cookie and dive into the chocolate." Moaning as she took a bite, her gaze flicked to the mantle. After swallowing, she gave a sigh. "You decided not to display it. Good."

I didn't have to ask what she meant. For a second I almost corrected her, clarifying that I'd merely taken the frame with me that day to photocopy and hadn't put it back. "For now, at least."

It looked like she was about to say something, then instead took another bite of the cookie.

Barry jumped in, never pausing in his attention to Watson as he spoke. "We brought our toothbrushes and stuff with us. It's all in the van. We figured we can hunker down in the guestroom. Strength in numbers and such."

"No!" I gaped at Barry, then turned toward Mom, though why I was surprised I had no idea. Like I'd expect anything less from either of them. "You said it yourself. The police are driving by. Checking on us. We couldn't be safer."

"We're not asking, Fred." She patted my knee and finished with a little smack. "It's a done deal. We're staying."

I started to argue but stopped myself. It would only cause Mom more worry if she was somewhere else. And she wasn't wrong: there was strength in numbers, or at least comfort in it. However, if Dean showed up with a gun, having Mom and Barry there simply meant two more victims. And *that* thought made me start to argue again, but once more I stopped myself. Though she displayed it much less frequently than my own, Mom's stubbornness was no less ironclad. "Well, thank you. It will be nice to have you here, though I hate that you have to do so."

"Hear that, bud?" Leo ruffled Watson in excitement. "Slumber party! You get to be with Barry all night!" Leo shot a wink at Barry. "We could do a photo for your Christmas card. You and your tie-dyed pajamas with Watson."

Barry winked right back. "What makes you think I sleep in pajamas?"

Leo flinched and barked out a laugh. "Well... okay then. That might be a look that's not appreciated for Christmas cards."

Barry sucked in a mock-offended gasp. "If I didn't know better, I'd say you were insulting my physique, Leo Lopez. We can't all have the body of a park ranger, but I'll let you know that I am holding up just fine for my age, thank you very much."

"Oh my Lord." I half laughed, half gagged. "I don't want to hear this conversation, much less think about it." I pointed at my stepfather. "You've been hanging out with Percival too much."

"Oh, that's definitely true." Barry nodded. "Why, just the other day, I caught myself humming a Judy Garland song."

For the first time that night, Mom chuckled, and she sent Barry an adoring smile. "No worse than what you were singing this morning. Something about being a bad boy."

"Bad guy." He sighed and rolled his eyes my way. "Britney had me listen to her favorite singer when we had our grandfather-granddaughter date the other night. It's been stuck in my head ever since. Billie something or other..."

"Eilish," Leo offered up casually as if barely aware of speaking, then flinched when all eyes turned toward him. "What?" He shrugged. "I'm in my midthirties. I'm still hip."

"Pretty sure if you refer to yourself as hip, you're not." My heart warmed as Leo responded with a scowl before I looked back to Mom and Barry. "It is nice to have you both here. I've been so caught up in my head all day that I think I'm about to break." Despite my best effort, with that comment I sank back into it. "I can just feel it boiling all around me. Something's happening. Beulah was blatant, nearly, with who she really is. And Simone is hinting that the end was near with the Irons family, or... something." I shot them a beseeching look. "I know I've driven everybody crazy, made everyone think I'm obsessed. But—"

"But it's time to let it go." Mom's words were firm as she atypically cut me off. She nodded when I looked toward her in surprise, then doubled down. "It is, Fred. It's time to let all the Irons family stuff go. No matter if you're right or wrong about everything bubbling up. Don't stay in the pot, get out of it. Let others handle it. If you're right about Beulah and Dean, they might back off if you do."

I stared at her, confused. "Mom... we could be so close to finding out who killed Dad, taking down the organization he died fighting. Or at least a step closer."

"Or..." Her gaze grew harder still, and she refused to let me look away. "*You* die trying. I've asked you before to be careful. Maybe I've not been clear enough. I always said I knew you had too much of your father in you to let it go. But..." She swallowed and leaned forward. "Let. It. Go."

Watson whimpered, pulling my attention away from her for a moment. He sat between Barry and Leo, who were both looking at us as if they were wondering what they were supposed to do. Watson didn't seem distraught, but more curious, maybe feeling my tension, or maybe at the concerned tone from his grandmother, which he'd never heard before.

I refocused on Mom. "I can't. Especially when we might be this close." I nearly brought up that it wasn't even going to be an option if Dean had in mind what I thought, then decided that was best left unsaid. "Dad would want this finished. We both know that."

"No!" Mom nearly shouted and pounded her thin fist on her leg. "No. Charles would want you *alive*. He would've sacrificed anything for you, you know that. Trust me." Shooting forward, she grabbed my hand so hard it almost hurt. "Your father would say the very same thing I'm saying right now. Let someone else handle this. He chose to be a detective. You didn't. It was his job. It isn't yours. He would *not* want you to fight this battle, and I should have put my foot down ages ago."

"Mom..." I put my other hand over where hers clasped mine. "You said yourself that Dad would be proud of all I've done here. That I've helped—"

"He is," she interrupted once more. "I have no

doubt about that. But he would be the first one to tell you to back off from this."

I considered just for a second and shook my head. "I don't think he would."

"Then *I* am!" Her voice shot up again, and though he didn't growl, Watson left two of his favorite men to come sit at my feet. Mom didn't seem to notice and she stayed laser-focused on me. "*I* am telling you to back off. Begging. Do it for me. Let someone else handle this. I already lost my husband, I'm *not* going to lose my daughter. And I don't care if that makes me selfish. I don't want you sacrificing yourself to get answers, not even for Charles's death."

I started to answer that, but she shook her head.

"I mean it, Fred. I'd rather have no answers and no justice for Charles's murder than have you dead in order to get it." She lifted her chin defiantly. "And think what you want, but I know, *I know* Charles would agree with me on that."

"Phyllis." Barry came over. Wedging himself on the edge of the couch, he wrapped an arm around my mom. She tried to pull away, but he held a little tighter. "Sweetheart. Fred is going to be safe. We're all with her. The police department is making the rounds. The FBI is here. She's safe." To my surprise, he looked at me as well. "Although, your mom's right, you *do* have to let this go. I know I'm not your dad, I can't speak for Charles. But if it was me, I'd want Zelda and Verona to just live, no matter what." He softened a little. "The same is true for you. I love you as much as I do my own girls. I want you to live."

Leo joined us, and he put a hand on my shoulder as he stood beside me. He didn't chime in on their display, nor did he rebuke them. He simply squeezed my shoulder and let his hand rest there, offering support, wordlessly letting me know that he'd go down whatever path I chose, that he'd be there to keep me safe.

It was that thought that clarified things—the idea that Leo would do anything to try to keep me safe. Then the thought, once more, that Mom and Barry were in my house at that very moment because *they* wanted to keep me safe and were willing to put themselves in harm's way to do so.

For some reason I felt Watson's attention on me, and I glanced down, staring into his brown eyes. He wasn't making any promises, didn't offer any advice about my murdered father or vengeance, justice, truth, or anything. He just stared up at me, gaze questioning yet full of love, devotion, and probably on the verge of begging for a treat...

completely unaware I was putting him in harm's way as well.

I took a shaky breath and held it, then glanced toward the framed photocopy on the mantle. It wasn't there, I'd forgotten.

Maybe it was too late, maybe it wasn't. But either way...

I squeezed my eyes shut and breathed out before looking at those I loved the most, then settling firmly on Mom. "Okay." I nodded, but the flash of hope in her eyes quickly shifted to skepticism. "Okay. I will. I'll... let it go."

A couple of hours passed before we all went to bed. Though they weren't strained, there was an odd tension in the air. Despite myself, I couldn't help but experience a sense of loss, of failure. Of letting Dad down.

I lay there, Leo's deep easy breathing on one side, and Watson's snores as he slept on the floor on the other. Sleep didn't come. It felt like more hours passed, weeks maybe.

Finally, I slid out of bed, not disturbing the deep breathing nor the snores. After tiptoeing out of the bedroom, I passed the guest room and retrieved the framed photocopy from my purse. Instead of turning on the lights or starting the fire—afraid of waking someone up—I took it to the window. Outside, the night sky was clear, filled with stars, giving just enough illumination to look at the photo.

I stared at the younger version of Beulah and her deceased husband, my certainty growing. Were they both part of it, or just Beulah? Not that it mattered, their children clearly were and Tony was long dead. I shifted to my great-grandmother. Had she been involved? Did Evelyn have ties to the Irons family, had she made choices that led to my father's murder, even after her death?

Finally, I settled on my mom and dad. Both so young, so beautiful. Not knowing within a few years of that photo they'd have a daughter. Unaware that one day Dad would be killed. That Mom would be a detective's widow and then start a new life... or resume her old one—in Estes and with her childhood sweetheart.

From the darkness, Watson padded toward me and sat at my feet, pulling my attention away.

"Hey." I reached down and stroked his face as I whispered, "Sorry to wake you, but thanks for joining me."

He offered my hand a quick lick and curled up at my feet, falling back to sleep instantly.

I returned my attention to the photo, to my parents, to my dad. I knew if he were alive, if he were me, he wouldn't rest till he figured it out. But I also knew Mom was right—he'd want me to live. And he'd never want me to put Mom in danger. I ran a fingertip over his face, the coolness of the glass not allowing me to pretend it was his cheek. "Sorry, Dad." I didn't know what I was apologizing for. For not fitting the puzzle pieces together quickly enough? For putting Mom and myself in danger? For giving up? For failing?

If I was waiting for the sound of his distant voice to offer some reassurance, I was deprived. There wasn't even an ease or settling in my chest as if receiving his blessing. Instead, just the sound of Watson snoring between gusts of the August breeze through the forest. Clutching the photo to my chest, I leaned my head against the windowpane, staring out into the night.

Nestled among endless stars, the moon shone bright, highlighting what little snow remained at the very peaks of the mountains, glistening off the tops of pines while dancing over the quaking leaves of the aspens. If I was looking for answers, I didn't find any there, either.

"It's just me, don't be startled."

Though Leo's whisper was warm and gentle, it still made me jump. I turned to him with a laugh. "Well, you're the best-looking heart attack I've ever had."

Leo chuckled. "Sorry." He offered a quick ruffle to Watson's head, who'd glanced up at his approach, then looked at me. "You okay?"

Instead of giving the obligatory affirmative, I paused before answering. "I... have no idea." I shrugged, turned back toward the window, toward the night.

Wordlessly, Leo stepped nearer and wrapped his arms around my chest so his own was pressed against my back, and he stared into the dark with me.

I don't know how much time passed, enough that the gentle swaying of the trees acted like a lullaby, soothing me, making my eyes flutter and sleep draw near.

All that evaporated in a flash when a movement caught my attention at the edge of the clearing, and I jolted.

"What?" Leo stiffened with a little start. "Do you see something?"

"I'm... not sure... I..." Straining to see into the dark, I leaned closer yet, bumping my head on the windowpane.

I must've been imagining it. There was nothing there. Still, I wished the next round of checks would happen, the lights from the police cruiser would sweep over the tree line, revealing its emptiness or highlighting Dean's hulking frame, either one. Just as long as I'd know what was coming.

Besides, there was constant movement in the woods. It was nothing to see herds of elk and deer wander through. Even bear and mountain lions were frequent enough they were no longer a surprise.

I started to turn around and suggest we go to bed, when I saw it again. A movement.

At Leo's stiffening once more, I realized he'd seen it as well. "Is that...?"

"A person? I think so." I strained even more, not that it did any good. A bear standing upright could look like a human from a distance. "It might just be a—"

Whatever else it might be swept away as a figure moved just a step or two so its silhouette was discernible from the surrounding trees. It *was* a person. Far enough away I couldn't tell the size but seemingly large enough to suggest a man.

"Dean." Leo released me, anger filling his voice. He headed to the door. "I'm ending this. Right now."

"No." I grabbed his hand, stopping him. "No. Stay here. We call Susan, we call the police." Truth be told, if I'd been by myself, I probably would've had the same reaction—gone right out into the night and had the confrontation straight-on. Funny how the fear of losing someone else gave you more sense.

For a second it seemed like he was going to argue, then Leo swiveled to get his phone.

I looked back to the night, fearing I'd see the man running our way, or worse yet turn around and have Dean's face right there by the window. But there was nothing. All was clear. Just the gently swaying trees, just the mountains and starlight. Nothing else.

Flecks of cardamom, cinnamon, and cloves swirled in the caramel-hued liquid, and the aroma of their spices blended with that of the espresso as I stared down into the depths of the Cozy Corgi mug. Typically, the first dirty chai of the morning, especially when served before daybreak, would prompt the arrival of synapses in my brain finally igniting. On this rare occasion, the jolt of the jumpstart wasn't required. With the abundance of synapses firing all night long, it was a miracle my brain wasn't on fire, and considering my heart rate had been elevated for countless hours, the shots of espresso in the dirty chai probably weren't recommended. I took a sip anyway, a long one, and felt the warm comfort of my addiction offer its loving embrace.

Watson had made it up to the bakery on the second level of the Cozy Corgi, though hadn't bothered to take refuge in his recently constructed little apartment under the merchandise shelving, but instead lay sprawled in the middle of the bakery floor, his exhausted snores offering a comfort all of their own. Poor little guy hadn't slept any more than the rest of us.

Katie smiled at me as I set the mug down. How her brown eyes managed to be so bright and clear at 4:45 a.m. escaped me; although, she was used to being at the bookshop and bakery that time of day. "Let me know when you're halfway through that one, and I'll get your second one brewing." She refocused on Leo beside me at the espresso bar. "You sure you don't want anything? Pumpkin spice latte, hot chocolate?"

"I'm already wound so tight I'm about to explode. Nothing with even the hint of caffeine for me. Thank you." He rested a hand on my back. "I'm going to call in. There's no reason for—"

"No." I swiveled to him, my voice sharper than I'd intended, and I took a second to adjust before attempting again. "No. Thank you, but like I've already said, it's pointless. There's no reason for you to be here all day. I've promised I won't leave the bookshop. I'll be with Katie, Ben, Nick—Watson, of course. And while I love to be with you, I need today to feel as normal as possible." I also wanted him away from *me*, same with my parents, just in case. If I could figure out a way, I'd get Katie and the Pacheco twins away as well. I couldn't help feeling anyone close to me was a target, but I'd yet to come up with a move manipulative enough to achieve keeping them away without raising suspicion. Maybe the dirty chais would help. "You're supposed to be on the mountain by six. Please do that."

Though every bit as strong as me, Leo wasn't as stubborn, at least not to a fault. But I could see it rise in his honey-brown eyes as he started to shake his head.

"Please." To my surprise, the crystal clear pleading in my voice wasn't manipulative or faked at all.

Even so, it worked. And though it looked like it gave him a bad taste in his mouth, Leo nodded. "Fine. But if you don't answer a call or text once, even for two minutes, I'm heading this way, *with* the cavalry." He straightened before I could reply and glanced at Katie. "You think Joe is awake?"

Though her eyes narrowed, Katie's tone was pleasant enough. "He doesn't keep baker's hours, but he'll be awake by six, and at Rocky Mountain Imprints by eight." Katie's T-shirt-maker boyfriend was roughly the size of a Mack truck.

"I'll give him a call. I bet he'll want to start work early." Leo settled a little bit. "And I'd also wager he'll probably have a craving for pastries every hour, on the hour."

"Leo." I didn't bother to keep my tone light. "Don't you think that's a little misogynistic? Katie and I can take care of ourselves."

"Plus, Smokey Bear" —Katie took up the cause— "you said yourself Susan is still going to have the police come by, *and* we've got Nick here, and Ben will show up soon, so..." Her eyes narrowed once more. "Wait... that argument is a little misogynistic in and of itself."

"Uhm..." Nick raised a hand—as if he were in school—from where he was slicing rolled-up dough into thick cinnamon roll portions. "Ben and I aren't exactly martial arts experts. I, for one, vote for Joe to come by as much as he likes."

"That's all beside the point. I don't need a man to..." My words fell away as I saw Leo harden, and I was certain he'd soon declare he was calling off work and staying right by my side, as if he were attached by Velcro. "Fine." I was too tired to argue, and... honestly, in Leo's case, I'd do the same, have him surrounded by an army if possible.

He relaxed. "Thanks." Then a new thought hit

him and he grinned. "I didn't promise you I wouldn't take off early. So we'll just have to see how that goes." With a satisfied smirk, he turned to Katie. "You know what, I think I would like a pumpkin spice latte. And one of those salted chocolate pool cookies, even though I finished them off at Fred's less than two hours ago."

Katie and I exchanged glances. I could tell she was secretly amused, but her tone turned serious and she angled toward the espresso machine. "Maybe it's all for nothing. You are both on edge. As much as I love your cabin, you can't deny you're in the middle of the woods, isolated. That by itself could be creepy at the best of times in the middle of the night, let alone when you're already worried about being targeted by the Irons family. The police didn't find anything. So maybe you were just seeing—"

"No." Leo and I spoke in unison, loud enough that Watson grunted and lifted his head from the floor to look our way. "It's okay, buddy."

Ever tuned to him, Leo cooed, "Go back to sleep."

I took over. "Someone was there. I have no doubt. I couldn't see their face, but it was a person, a human. And they could see us. You could feel it."

Refocusing on us, Leo nodded. "As great as they

are, the police didn't get there for a good five minutes. It wasn't like there was snow to see footprints, and even by moonlight, as much as Fred, Watson, and I hike around those woods, there wouldn't even be a clear trail of disturbance to track. Dean could have been anywhere."

"You said the police were there for over an hour." Katie put the final touches on the latte and slid it toward Leo. "Surely they would've found something." I could hear in her voice that she wasn't really arguing or disagreeing, just wishing it not to be true.

The police *had* searched the woods. Even Susan joined them—though about twenty minutes later than Jackson and Lin, coming in off-shift from her home to check things out herself. Not too long ago, that act of care would've surprised me, or I would've chalked it up to her simply being a thorough detective. While that was true, I knew for her at this point, it was personal, and not just because of her own history with the Irons family seeping into her police department. She went so far as to have officers escort Mom and Barry back to their house and Leo and me to the Cozy Corgi when it became clear none of us were going to sleep anymore.

Instead of debating if there really had been someone in the woods, I returned to what had plagued me all night long. "I don't understand why Dean was there. It just doesn't make sense."

Leo joined in—we'd all rehashed enough that by this point it nearly felt like following a script, though his tone suggested he'd been mulling it over again that very moment. "It had to be an intimidation factor, only a warning."

I followed my lines, just as I had before. "But at that time of night? It was only a fluke I was awake. Why would he be standing there at that hour when I should've been sleeping?"

Though Katie hadn't been privy to our conversation earlier, she filled in Susan's role, saying the sentiment almost verbatim. "But if Dean wasn't there to intimidate, then why didn't he attack?"

"Because he saw us." Leo and I spoke again, and we both chuckled, though there was no humor in it.

It was the explanation we'd landed on. I took over for Katie. "Like I said a second ago, I should've been asleep, we all should have been. Dean was planning to sneak in and dispatch me in the middle of the night, and arriving to find us standing at the window ruined his advantage of surprise. Now he'd have a fight on his hands, resistance."

"I haven't interacted with him"—Nick spoke up from where he was placing the cinnamon rolls in a tray, proving that he was both listening and quick-witted, which wasn't news—"but from the size of him, and the coldness in his eyes, I don't think he'd run away from a fight. In fact, I think he'd enjoy it."

Katie nodded with him, not missing a beat. "I hate to say it, but I think I agree."

"Yeah, us too." Leo sounded almost hopeless. "Which means none of it makes sense."

"It would also be a pretty big coincidence." That bothered me more than any other part of it. "We *just happened* to be at the window the very moment Dean decided to attack?"

"If there was really a person standing at the edge of your woods looking into your window, no matter who it was, the timing has to be a coincidence. Unless they were just standing there for hours." Katie waved it off. "I know you don't like coincidences, Fred, me neither, but they do exist, even if overused as explanations."

I opened my mouth to argue, then glanced to Leo and felt my shoulders slump. "Huh, I can't argue with that."

Katie winked. "See, I knew you were a smart one."

We sat there rehashing and rehashing and rehashing, long past when Leo left for his shift at the national park, past when the sun rose over the mountains and spread its pink glow over the downtown shops outside the windows, past Ben arriving and getting the bookshop ready to open.

When the breakfast rush arrived, Watson woke and disappeared into his little apartment, not even bothering to beg for a treat before attempting to catch up on the sleep he missed.

I planned on going to the mystery room, forcing myself to arrange the recently arrived mystery books, but I didn't. I felt too heavy, tired... frozen. I stayed where I was, the abundance of caffeine from the endless stream of dirty chais seemingly having no effect. Katie and Nick attended to the locals, getting their coffees, espressos, lattes, cinnamon rolls, scones, bear claws, all of it continuing on as normal.

Until Anna Hanson—clad in a mauve muumuu of a dress, with her scroungy white dog, Winston, yipping as he was clutched above her breast—shared what might've been the juiciest gossip to ever leave her lips, which was saying something. The fact that the news arrived from her, in and of itself almost made the morning normal. As she reached me at the espresso bar, she had to pause for a moment to catch her breath; clearly she'd rushed across the street and not slowed in her trajectory up the steps to the bakery. "Did you hear?"

I didn't get a chance to reply before Katie was on the other side of the marble counter once more, leaning nearer.

Anna didn't have to wait for more than a second for the entirety of the bakery parishioners to hush and lean closer as well, everyone knowing that if Anna Hanson made such an entrance, she was about to offer something juicy.

Apparently feeling the attention on her, Anna glanced around, then took another labored breath before lifting her voice. "Simone Pryce, of the FBI..." She hesitated, just for a second, to glare at me then dipping to whisper, "Did *you* know that Pink Panthers floozy was an undercover FBI agent and not tell me?" Without waiting for a reply, she increased her volume yet again and lifted her chin, as if allowing a spotlight to catch her best angles. "The FBI just raided Mountain Memories and arrested Beulah Gerber!" Finishing with a flourish, she lifted the hand that was free of Winston.

At the commotion, Watson trundled out—clearly still exhausted, judging from his lumbering pace—and spared a moment to glance up to the dog in Anna's arms and give a warning growl, as if to say

Grandpa ain't in the mood today, kid, then came to sit at my feet.

I couldn't answer her, or even try. Instead I swiveled and looked out the window, craning to see as far as I could along Elkhorn Avenue toward Mountain Memories. More questions than my mind could handle flooded through me, overwhelming the already exhausted synapses. *Why then? Why wait for morning? Why Mountain Memories? Why so public?* I gave up. I couldn't see the scrapbook shop, not from that angle, though people were swarming that way, proving Anna was onto something. I turned back around, feeling shellshocked. Simone *had* suggested things were near the end with the Irons family, but I never dreamed they were *that* close. Nor that she'd blow her cover.

Proving she was more on her game than myself, Katie was the first to question Anna. "You said they arrested Beulah? *Only* Beulah?"

Being the reigning queen of gossip—or at least tied for that title with Percival—and requiring no explanation, Anna practically wriggled with pleasure as she replied, allowing her tone to take on a scandalous air that was evident even over Winston's continued yipping. "*Only* Beulah. That grandson of hers fired a shot, apparently hit Simone in the shoulder, and then took off."

The entire bakery erupted into questions and speculation as if a switch had been flicked.

"*I* think the two of..." Anna's voice trailed off as she realized her theoretical spotlight had dimmed and turned back to us with a disappointed scowl that we were the only two who'd hear her speculations. "I think the two of them must've been smuggling something. Probably Dean. He shows up and gets that poor dear into trouble. Like she hadn't been through enough with that sister of his."

Katie and I jumped over Anna's theories, both simultaneously asking questions, Katie's "Dean escaped?" colliding with my "Simone was shot?"

Anna nodded in the affirmative to both. "Yes. I was picking up some cupcakes from Patty Proctor..." She cast Katie an apologetic grimace. "Sorry, dear. I wasn't trying to cheat on you. That's when I saw the *whole* thing." She paused, just for a heartbeat. "Well, not the whole thing. And strangely, considering I was so close, didn't *hear* any of it. But I was still inside Patty Cakes when they led Beulah from the shop in cuffs. I had no idea anything was even going on. There were only two black cars out there. Granted"—she was practically speed-talking at this point—"looking back, they were rather shiny and official looking, not at all touristy. But still. Not like there was the wailing of sirens or the convergence of ten thousand FBI cars like one sees in the movies. Didn't even hear a gunshot. Of course I rushed right out when I saw them taking Beulah. It was only then that I noticed Simone was in uniform—and *not* that garish Pink Panthers uniform, and bleeding. Of course she practically bit my head off when I asked what was going on. But I overheard enough to figure out that Dean was the one that shot her and he got away."

I was speechless and oddly numb.

Anna continued, her scandalized tone shifting to accusatory. "What do you know, Winifred Page? You don't look at all shocked Beulah's been arrested."

I was numb enough that when I felt my phone vibrate, I barely noticed. When I did, instead of answering Anna, I pulled it out, expecting it to be Leo. Susan's name filled the screen. I answered, lifting it to my ear. "Hey. I just heard—"

"Are you okay?" Susan cut me off, and though she'd had just as little sleep as me, there wasn't an ounce of exhaustion in her tone. "Where are you? Are you safe?"

"Am I..." Trying to figure things out, I paused,

until Susan growled. "Yes. Yes, I'm fine. I'm at the Cozy Corgi."

She breathed out a relieved sigh. "Good. Stay there."

"Susan..." As I spoke, the puzzle pieces clicked. "You're worried Dean is going to head toward me after he escaped?"

Susan hesitated just then, requiring me to prompt her that time. When she finally spoke, her voice was a whisper, as if she knew I was surrounded on the other side of the phone. "Maybe... Something is happening. There have been two murders during the night. Two... *families* murdered."

Everything moved in a whirlwind, so quickly I wasn't able to get my bearings as the world seemed to shift under my feet. On Susan's directives, the Cozy Corgi was closed. Her partner, Officer Campbell Clifton Cabot, had arrived, sidearm at the ready, to deliver the edict. Anna had put up a bit of a stink at being asked to leave, during which she made some disparaging remarks about Officer Cabot's complexion, but had finally complied. Katie and I sent the twins home, and less than fifteen minutes after Anna's stormy exit, Leo and Joe were both present.

As ever, Katie put first things first and whipped up drinks and a tray of pastries. She laid everything out as the five of us settled down at the tables near the rear of the bakery, beside Watson's fancy little apartment.

Whether finally caught up on sleep or simply because he was near Leo again, Watson rejected his secluded napping space and sat at high alert close to Leo's feet.

Before we started to talk, nearly everyone seemingly as numb as I felt, there was a knock below. Watson barked, shifting instantly into a growling rottweiler imitation.

Officer Cabot jumped to his feet, hand going to his pistol, then laughed as a blush rose to his cheeks. "If that was Dean at the door, he probably wouldn't knock." He scrunched up his nose. "Although if it was Detective Green, she would've pounded it a lot harder."

"I'll come with you." Leo made to stand, as did Joe.

Campbell waved them off. "I'm okay. Thanks."

Leo and Joe exchanged a glance, and as one, they sat back down. Neither wanted to insult Campbell by seeming like he couldn't handle it on his own.

To my surprise, Watson plodded along after Cabot, but remained at the top of the steps, continuing to growl as he descended into the bookshop. Before Campbell would've had a chance to cross to the door, Watson stiffened, his growl cutting off abruptly, and he spun on his heels and raced back toward us.

Fear flitted through me, and I started to slide off

the bench to gather him up, when Watson ran right past me, past Leo, and darted through the little doggy door that led to his apartment. I stared at him through the one-way glass. My little furball didn't always display overt bravery, but he wasn't exactly the biggest coward in the world, either.

The frantic clattering over the hardwood drifting up from the bookstore solved the mystery quickly enough.

Leo chuckled.

Katie grinned. "Paulie's here."

Joe looked confused, but his furrowed brow smoothed as two corgis—one red and white like Watson, the other a tricolor—rounded the corner of the steps and tumbled over each other into the bakery. As one, tongues lolling in frantic happiness, they pranced to us like a school of furry dolphins over the waves, and as Watson had done before, ignored us entirely as they both tried to cram through the doggy door.

Despite myself, despite everything, I laughed as Watson growled from inside and bared his fangs from his position on his little sofa. To my knowledge, Flotsam and Jetsam hadn't been in the bakery since Watson had acquired his little apartment, but it seemed they were more astute than I'd given them credit for.

"Help me." Katie nudged Joe. "I love those two knuckleheads, but they're either going to tear up the doggy door or ruin the floors. And I *don't* want to have to go through another bakery remodel." If the corgis were distraught about not gaining entrance into Watson's apartment, they didn't let on, as each of them lathered Katie and Joe's faces in unbridled licks and kisses.

When Paulie Bezor entered the bakery with Office Cabot at his side, only the faintest smile flickered over his lips as he observed his boys with Katie and Joe before he turned his worried brown gaze on me. "It's the Irons family."

"I know." Instinct took over, and I stood and fell into his embrace, which was rare for us though we were dear friends. Paulie held on to me so tightly it nearly hurt. As he began to tremble, I squeezed my arms snugger around him. "It's okay. Are you... okay?"

Katie and Leo gathered near, concern over their faces as Paulie nodded into my shoulder. At her closeness, Jetsam tried to lick his master from Katie's arms, but Paulie didn't notice.

Paulie's life had been affected by the Irons

family as much as mine, though in a different way. He'd moved to Estes before I had and became a pet-shop owner as part of a witness protection relocation program. But though he'd come to the town for safety, he'd only found more danger as the corrupt Chief Briggs and my ex, Detective Branson Wexler, used him under duress for their own nefarious reasons as part of the Irons family.

Finally, Paulie pulled back and looked up at me. "Remember I told you that I knew some of the other people in town were part of the Irons family and that I'd tell you if I ever thought your life was in danger?"

I nearly laughed at the idea that I could forget that. "Of course."

His gaze grew even more serious. "I didn't know about Beulah, I swear. I would've—"

"I know that." I pulled him tight once more. "Paulie, I *know* that. Don't you worry. Don't think twice about—"

"I knew about Clint Fuller. He would come in from time to time, most recently less than a week ago, just to make sure I knew I was still expected to keep my mouth shut." Paulie cleared his throat. "But I never saw any connection to you."

"There wasn't one." I attempted a smile of comfort. "I never even met him."

"The *postmaster* was part of the Irons family?" Leo had placed a supportive hand on Paulie's shoulder but shot a glance my way. "There's no way that's not connected to Beulah's arrest. Clint Fuller and his wife murdered the night before she was taken in by the FBI?"

Campbell didn't give me a chance to respond before he stepped up to Paulie, his tone conveying hurt and a flash of anger I hadn't heard from him before. "Mr. Fuller threatened you *last week* and you didn't say anything? You didn't tell me?"

Paulie pulled the rest of the way from me, ending the hug, and gave Officer Cabot's hand a quick squeeze. "I'm sorry. I didn't want to lie. But I wanted to keep you safe too. Just like Fred."

"That's *my* job. *I* keep people safe." Campbell looked like he was going to say more but then didn't. After a second he spoke, as if to himself. "And Susan was right." He glanced at Leo. "Like you said, then both of the families murdered last night were probably part of the Irons family. But Boler—"

"That means there was another dirty police officer." Katie looked horror-stricken. "Jack Boler... I..."

"Right?" Joe shook his head and put his arm over Katie's shoulder as her words trailed off. "I never would've guessed."

"Me neither." Leo's expression darkened even further. "Clint was always arrogant, so full of himself that I can't say I am all that surprised. But Jack seemed like a good guy. He and his wife."

I didn't think I'd met them either, at least no more than passing Officer Boler in the hallways of the police station. Though maybe his wife had come to the bookshop once, but I wasn't certain. I looked to Paulie. "Did you ever have any interactions with Officer Boler? Can we confirm he's definitely Irons family?"

Paulie shook his head. "Never. I don't know if I've even met him."

"So we can't say for certain they're all connected." I thought back to what Katie had said about coincidences at the espresso bar. "Although, I'm willing to bet they are."

"Here—" Katie transferred the still wriggling Jetsam to Paulie before patting a spot at the table for Paulie, and then headed toward the pastry counter. "—I'm gonna get you a lemon bar, I know you like those. And a praline latte."

By the time Katie returned with a latte, Flotsam and Jetsam had taken sleeping sentinel on either side of the dog door. Watson stayed quiet inside, keeping his gaze firmly on that little entrance, waiting to defend his home against overly enthusiastic visitors.

Before we could launch into a debate about the two murdered couples, Officer Cabot's phone rang. He lifted it, grunted a couple of times, and finished with a "Yes, ma'am." After, he looked at us, his voice grave. "Another murder. Not a family this time, just one man." He focused on Leo. "Jackson and Lin just found Steve Masters dead in his living room. Shot once in the head, like the others."

Leo flinched so hard it looked like it hurt. "Steve?"

It was a moment before I connected the name. Steve Masters, the handsome older ranger I'd met as Leo and I had left Rocky Mountain Pie the other night.

Leo's shock faded almost instantly as a dark shadow entered his eyes, and his voice became a growl. "That explains a lot." His teeth clenched and a muscle in his jaw twitched before he spoke again, looking at me instead of Campbell. "He would've helped out with some of the trafficking of poached animals when Branson, Briggs, and Etta were involved. He just didn't get caught. With Steve's position and reputation, no one would've looked twice. He wasn't exactly a nice guy, but he was a great ranger, at least presented like one."

"Leo…" Another moment from Rocky Mountain Pie arrived before I could decide if I needed to offer condolences or check if Leo was okay from the death of a coworker. "*Dean* was walking in when we left the other night, remember? We practically ran into him."

"One more bit of proof." Leo was instantly on the same page. "Circumstantial at best, but enough for me, given the situation. Maybe he was meeting Steve, having a handoff, something…"

"I don't get it. So we're saying what, exactly…?" Though utterly atypical, Katie sat there looking confused, for once not raising her hand like she was desperate to answer every question. "That Beulah knew she was going to get arrested today so she sent Dean out to kill the remaining Irons family members beforehand?" She glanced at Campbell. "Or that this is a possible string of failed FBI raids."

Cabot shook his head before I could respond. "No. Mr. Masters was killed in his living room, but it wasn't a shootout. The other two families were shot in their beds. That's not FBI arrests, that's a hit."

"I agree." I shivered.

"Can we please quit calling them families?" Joe

sounded a little nauseous. "I get that Clint and Sarah, and Jack and his wife were all killed, and that they were families, but... I hear the word *families* and I think of kids." His hound dog face looked toward Campbell once more. "Clint and Sarah didn't have children. Please tell me Jack and Amy didn't either."

"No." Campbell looked like he was going to be sick right along with Joe. "No kids. Thank God."

Another thing came back to me, and I took a second to sit with it, make sure I was remembering correctly. Though Katie and I had just looked through them the previous afternoon, the detail was scanned over in the search for proof of Beulah. "Remember those five Irons family tomes we got from Jake Jazz last Christmas, all the stuff he found or speculated about the Irons family?" When the group looked at me, I continued. "It was just scrawled in passing somewhere. But he mentioned the Irons family preferred to have members who are either childless or single. Jake had written that he thought the Irons family felt kids, and even spouses, opened up a person for weakness, like they were tools which could be used against them and come back and hurt the Irons family itself."

"Well... this would be more proof of that." Leo let out a long breath, then took a drink of his newly made pumpkin spice latte. "That goes for the others we found over the years—Briggs, Branson, Etta."

"Alexandria, that fits for her as well." Katie spoke up, sounding more like herself and happy to contribute to the trivia as she referenced a woman killed at Baldpate Inn during my uncles' snowed-in anniversary party. "And Danielle, who worked at the pot shop in Lyons. Oh, and that sweet kid who worked there before her."

"The Green Munchies and Eddie." Even after nearly three years had passed, my heart still ached for young, sweet Eddie, who Branson had killed. "Yes, that fits for both of them too."

Over the next two hours, Watson remained firmly in his apartment as his two guards snored away by the door, while the rest of us drank insane amounts of caffeine and ate pounds of pastry while we speculated theories, motives, and guessed at what came next.

During that time, the list of victims murdered during the night before grew to six households. One by one, Susan called in with each killing. After the discovery of Officer Boler, was Doctor Grunt and her husband, John. Next was Joyce Williams, a single pharmacist. And finally, a name that Katie and I not only recognized but knew: Benjamin Marshall, a young man who owned Shutterbug, a camera shop downtown and had been a member of Myrtle Bantam's Feathered Friends Brigade. I'd considered him as a murder suspect a couple of years before. Apparently I hadn't been entirely wrong.

Thankfully, as Joe had wished, and Jake Jazz had figured out, each home was occupied by either single people or couples. None had children. Only Steve Masters had been in his living room. All the rest had been asleep in their beds.

By midafternoon, as much as I loved the Cozy Corgi and found both the bookshop and the bakery one of the coziest places to be, I began to feel claustrophobic. By the way everyone was pacing, drumming their fingers on the tabletops, or looking ready to explode, it was a common sensation. Even the dogs picked up on it and behaved accordingly, which wasn't overly surprising for Watson, but to see Flotsam and Jetsam sitting in absolute stillness, their brown eyes trained fully on their dad, was enough to signal the arrival of the horsemen of the apocalypse.

For Watson's part, as much as he loved Leo, he stayed by my side. After hours in the bakery, I attempted book categorization in the mystery room. But my heart wasn't in it, and I only lasted fifteen minutes. Before long, I was back upstairs with everyone else, eating so many pastries they began to taste stale, and even the unending supply of dirty chais started to lose its allure.

When Susan and Simone were led up the stairs by Officer Cabot a few minutes after four in the afternoon, both of them looked like they'd gotten the worse end of the stick compared to those of us hunkering down in the Cozy Corgi. The two of them couldn't be more different—Susan with her tall, muscular frame, looking like she'd just stepped off *American Gladiators* in her rumpled police uniform, and Simone with her Barbie-doll figure, model face, and equally as rumpled dark blue FBI jacket. As one, they plopped down in the same section of tables we'd occupied all day, though on opposite ends, and each looked like they were ready to pass out, if not for the angry glares they kept shooting at each other.

"Coffee. Black." Susan didn't bother even muttering a greeting, or to tear her stare away from Simone as she issued the command to Katie. "And food. I don't care what it is. Just make it huge."

For a second, it looked like Katie was going to argue, but she knew Susan almost as well as I did, and was aware that would only slow things down. "You got it." She addressed Simone. "Would you care for anything?"

"Just a skinny nonfat latte." She barely offered a smile, though unlike Susan, she actually looked at Katie. "And do you have any fruit not baked or filled with sugar?"

Susan let out a derisive snort but didn't offer any commentary.

"You bet." Katie was already heading toward the kitchen. "We peel all of our own apples, of course, for the apple pastries. I'll bring you a couple of those."

Paulie jumped up. "Here. I'll help you."

"Thank you." Simone kept her weak smile on Katie's retreating form for a second before shooting a warning glare at Susan, then turned to address us as a group. The motion caused her to flinch, and though I was certain her wounded shoulder was screaming in pain, the small movement was her only tell. "I'm sure you're all ready to get out of here. It's been a long day. But it was Officer Green's idea to—"

"*Detective.*" Susan's growl of a whisper was so ferocious, Watson joined in, promptly followed by Flotsam and Jetsam echoing as well.

Simone glanced at the corgis, then shot an eye roll toward Susan, who was now flanked by Campbell. "Oh, right." Again she looked back at Joe,

Paulie, Leo, and me. "*Detective* Green's idea to keep you here under police protection, while I got everything sorted out with the Irons family."

Susan mumbled, her words indiscernible, but I was willing to bet it was in Simone's solitary reference to getting things sorted out.

Simone ignored her. "While I can't give you unlimited details, of course, as much of it's classified, I agree with Officer—" She closed her eyes, the copper hue of the eye shadow over her deep brown skin setting her apart from Susan's makeup-free sun-kissed complexion as well. "—excuse me, *Detective* Green, that all of you are entitled to some details, considering each of your lives has been affected by the Irons family." She halted at Joe. "Though, not you. Why are you here?"

"He's with me," Katie called out from the far side of the bakery where she worked at the espresso machine. "He's staying. And we waited all day for an explanation, so give me another two minutes to get your latte and apples before you start."

Susan grunted and finally looked away from Simone to shoot an approving glance toward the open-air kitchen.

It took all my effort not to tell Katie to forget the

coffee, latte, and apples. We'd all waited the afternoon, but really, we'd all waited years for these answers. As if sensing my mood, Leo slipped his hand into mine with a supportive squeeze at the exact same moment Watson pressed against my leg.

In the time it took Katie to finish up, I remembered I wasn't the only one who'd been waiting years. I addressed Susan instead of Simone. "I don't want to hold things up, but can I call Mom? She deserves to—"

"No." Simone's tone was abrupt, and though she apologized within the next breath, it didn't change. "I'm sorry. I shouldn't even be taking the time I am right now. I'm only doing it as a courtesy."

"And I made it perfectly clear you didn't need to. I'm more than capable of..." Susan quit speaking when Simone cocked an eyebrow her way. She didn't seem cowed... If anything, Susan looked as if it was taking all of her willpower to not add one more murder victim to the day's list.

Katie and Paulie came back with the drinks, along with the apples for Simone and a large platter of assorted cookies and pastries for Susan.

Thankfully, Simone barely took a sip before tossing her long braids over her shoulder and launching in. "The Irons family is coming down today, worldwide. In truth, though Beulah is the head honcho of this whole rigmarole, snagging her was the easiest and least dangerous of all of it." The smile that played on her face was different than any I'd seen before. Smaller, more professional, as if now that she'd traded her Pink Panthers jacket for the FBI version she was letting the Simone Pryce façade fade away. With that thought, I recalled I didn't know her real name. "After all of it, Beulah was a little cocky where she was concerned. So confident it would never come to roost where she lived, that she'd crossed every t and dotted every i."

"It's still crazy that *Beulah* was really the ringleader... or... founder of the whole thing." Katie plopped down beside Joe.

"That scrapbooking grandma being the *leader* of a worldwide, deadly crime organization would've been my last guess." Joe shook his head in wonder, maybe skepticism.

"She was." Simone gave a tight nod and seemed annoyed Joe had the audacity to speak when he wasn't actually involved in any of it. "And now she's been arrested."

When Simone paused, I only waited a heartbeat and didn't bother reminding myself to hold my temper or refrain from sticking my foot in my mouth. "I'm sorry, I'm going to need more than that. We've already figured out that much, so don't think for a second that you'll toss us scraps and we'll be satisfied. I want to know it all. How do you know it's happening worldwide? And how, where...?"

Susan chuckled.

Simone glowered for a moment, the notion of refusing clear on her expression, then filled my demand, mostly. "I know because *I'm* part of the FBI, and unlike how things operate here—both in the police department and through the snooping around of some of Estes Park's citizens, we've been working on this well over a decade. While it may all seem sudden to you, I can promise it isn't." She cleared her throat, almost like a kindergarten teacher preparing for story time, though her tone was much more matter of fact, as if giving the most pared-down school report imaginable. "Beulah and Tony were doing pretty well as a couple. They had five young children, a nice house, plenty of money. Then Tony lost his job, and along with it, apparently, his motivation to get a new one. Beulah, at her wit's end, finally took matters into her own hands and discovered she had a knack for crime and ironclad leadership."

"I wonder if—" I stopped at Simone's glare,

though not because of it. The notion that perhaps Beulah had been lamenting to my great-grandmother and she'd somehow promoted or inspired such a plan was beside the point, at least at the moment.

Simone continued without any more of a pause. "Her skills at both matured over time, although quickly, considering. What started off local and small grew—again, quickly. Specifically trafficking in stolen goods, drugs, and over the years, expanding to animals, both the exotic and the poached variety. The only thing they didn't traffic was humans, which, maybe indicates the old woman still has part of her soul intact. They had their hands in almost every moneymaking scheme through a web of contacts that grew over the years, people in positions of power who are either members or were black-mailed into participation. The smartest thing she did was wrap the whole thing in secrecy. Ninety-nine percent of those in the Irons family had limited knowledge of who else was involved. So when one cell was compromised, very little damage was inflicted."

That fit with the details Branson had given me when he... left... the organization. Again I wanted to ask how the FBI got the details of Beulah's initial plan, but once more focused on the issue at hand.

"Then how did that secrecy system break down? How did Beulah get exposed?"

Simone opened her mouth, then paused and glanced at Susan, who was midbite of an almond croissant and simply glared. Finally, she looked back at me. "As I told you, there's plenty that I won't be allowed to say, and that's honestly none of your business."

"Mine either." Susan shot me a furious expression, then took another bite of the croissant. "Apparently."

"Have you apprehended Dean yet?" Leo finally spoke up, and it didn't surprise me that he was less curious about the inner workings of the Irons family than the practicality of the man who stood outside my window last night being at large.

"No... not yet. We've every reason to believe he's left town, that Fred is safe." For the first time, Simone faltered, her hand lifting toward her wounded shoulder, but then dropping back to the table. "Three of Beulah's children were also taken in, at the exact same time as Beulah herself. Two of them—Irene and Oliver—have yet to be apprehended. Though we've taken in numerous accomplices in both of those locations."

"Oliver." I sat up straighter, moving so fast I accidentally kicked Watson with the side of my boot. At his grunt, I reached down to stroke his side by way of apology but didn't look away from Simone. "Dean's father, in Kansas City."

"Exactly." Simone gave a sharp nod. "We suspect Dean will go to him, either to offer protection or for guidance. We have every reason to believe we'll apprehend both of them shortly."

"But you're speculating." Leo leaned forward, aggression all over his posture as he addressed Simone. "Or do you have proof that Dean definitely is no longer in Estes."

"No, no proof." If she was either impressed or intimidated by Leo's tone, Simone didn't let on. "Here again. We're a little more skilled at knowing how these things work. You can trust me."

"Skilled?" Leo's growl was worthy of Susan's typical timbre. "*Six* households were murdered last night. Was that through the skilled work of the FBI... shooting people in their beds? If not, such a massacre would indicate that things aren't nearly as much in your control as you'd like us to believe."

Joe grunted his agreement and pulled Katie closer.

"It will be a few days before things are

completely smoothed out." Simone sloughed it off, though there was some change in her expression, some cloud behind her eyes I couldn't discern the meaning of. "Taking down a worldwide organization like the Irons family doesn't come without a few glitches."

"*Glitches?*" I'd only heard Leo sound deadly a handful of times, but that tone was there again. "Dean was outside Fred's window on the very night a host of people were shot in their beds. Would *she* have just been another glitch?"

"Fred is safe. And she'll stay that way. You *all* will." Again, Simone sounded off, but I couldn't read the meaning in it. She'd told us she wasn't going to be upfront about everything, was that it? Just her putting up walls to keep classified information classified—or was there more?

"Yes, she *will* say safe." Susan's tone matched Leo's. "Though that won't be thanks to you, now that you've got your little trophy and you're prancing out of town."

"You're leaving?" Maybe that should have been obvious, but for some reason it surprised me.

"Yes. My job here is done." For the first time, I thought I heard regret in her words, and she sounded more like the Simone I'd come to know and respect. "It's almost tempting, the idea of hanging up the hat and only being a potter, continuing on with Carla at the Koffee Kiln, but..." She shook her head. "No. Bringing in Beulah, like Susan said, is a big trophy. I want to take advantage of that, and I can't do so in this little mountain town."

"Why is it called the Irons family?" Paulie spoke up, sounding as if he'd been a million miles away. "If Beulah is the ringleader and her last name is Gerber, then Irons doesn't make much sense. Although..." He shrugged and tilted his head, clearly talking to himself at that point. "If you're going to run a secret crime organization, I don't suppose you'd name it after yourself."

"It wouldn't last very long if it she'd named it the Beulah Gerber Crime Dynasty or something." Officer Cabot chuckled, sounding very uncoplike. At Susan's glare, he straightened.

Paulie chuckled as well and seemed to come to Campbell's aid. "However, the BGCD has a nice ring to it, she could've gone with that."

"Not far off." Simone latched onto the topic change like a drowning woman to a life preserver. "The Irons family—"

"Is an acronym!" Katie sprang forward, her hand

raised as she spoke, finally sounding like the Hermione Granger of the Scooby Gang once more. "I can't believe we didn't tell you already today. Fred and I figured it out last night." She lowered her hand but increased her speed. "Each letter stands for one of her children. Irene, who's in Russia. Rosalind, in Boston. Oliver, Dean and Ebony's dad. Nicholas, in Japan, and Simon, in England."

"What we still need to—"

"Well. Sounds like you've got all the answers after all." Instead of sounding impressed, Simone looked thoroughly annoyed as she stood, cutting me off, and dusted her hands as if she'd been the one eating pastries instead of Susan. I hadn't even noticed if she'd taken a drink of her latte or a bite of the apples. "I need to get back to my team. I simply wanted to give you the courtesy of officially answering what I could." She attempted what appeared to be a genuine smile. "I'll say goodbye before I leave town." With that she turned and walked out of the bakery.

The rest of us sat—dumbfounded, furious, worried, drained, or any combination thereof, depending on which one of us was being considered. Finally, Katie looked over at me. "So... it's done?"

I shrugged. "I... guess so?" An unclear sensation

tumbled inside of me, but I couldn't tell what it was —relief... disappointment. "It seems a little anticlimactic."

"Tell that to all the people murdered last night." Paulie spoke in a whisper and shuddered.

TWELVE

After tearing off a large hunk of the crusty loaf of sourdough bread I'd brought home from the bakery, I dunked it into the steaming bowl of vegetarian stew, then took a bite and let the heat, carby goodness, and hardy flavors offer comfort. After savoring that for a moment, I opened my eyes, and instead of focusing on those around me, my gaze lifted to stare past the curtains with their flamboyance of flamingos strutting over tie-dyed print, into the night.

"Oh, Fred." Mom patted my hand from her place beside me at the seafoam-green kitchen table, then stood to walk over to the sink and pull the curtains shut. "You keep staring out there. You're both freaking me out and making yourself worry."

As if on cue, Watson growled from underneath the table, though at this point he sounded half-hearted, and a second later we heard the crunch of tires outside the house only to have them pause, then fade away.

"See? Safe as bugs in rugs." Mom brightened as she sat back down, patting my hand again. "The police are checking on us more now than they did last night."

"Well, I'd hope." Barry glowered, the purple and orange of his tie-dye tank top nearly making my eyes water as it did weird things with the yellow-and-green tie-dyed curtains directly over his shoulder. "Considering how many people were murdered in their sleep last night, and the man responsible is still at large."

Mom shot him a reproving glare and refocused on me. "The FBI is certain Dean headed to Kansas City to meet with his dad. I'm sure we're all overreacting."

Nonplussed, Barry winked at me. "Which is why she insisted we continue to sleep here indefinitely."

"Works for me. Free dinners!" Though Leo's voice was soft and warm, his eyes were still tight with tension. "Your skills in the kitchen are nearly on par with Katie's. I would have had no idea the stew was vegetarian if it hadn't been you who cooked it."

"Flattery will get you everywhere." That time, Barry shot a wink at Leo. "I didn't even attempt subterfuge. There's not a meat substitute in there, just a celebration of vegetables."

From under the table, a loud belch sounded, much more enthusiastic than Watson's exhaustive growl moments before.

"The compliment is appreciated." Barry glanced under the table, then reached out to pet Watson.

"I think Watson would be okay with you all staying indefinitely." Leo also peered beneath the table, smiling affectionately. "It's twice in the past couple of weeks you've made him a steak."

"It is delicious." Remembering my manners, I looked toward Barry. "The stew, not the steak. Although I'm sure that's good too." Of their own accord, my eyes focused toward the kitchen window, and only found pink flamingos instead of the night. I refocused on Mom. "You're welcome to stay as long as you want, you know that. But as you pointed out, there's no need. If Dean really has gone back to Kansas City, then—"

"Nope." Though polite, her tone left no room for argument. "Like I said, I'm certain everyone is safe as can be, but I'm your mother—it's my job to worry. And I'd like some sleep. If Barry and I were at home, I wouldn't get a wink, even though I know you're safe. But if I'm right in the next room, I'll probably sleep so hard my snoring will keep you awake."

"That's true. Phyllis snores like a banshee." Barry pulled a face. 'I swear, after our honeymoon night, I nearly called the priest for an annulment." His third wink went toward my mother. "Or an exorcism."

As ever, no matter what her mood or stress level, she relaxed at Barry's humor and waved him off. "You're horrible."

We'd put our phones away at the beginning of the meal, but now, barely five minutes into it, I slipped mine out of my pocket. As I did so, my fingers brushed against Dad's pendant, which my mother had made for him. I pulled out the small black stone with a star wrapped around it and set it on the table. At her request, he'd carried it with him, Mom believing the black tourmaline offered protection. He didn't have it the night he was killed, and Mom had recently found it in a box of his things and passed that protection on to me. Touching the star, I pictured his face, then refocused on the phone, opening the browser.

"Fred…" Mom's tone was both a plea and a chide. However, she knew a lost cause when she saw one and shook her head. "I wish I'd made curtains for that phone like I did your windows."

"I'll take a pair of those." Leo paused with a spoonful of stew at his lips. "That would make quite the statement when I'm guiding a tour on the trails and I pull out my phone with tie-dye flamingo curtains on it. Might increase the tips." Though he was playful, with his other hand he followed suit and got out his phone.

And Barry made three. "Let's all look. It'll be much more soothing over stew anyway."

"Fine." Mom sighed and laid her cell phone on the table as well. "Although it's only been ten minutes. What else could have happened?" She raised her hand quickly. "Never mind, I know better than to ask that."

As we all began to search on our browsers, another belch issued from beneath the table, which either meant Watson was thoroughly enjoying his steak, or he was ready for another round. Sure enough, his little feet padded on the kitchen floor as he trotted from person to person, looking up with his large, round chocolate eyes and pulling a puppy face that was impressive, considering his undercurrent grumpy demeanor.

Barry pulled a piece of broccoli from his bowl and offered it to Watson. "How about this? Care to be a vegetarian convert?"

Though I couldn't see Watson from my angle at the table, I caught a sniff then a snort of disgust, before his padding paws sounded again.

"Sorry, buddy." Leo reached down and ruffled Watson's fur. "No steak here. How about some asparagus?"

With another snort, Watson paused long enough to glare up at me, then trotted over toward the counter to stare longingly at the plate of cookies I'd brought home. He snorted once more and disappeared into the living room, doubtlessly to nap by the fire.

As we'd done while dinner was being prepared, we scoured the internet, and it was only a couple of moments before I found something new and sat a little straighter. "Here." I jammed my finger at the screen like I would a newspaper and accidentally opened a pop-up advertisement. After a snort of my own and a couple of adjustments, I was back to the article. "Nicholas Gerber, sixty, arrested in Yokohama, Japan." I scanned the article for anything new, then sighed. "All the same stuff—a breakdown of the Irons family that's as brief and clean-cut as what Simone offered us today, and warning of those at large."

Leo leaned closer, glancing at my screen and

giving a nod. "Listed them by name there too. Irene Gerber in Russia, and Oliver and Dean Gerber in Kansas City."

"In every article we found, it says Dean is in Kansas City. As if it's a sure thing." With a frustrated flick, I exited the article and went on the search for the next. "Maybe Simone is right about him. While my impression of Dean is that he's definitely a cold-blooded killer, he also seemed like a good-little-soldier type. That instead of questioning things on his own, he waits for a command and simply does what he's told. Without his grandmother to give those commands, maybe he truly did go directly to his father."

"Maybe that was the command. Either set up in advance or prearranged in case a crisis like this occurred." Mom's matter-of-fact tone proved, once again, that under her flighty, crystal-loving surface, she was the practical widow of a police officer.

"You might be right." I looked at her, feeling settled at the new explanation. "That does make sense, and it fits."

"And one more example of how he and Ebony couldn't have been more different," Leo chimed in again. "She had her own agenda. The way it sounds, Beulah raised her family with an iron fist and demanded complete adherence to her ways. From all we're finding, Ebony is the only one who bucked that system."

When Barry chuckled we all looked at him, baffled. With a blush, he shrugged and grinned at Leo. "You said Iron fist."

Leo cocked his head in confusion, but his expression cleared instantly, and he laughed. Mom and I joined in, before he explained, "Oh, right. Beulah, the matriarch of the Irons family ruling her children and grandchildren with an *iron* fist. Got it."

Barry shrugged again. "Simple pleasures, simple pleasures." As if to prove the point, he took a huge spoonful of stew and made a show of humming contentedly as he chewed.

Following his lead, I took a spoonful myself, then refocused on the screen, not entirely sure what I was searching for. I found some of it, partially, confirmation of Simone's assertions at the Cozy Corgi only a few hours before. What we'd witnessed on Elkhorn Avenue was just a small piece of a much bigger production that occurred simultaneously worldwide. There were countless reports of the Irons family being brought down. And though there was a couple of sentences about Beulah's arrest in Estes Park, because there'd actually been casualties in Boston when Rosalind was arrested and one injury to a detective in Manchester when Simon was apprehended, those stories took precedence. Beyond that, considering how significant the raids really were, every single report was cut-and-dried. Even the details of the six households murdered in Estes were bare-bones, all of them told the story of Beulah and her five children, who became a global underworld empire. I read through it again when I found yet another source, and some of the things that had been bugging me finally clicked into place.

I continued to scan the words as I spoke, partially addressing my family, partially simply talking out loud. "Almost reminds me of when I was a professor. I'd get these long, flowery reports from some of my students, but the substance of what they turned in could've been summed up in a paragraph. They used big words to try to fool me, and basically rewrote the same two or three sentiments a billion different ways to make it longer and feel more complete. It might look like they did all the work, but it was clear they hadn't. And..." That time, I did look up, scanning past Mom and Barry and settling on Leo. "It only happened a couple of times, but these? They all feel plagiarized. Even the structure of the articles are the same, with just a few words changed here and there.

It's basically the same article, over and over again. No different angles, no hard questions or dangling threads. No difficult questions about why all the people were shot in their beds here last night."

Leo considered, then nodded his agreement after a second or two. "You think Simone... or someone else, pushed out a narrative or talking points? Maybe even provided a script."

"Yeah. That's exactly what I think."

"Of course that's what happened." Once more, Mom sounded like a cop's wife. "Chances are it didn't come from Simone, but someone above her. This *is* the FBI, and a worldwide investigation that's gone on for years. One that took Charles's life." Mom leveled her gaze on me. "The FBI is going to control the account, especially when there's a couple of the big players still at large. Doesn't mean what we're seeing is untrue, but of course we're not getting all the details. I'm sure you didn't get them from Simone when she talked to you earlier. From what you said, she basically alluded to that. That there were things she couldn't or wouldn't tell you." Mom finished with a shrug, "That's how this goes. There were even cases your dad couldn't tell me most of the details about, and he knew he could trust me."

I nodded slowly, letting her words settle over me.

They felt right. "I think that's true, Mom. But..." Once more I looked toward the window and only found flamingos. "That would be good enough if I was the general public. If Dad hadn't died, if the Irons family hadn't touched our lives in a million different ways lately, between Branson, Ebony, and Dean. For us to stay safe, to be assured of it, I want to know the answers."

Mom glanced toward the living room, maybe Watson shifting in his sleep by the fireplace catching her eyes through the doorway. She lifted her voice, and though not unkind, she had her mother's tone that she rarely used with me. "If anything, we are safer than we've ever been. Even if Dean is still out there, and his father and aunt..." She waffled a hand in the air. "They're named, for the whole world to see. We're being protected by the police at the moment, and everything, as much as can be expected, is out in the open." That time, Mom reached out and touched Dad's stone. "This is what your father ended up giving his life for, to see the Irons family brought down, and that's happening." Again her gaze lifted to mine. "But this is the real world, love. Not every member of the Irons family will be caught, and we have to deal with that, live with it. It has to be enough that the organization is crumbling, being brought down. We should be thankful. More than ever. You've got what you've been searching for."

"But—"

"No." She shook her head firmly, cutting me off. "Didn't you learn the error of that from Garrett?"

At the unexpected mention of my ex-husband, I flinched.

She didn't hold back. "It never stopped with him, did it? Every goal Garrett had, as soon as he met it, he didn't take time to celebrate it. It was never enough. Soon as he was able to check it off, he made a bigger goal, then a bigger one, and it consumed him. Totally changed him from the kind man he was when you married him, to someone nearly unrecognizable within years. Changed him from the pure soul of a cop like your dad to... a career politician."

She wasn't wrong about him, but maybe it was the unexpectedness of Garrett arriving in the middle of the dinner table that made me unsure, and I shook my head, trying to make sense of it. "I don't see how Garrett has anything to do with—"

"The Irons family has come down." When Mom took my hand that time, she held on, squeezing tightly. "More than I ever would've believed could happen, and quicker and more thoroughly than what you probably even thought possible. Of anyone, *you* should be celebrating. It's done. It's time to live your life."

"But, Mom, I didn't—"

"It doesn't matter if *you're* not the one who put the puzzle pieces together. If you're not the one who avenged your dad." Her grip still iron-tight, she gave my hand a little shake. "Just because it didn't come from you doesn't mean it isn't correct. Not to mention that I have no doubt that you helped. Quite directly in some ways with Simone at times."

Again I flinched. I wasn't sure what I'd been about to say to Mom, but... had that been it? That *I* hadn't solved it so it couldn't be trusted. Was that my arrogance that I was the only one worthy of putting the pieces together? Or that to truly avenge my father, *I* had to do it all personally?

Mom continued to push on. "Let yourself sleep tonight. Then tomorrow morning, let's live. All of us. Barry will check in with some of the renters, there's been a couple saying there's repairs needed. I'll... start making some new necklaces to sell at Chakras. Leo can continue with revamping Chipmunk Mountain or giving a tour. And..." A smile curved at the corner of her lips as a solitary tear rolled down her face. "And you, my darling, can go be a bookshop owner, and that's it. Let Watson curl up and snore in his little sunbeam while you arrange all the books in the mystery room. Drink dirty chai after dirty chai, eat endless amounts of Katie's cookies, and every once in a while, slip your hand into your pocket and squeeze your father's amulet, feel his love and pride in you, and *live*. Just live."

As if sharing a brain, Barry stretched out a hand to put over my mother's, just as Leo took my other hand, the one not in my mother's grip. After a second, the two of them exchanged a glance and chuckled, then took each other's hands. In that moment the four of us formed an unbroken circle around the table. Both a partial family and a complete family in one.

I glanced at each of them in turn and even angled to look over into the living room where Watson, as expected, snored away by the fire.

It was enough. *More* than enough.

And yet...

After Mom and Barry shut the door to the guest room, I stood in a flannel nightgown by the living room window and stared out into the woods. A police cruiser had just made a circle, its beams falling over the house then the trees, showing nothing amiss before driving away. Just like the night before, Watson was at my feet within a few moments, and Leo was at my back, his chest against me as he peered over my shoulder. "See anything? Dean?"

I shook my head and continued to stare. It was well past twenty-four hours since I'd slept, and exhaustion had settled bone deep. My brain was fuzzy, my nerves shot, and I needed to go to bed. Even my dry eyes were screaming. After lifting a hand and rubbing them, I stared back out, searching for some clue in the trees of the mountains. White spots flickered through my vision, and I rubbed my eyes again, nearly swept away by an overwhelming rush of déjà vu.

Blinking, my vision cleared, and there was nothing more than the dark silhouette of rugged mountains and dense forest—barely even that, though, as clouds nearly obliterated the moon and stars. Still the déjà vu lingered, and after another blink or two, I sucked in a breath.

"What is it?" Leo's voice was tight as I stiffened.

At our feet, Watson sat up, ready for action.

"I..." It took a second to play through the connection, the whole thing had been long ago. Over a year and a half. "I was just staring out into the woods, and my vision went a little blurry, spotty, and..." I started to look at Leo, then stayed focused on the forest instead. "Remember at Baldpate Inn for my uncles' anniversary? When Alexandria was murdered, when Luca was murdered?"

"Of course." His voice warmed softly. "That was where I finally got to kiss you."

"True." A little peace entered at that memory, and I reached up to place my hand over his where it rested on my shoulder. "Remember that scene Luca recorded on his phone at the windows of the glassed-in porch, the one that got him killed."

"Of course." He repeated the words but lost the sweet sentiment they held before. "A video of Alexandria transporting something from Cordelia's knitting group's van from Willow Springs, in the middle of a blizzard."

"Alexandria *and* some shadowy form we never identified. We assumed it was another member of the Irons family meeting her out in the woods in the middle of the night." I gestured with my chin toward the tree line. "Just like this. Except with snow."

He didn't require any other explanation. "You're thinking Dean was that someone?"

"Maybe. It could've been anybody. I don't remember if the shadow was big enough to be him or not. It was hard to tell on that recording, considering the blizzard conditions and the lighting. But..."

"But you think it was Dean." Leo didn't question, just uttered it like a matter of fact.

I didn't answer, just nodded. In the long run, it really didn't matter. And I probably would never know with complete certainty, but yes. That missing puzzle piece finally clicked into place, and it seemed to fit perfectly. I made the next leap. "Dean might've been the one to kill Luca, not Alexandria. Either way I'm willing to bet Luca wasn't his first—or his last—kill. So it makes sense that Dean would be capable of murdering those people last night."

"But you don't think so." Again Leo didn't frame it as a question.

I already knew the answer, but I considered it for a few heartbeats anyway before replying, "If he did, and if he was the figure we saw staring back at us, then why kill all of them and *not* us?" I finally tore my eyes away from the trees, feeling like no one was going to step into the clearing that night, and focused on Leo. "Beyond that, like Katie said before, why murder all those people? If Beulah thought things were coming to a head and was attempting to clean up, that wouldn't have done it. If she knew the FBI was planning a raid today on her entire family, a lot more than Irene and Oliver and Dean would've escaped."

"You're right." The heaviness that settled over Leo was palpable, though his voice was barely audible. "But you said yourself, Beulah practically admitted it to you yesterday at Mountain Memories. That would indicate she knew change was coming."

"No." Suddenly I was certain. "That only means life was about to change for *me*. I was too close, too suspicious, too... something. Beulah flaunted it in my face to scare me. But it wasn't an idle threat, just taunting me, knowing my end was nearly up. I'm not sure if Dean was out in the woods last night. If he was, then it still doesn't make sense that we're all here, but it makes even less sense that he was behind the massacre and Beulah still got captured, as well as much of their family... not to mention their Irons family empire crumbled."

"Then who?" Leo glanced back out the window. "Who murdered all those people?"

"Branson." His name came forth like a clairvoyant proclamation. But the truth of it settled in my gut. "Branson was watching us last night, and that's why we're still alive. He wasn't here to kill us, only to—"

"Spy on you. Again." Once more Leo's dark tone

took on that rarely murderous tint. "And... *that* monster? Yeah... I can see him pulling off the massacre, easily."

"Me too." I had no doubt. My blood chilled, even more than at the thought of Dean Gerber. Branson had sworn to never hurt me, and for a long time I believed him. I didn't anymore—at least I was no longer convinced, even if Branson was sure of it himself. "Me too."

THIRTEEN

Whether because my gut settled, knowing I'd landed on the truth of it being Branson in the woods, or nothing more than pure and utter exhaustion, I slept. I didn't even remember my head hitting the pillow. I wasn't aware of Leo's breathing slowing as sleep took him, or even Watson's gentle snoring. I had no dreams, not even a moment in the middle of the night where I needed to get up to use the restroom. It was pure, unadulterated oblivion. The result was that I woke up calm, clear-eyed, and with my brain sharp enough it didn't even require a dirty chai for a kickstart.

In truth, Branson was a thousand times more terrifying than Dean Gerber could ever be. Dean might be a cold-blooded killer, but he had more of an animalistic feel to him, more of a trained attack dog. Granted those could be dangerous, as they could strike without warning or reason—and Dean definitely had reasons—but there was no way to predict or figure them out. Due to that, there was a powerlessness in all of it, but knowing it had been *Branson*... even if he was more dangerous, made me feel like I had the upper hand, or at least some power. Branson was about as far away from someone else's attack dog as I could imagine. Everything he did was thought through, intentional and reasoned. And as a result, he could be figured out. There would be clues to find, puzzle pieces to put together, some dark, nefarious plan to unravel. And *that* I could do.

The other result was that Leo absolutely refused to consider leaving my side. I argued for about thirty seconds before knowing I would be the exact same— that *in fact*, I did feel the exact same. If either one of us was in danger from Branson, it was Leo, and I wanted *him* with *me*.

Leo joined Watson and me on our morning stroll through the woods, both of us with thermoses of coffee in hand. Part of me wished Leo would stay back. If Branson was in the woods watching, he was more likely to make himself known if I was alone, but I didn't ask. It wouldn't have been fair or smart. There was no sign Branson had been there, not that I expected there to be. Especially after the police had searched the nearby woods the day before, disturbing any trail that might've been left. It didn't really matter: if Branson didn't want to be found, he wouldn't be. Just like him standing there staring back at us in the night. I wasn't sure about that. Had he wanted me to see him and remained there until I did, taking the chance I'd be up in the middle of the night? Or had I caught him and he'd simply decided to flaunt his presence? I wasn't certain, nor did I know if it mattered.

Susan didn't answer her cell, but to my surprise, dispatch told me where she was when I called the station. I doubted she would've appreciated that fact very much, but as her location was the second stop on my list, I figured we might as well head there, kill two birds with one stone.

While the typical morning rush at the Koffee Kiln was sizable—it was nothing compared to what happened at the Cozy Corgi Bakery, thanks to Katie's baking—the fact that it had a Closed sign and the front door was locked meant that Katie was going to have more of a crowd than normal.

When Carla unlocked and threw open the door after I knocked, that fact hadn't escaped her either.

"Come down here to gloat? First you steal my baker, and then you make it where I can't even open for *my* customers?"

"Carla, you didn't even let Katie—" I bit my tongue halfway through, deciding not to point out that Carla had never allowed Katie to bake, which was part of the reason she left to begin with. While even on the best day I could expect to be greeted with fangs from Carla Beaker, her red-rimmed, puffy eyes told me this was far from the best day. It was further proven by her stepping back and holding the door for all three of us without even making a comment about Watson's presence. It seemed that after her initial insult, Carla had no fight left. She didn't even mutter as she relocked the door.

Simone sat at one of the tables nearest the pastry display, a steaming mug of coffee in her hands and what looked to be a pumpkin scone plated in front of her. Susan stood opposite, with her black-booted foot propped up on the chair, and she leaned forward with her elbow resting on her knee, towering over Simone. As one they looked over and gave matching expressions of resigned annoyance.

"How in the world did you know I was here?" Susan shot a glare at Officer Cabot, who was twinkling his fingers toward Watson, before stiffening back to attention. "Did she text you?"

Simone didn't give Campbell a chance to respond as she pointed her finger from us back to the door. "Turn yourself around, Winifred Page. If there is ever official FBI business, this is it."

Watson padded forward, looking like he was heading toward Campbell, but angled slightly more toward the pastry case.

"Did *you* know?" As Simone had just done, Carla didn't give time for a response to the question either, and when she looked at me, there was a pleading look in her blue eyes. "Did you know Simone was undercover this whole time? Did *she* tell *you*?"

"Carla..." The pleading in Simone's voice matched Carla's expression.

"I'm not asking you," Carla bit out at Simone before looking back at me. "Did she tell you?"

Watson pulled slightly at the end of his leash, nearly reaching the array of pastries, clearly not caring they weren't as scrumptious as Katie's.

"I found out." Ignoring Watson, I softened my voice, understanding the state Carla was in—discovering that her friend and business partner wasn't who she believed she was. I'd had a similar experience at the end of my publishing-company days. "She didn't tell me because she wanted to."

Carla let out a sigh of relief at that, but her face tightened again just as instantly. "But you *did* know."

Leo stepped forward, clearly getting ready to offer comfort. "Carla—"

"Back off, Boy Scout," Carla snarled, but stayed focused on me, tears glistening in her eyes. "You... you... take *everything* from me." She whirled and stormed off toward the back room but paused once more where Watson was straining toward the pastry case and let out a scream, causing him to flinch away. "You know what, dog, your mom has made it perfectly clear that the items in the store are nothing more than dog treats anyway." Again she glared back at me. "What was it? My scones are dry, was that it?"

Leo hurried forward as if Carla might attack Watson, and at the same moment, Simone stood, heading toward them as well, though focused on her friend. "Carla, please—"

Not listening to either, Carla darted behind the pastry case, grabbed a tray of scones and lifted it in the air, then treated the tray as a catapult and shot the scones out into the bakery, one of them bouncing off the side of Susan's head, another hitting my shoulder as they rained down onto the floor. "Well, here you go, *corgi*, here you go!" Voice cracking, Carla whirled once more and ran down the hall, and slammed the door shut with a sob. I wasn't sure if she disappeared into the restroom, the office, or where the pottery was fired, but there was another loud crash, like some object being thrown, then nothing.

All of us—Simone, Susan, Campbell, Leo, and myself—stood frozen as if equally assaulted, embarrassed, and hurting for Carla.

At some point in the melee, it seemed I dropped Watson's leash, and he was about as far from frozen as a corgi could get. With his best impression of Hungry Hungry Hippos, my grumpy little man shifted into high gear and went to town on the scones covering the floor.

Actually the hippo analogy wasn't quite right, more like a frantic vacuum cleaner—a stubborn, surprisingly agile, vacuum cleaner.

Refusing to acknowledge either of our existences or our commands and pleas to stop, Watson ran full tilt from scone to scone, scarfing them down in an explosion of crumbs, all the while darting under tables and chair legs as we attempted to catch him, easily wriggling out of our grasps and devouring another scone.

He made it through at least four scones before he

made his fatal mistake and lunged for a white chocolate and raspberry offering beside Susan's boot. Proving to be more agile than she looked as well, Susan shot down one muscular arm and scooped Watson up to her chest, eliciting a cloud of corgi hair at the sudden motion.

Proving that old fears died hard, my heart stopped just for a second as I expected her to squeeze him so tightly he'd pop. Instead Detective Susan Green, with her hair pulled so tight into her short ponytail that it threatened to rip out her temples under her police cap, grinned at Watson, and when she offered him her trademark insult of "fleabag," there was more than a hint of admiration and affection in her tone. Catching herself, she looked up quickly, cleared her throat, then held Watson out with both arms extended, like she held an unwanted baby, toward Leo. "Take this fat thing, will you? My uniform is so covered with hair I might as well burn it. Dry cleaning will be pointless."

Leo obliged, holding Watson to his chest as he squirmed and tried to get back down to the scone smorgasbord.

Susan snapped her fingers at her partner. "Cabot. Clean this place up." Without waiting for a reply, she looked back at me, and for a second I thought she was going to return to her original question of how I knew where she was. Instead, with a heavy sigh, she plopped down in the chair she'd been using as a foot perch and motioned to the empty seats around it. "Well... why fight it?"

"No... I'm not doing this." Simone shook her head, the coils of her braids clicking musically as she looked down the hallway.

"Handle your ruined relationship with Carla later. That's your own fault." Susan gestured again, that time toward the chair Simone had occupied only moments before. "Sit and get this conversation done. You know it's the only way I'll stop. And as I was telling you before Fred got here, you owe me answers. And..." Another sigh. "You do owe Fred as well."

Proving Susan was just as powerful as she thought she was, Simone did as she was commanded.

Leo went toward Campbell. "Here, let me help. You don't have to—"

"It's all good." Grinning, Campbell shot an adoring gaze at Susan. "Got my orders. You be with Fred."

Less than thirty seconds later, Susan, Simone, Leo, and I were gathered around the table. Watson was back on his leash and under Leo's chair. He was clearly thoroughly convinced we hadn't noticed him snag half of Simone's pumpkin scone that had fallen off her plate in the chaos, and I didn't see any reason to ruin his final snack.

I was so used to Susan launching in, that it surprised me when Simone started off, pulling my attention away from Watson. "Let me guess, you've got another theory. Never mind that you were in here two seconds ago telling me Beulah was the ringleader of the Irons family. Never mind that you were annoyingly correct—*which* I already knew and told you I was already handling. But I'm willing to bet *now* you're going to tell me I have the wrong person. That Beulah was innocent. That someone else is behind the whole thing."

"No." Despite the seriousness, I couldn't hold back a chuckle. "Well, maybe a little. More that there's someone *else* involved, besides Beulah and Dean."

"Duh." Simone was clearly done with me, her attitude back to how it had been when I'd first discovered she was undercover. "The Irons family was hardly a two-person operation. And it's not up for debate. I have... *we* have a lovely little rat who squealed everything we need to put Beulah Gerber away for the next five centuries. That was nailed in stone and finalized before we even scheduled a time for the mass arrests."

"No," I repeated. "That's not what I mean. I believe Beulah is either behind it all or part of it. *I'm* talking about the massacre that happened with the other Irons family members in town. It wasn't Dean."

Simone rolled her beautiful dark eyes, at the same moment Susan's pale blue gaze narrowed on me. "Branson."

Leo and I both flinched as one.

Susan smirked and stayed focused on me as she cocked her brow. "See? You're not the only one who can steal a big reveal." She refocused on Simone. "It's the way they were killed, all with a single bullet. That has Branson's style all over it—clean, efficient, cold, and utterly heartless."

"And this is why the FBI is in charge of things like this, and not some Podunk Barney Fife." Taking her life in her hands, Simone gave another eye roll, this time toward Susan. "That *style*, as you say, is hardly unique to Branson Wexler. I know this town has made him out to be the big bad of all big bads, but he's just another dog who was well-trained. That's all. Any assassin for the Irons family would have that same efficient method, plain and simple."

"It was Branson." I waited until Simone looked at me. I was already convinced, but hearing her refer to him like a guard dog, as I saw Dean only confirmed she didn't have an adequate grasp of Branson. "It was. And he was the one in the woods outside my house the other night. Not Dean."

"That was my other thought," Susan picked up, proving she was every bit as quick and smart as I'd come to believe. "That's the only thing that makes sense. If it was Dean, and he was the one responsible for killing all the others that night, he would've done the same to Fred, to Leo, to the whole family under her roof. *Branson* wouldn't have. He's so head over heels for Fred, he'll never hurt her. Or her family."

"I'm not so sure of that." Leo's tone was heavy, fearful. "I think he believes that himself, but that doesn't make it true."

Susan started to argue, then paled.

Simone let out a long-suffering sigh and lowered her head slightly to rub her temples with her fingers. "I swear you people drive me crazy. You think the whole world revolves around you." She glared at me. "More specifically, around Fred." She straightened slightly. "Don't get me wrong, Winifred. I like you. I respect you. You're smart, good, determined. You drive me nuts, but I like you. But you aren't the star of everyone's show like you think you are, like you've got half the town convinced you are."

"She's the star of Branson's." Leo's fist clenched, unclenched, then tightened again on the tabletop. "It was him that night."

"Okay." Simone checked her watch. "I'm giving this five more minutes and then I'm done humoring you. *All* of you." She refocused on Susan for a flash, then me. "Let's say Branson was outside your cabin. Why was he here? He's not even part of the Irons family anymore. He's admitted that to you, Fred. And it's well-documented within all the intel we found on him and the Irons family lately. So... why did he kill all those people? Don't give me the reason it was because of Fred."

"Revenge," Leo and Susan said at the same time, and they shared a quick glance of acknowledgment.

"But isn't that curious timing?" Simone didn't even have to consider. "Branson just happens to show up for revenge the very night before the Irons family falls?" Though she'd been looking at Leo and Susan, Simone turned to me once more. "How many times have I heard you talk about your disbelief in coincidence—which is funny since you're so adamant about your gut instincts?"

I let the insult slide. "I don't think it's a coincidence, I think there's more going on here. I think..." I hadn't quite gotten that far but went with it—with instinct, as Simone called it, with my gut. "But somehow he's involved. Maybe he helped bring them down, maybe he knew what the FBI was doing and decided to take vengeance before they merely got handled by the law."

"That makes as much sense as anything." Susan started to nod and glanced at me. "But... if Branson is here getting vengeance, then wouldn't Angus be dead? The last time Branson was in town, he hung Raul Acosta in the middle of Angus's store, a clear threat."

"Great, *now* what? *Angus Witt* is the real leader of the Irons family and Beulah was just the scapegoat?" Scorn dripped from Simone's words as she checked her watch once more then narrowed in on me. "You really think Branson has access to the FBI? That he's got a little mole in the *Federal Bureau of Investigations*? You really do have him built up in your mind." She whipped toward Leo, her tone shifting to mocking. "You might want to have some concerns that your girlfriend has such a grandiose perception of her ex."

My temper, which could ignite easily at times, flared so bright and hot that I felt beads of sweat break out of my forehead. But maybe it was because I saw that same sentiment mirrored over Leo's furious face that I paused just long enough for synapses to fire below the rage, calming me instantly with a bucket of ice. Instead of responding, I leaned back in my chair and stared at Simone in realization.

"Are you really going to sit there and pretend there're no leaks in the FBI? That there aren't Irons family members *in* the FBI?" It was Susan who spoke, and her words were just as belittling as Simone's. "*I* read the papers too, you know. One of those arrested in Kansas City was an FBI agent."

"And he's *arrested*." Simone stood, her chair scraping, clearly done with the conversation. "Either way, get over your obsession with Branson Wexler, all of you. It's pathetic."

Watson emerged from under my chair at the commotion but didn't growl.

I lowered my hand to his head as I stared at Simone, the realization solidifying. While her scorn and hostility felt familiar, she'd only displayed that for a fraction of our interactions, even after uncovering her secret. It was never with such arrogance or cruelty. That wasn't her. Not really, undercover or not.

She flinched slightly as she caught me staring. "What?"

"What's going on, Simone?" I refused to let her look away. "Are you in danger? Is Branson threatening you?"

She flinched again, her lips moving wordlessly for a moment, and then the anger flared once more. "See? Obsessed. It's gross." She shot the insult toward Leo again. "Really, dude. What kind of man is okay with his girlfriend being clearly consumed with another guy?" Then back to me. "You just can't handle not being the center of the universe, can you, Winifred? You made it your mission to save the world from the Irons family for years, and you just can't accept that *I'm* the one who helped bring it down, and not you." She laughed. "I'm sorry I did what you couldn't." With a final sigh, she turned and rounded the table, then paused, clearly torn in her desire to head toward the back to find Carla. Instead, she walked to the front door, unlocked it, and stepped out into the morning sunlight on Elkhorn Avenue, one last insult drifting in before the door closed behind her. "I can't wait to be away from all of you."

I'd planned on jumping right into the thick of things with Angus when we walked down to Knit Witt, but I hadn't counted on two things.

First, despite the tourist season slowing due to school being back in session, Angus had customers and was kneeling beside a young woman talking gently to her child, a little boy who was probably six or seven. His green gaze flicked to me and twinkled in acknowledgment; clearly he'd been expecting me. "Give me a couple of moments, dear Winifred." He then refocused on the boy, putting his arms gently around the child and guiding the small hands fumbling with knitting needles.

Second, was Leo. I'd forgotten he hadn't been in the knitting shop, and no matter what was going on, he was at heart a park ranger. He stopped dead in his tracks the moment he walked into the store and gaped at the knitted Samson display, then walked slowly toward it as if approaching a deity. Though Watson had already seen the elk, a little wariness seemed to linger in his curiosity as he trotted along at Leo's side, sniffing the air with a confused expression—doubtlessly smelling wool and human, and an abundant lack of elk scent.

I was glad for the distractions now that I was inside the beautiful modern, sleek store with walls of soft steel blue, floors and ceiling in a matching deep, shiny mahogany, and everything in between skeins of every hue of the rainbow and every type of material imaginable. At one point, when I'd browsed, I found one spool priced for eight hundred dollars. I wasn't sure why that memory flickered through my mind, just another puzzle piece of Angus Witt and his knitting shop. Maybe it revealed a telling aspect of his personality; maybe it didn't. My gaze followed Leo as he repeated my instincts when I'd seen Sampson and reverently reached out a hand to touch. The masterfully knitted elk *did* say a lot about Angus Witt—it screamed of patience, dedication, determination, artistry, and skill. Of perfection.

The way he interacted with the mother and child was revealing as well. Angus was kind, gentle, caring, and again, patient. Nothing in the shop nor in the vast majority of interactions with the man ever suggested he was anything other than just that. It'd only been in flashes, and times when someone else dear to him was in trouble, or he was being directly threatened, that I caught the glimpse of fangs sharper than any pair of knitting needles.

Susan hadn't put up a fight, had in fact agreed when I suggested I speak to Angus without her. She had a tendency to lose her patience with Angus... with most people. But now I was there, with him in front of me, I wasn't certain why I'd come. Had it been to warn him that Branson was in town, seeking revenge? Or to accuse him of being part of the Irons family despite his recent denial?

Several minutes later, as he wrapped up a child-size knitting kit and beginner's instruction book, then sent the mother and son on their way, I decided it was both.

"I told Winifred to let you know I acquired the antlers in a humane way. The magnificent beast who crafted these dropped them by a trail I frequent. I merely retrieved them." Angus crossed to the elk and lifted his hand, touching the spiky crown. "All on the up-and-up, but I hope you approve of him. If Samson here can fool a park ranger, then I'll count that a success."

Leo cleared his throat. "I'm sure you know that collecting fallen antlers is illegal and can come with a fifty-dollar fine, plus an eighteen-dollar surcharge."

Angus chuckled warmly. "Would you like that in credit card or cash?"

Leo barely spared him a glance, as if it was painful to look away from Samson's beauty. "I don't know if I've ever seen anything more stunning."

"Then... success?" Angus lifted his brows.

"Yeah." Leo gave the elk another tender stroke. "I don't know what your plan is for him, but I'm certain he'll fetch top dollar. A donation to fight poaching would be appreciated."

That time, Angus cocked his head. "Was that in addition to the sixty-eight dollars already mentioned, or as a way to acquire a get-out-of-jail-free card?" He chuckled good-naturedly again and reached out and squeezed Leo's arm, his hand looking small and aged against Leo's thick shoulder. "I think it's a beautiful idea. Though Sampson won't be for sale, I don't believe. He will be making the museum rounds. But I'll still make a donation. And also have a mention of where others can participate in the fight against animal trafficking and poaching on the display plaque that travels with him."

"That would be a help, thank you." Leo finally looked away from Samson, as if coming out of a spell, and shot me an embarrassed smile.

"And you, handsome man." Angus knelt as he had with the small child, one of his knees popping, and extended a hand toward Watson as he so often did. "Good to see you again on this fine day."

I never knew what reaction Watson would have to Angus. Sometimes it was completely ignoring him, a curious sniff, or every once in a while, a little lick. That time he sniffed the back of Angus's hand, then quickly swung his head back toward the hoof of the elk, took in a deep breath, and returned to Angus's hand, sniffing again. Suddenly realizing what he was doing, I marveled at him. Having put the pieces together that this elk was no elk and was somehow part of the old man, Watson turned away from Angus and the elk, losing interest, and trotted halfway between Leo and me and sat.

"He is a spectacular creature, that dog." Angus stood again, using one hand on his knee, which issued another pop, and then crossed his arms casually over the thick pale blue cable-knit sweater. "I think after Samson is gone, I should do a life-sized

Watson." He grinned at me. "The other one I knitted for you could fit in your hand."

"But he was every bit as lifelike." Despite my suspicions, I smiled. "He's still on my mantle. Always will be."

"And more compliments." Angus looked like he was about to continue speaking but paused, glancing toward the front door. "Excuse me. Traffic is slow, but you can never be sure. I doubt you're here for knitting instruction." Uncrossing his arms, he went to the door, locked it, and then returned to us. "Now, what can I do for you? Am I defending myself against being a member of the Irons family, giving you my whereabouts during the massacre, or have you decided I know details about your great-grandmother that I'm not sharing?"

I sighed, and despite myself, smiled. A glance at Leo's expression told me he was feeling the exact same thing. "How do you do it? No matter how long I live, Angus Witt, I will never figure out how to have the ease and grace that you display. You make it sound as if being accused of murder or being part of an evil crime syndicate is no more offensive than being asked to register to vote. And you manage to do so with affection in your tone."

"That's because it's genuine." There was that

smile. "I've told you countless times, Winifred, I admire you immensely. I care for you a great deal." His green gaze dipped warmly to Watson and then up to Leo. "I admire you too, of course, Mr. Lopez. You're a good man, but you're lucky to have been chosen by this woman, and you know it."

"Yes, I do." Leo shot me a look that confirmed everything Angus had just said, then refocused on Angus with a discerning stare. "And Fred is right. Your skills, with the needles *and* charm, serve you well."

"They do." He nodded, then took a couple of steps to the side to lean with casual elegance against the counter, as if he might just be the slightest bit tired. Then he offered me yet another smile. "What questions can I answer for you, Winifred? As ever, I will be as honest as I can."

I gave him a smile back. "That doesn't necessarily mean you'll be honest."

He chuckled warmly. "No, I suppose it doesn't."

Where did I want to start, and if he lied... *when* he lied, would I recognize it?

"Branson was outside my cabin the other night. At first I thought it was Dean." I watched him carefully for any flinch. There was nothing. "It wasn't."

"Thank goodness for that." Angus sounded sincere. "As I told you just the other day, Dean isn't harmless like Ebony. I do want you safe. If you're correct that Branson is in town, then you probably are safe. Even from Dean." He looked toward Leo. "Not that you can't offer adequate protection, young man."

I bristled at that but let it go. "Are you safe, Angus, if Branson is in town?"

"Because of his display of Raul?" He glanced toward the ceiling above where Samson stood, as if he could still see the chef and owner of the fancy Italian restaurant and Irons family member wannabe hanging from a noose, before finally looking back at me. "From what I know of Branson, I'd say you're the only one truly safe if he's in town. And Watson. Possibly Leo and the rest you love, but I wouldn't place money on that."

I wasn't sure if that was an answer or not. "Have you had contact from him? Any threats or otherwise?"

The briefest of sneers curled his upper lip, hinting at those hidden fangs. "The only threats I've had recently were of the Dean Gerber variety, so... not all that impressive, but deadly nonetheless." His charm slid back into place. "Unfortunately, if

Branson is in town, he doesn't offer *me* any protection against Dean."

"Do you need it?" I narrowed in on his eyes, searching. "Do you need protection from Dean, from Branson?"

Whether intentional or not, Angus didn't hide the steel or the hint of arrogance that flashed. "I can handle myself, thank you for your concern."

I took another tactic. "I think Branson struck a deal with Simone to turn in members of the Irons family. He might pose a threat for you that way."

"Though I know of Branson's reputation, I never had any dealings with the man. Besides, I told you last time, Fred. I'm not part of the Irons family." Anger again, and then... was I reading him correctly? Sadness? "Like you, I was betrayed, lied to. Just as the whole town was. Beulah Gerber has been my friend for decades. My dear, dear friend. She wasn't who I believed her to be. Wasn't who any of us believed her to be."

His words from our last conversation flitted in the back of my mind—*I've discovered that gold, at least—or wool, actually—will not betray you. But even those you count as family, not only can, but will. It's just a matter of time.*

Despite myself, I took a step back. Maybe it

should've been obvious long before, but it was sunshine-bright in that moment. "You struck a deal with Simone. *You* betrayed Beulah."

Leo shot me a wide-eyed glance but didn't say anything.

"Like I told you before, Winifred. Beulah wasn't who I believed her to be." Again there seemed to be sadness in his eyes. "*I* was the one betrayed after all these decades. Not her."

The truth of his words was evident. However, it was *his* truth. *His* perspective of reality, not *the* truth.

"So..." Maybe it didn't matter, and maybe it was pushing my luck. Though I didn't think he would hurt me, I instinctively took a step forward and then to the side, partially blocking Watson in a protective stance. It didn't do much good as Watson, true to his stubborn nature, peered around the edge of my skirt. "So are you in danger with Branson in town, or is it a case of strange bedfellows?"

"The man is handsome, but no, no bedfellow for me. You've met my type." He winked, making a joke of the literal interpretation while reminding me of his relationship with the young and gorgeous Alexandria, killed at Baldpate Inn. One more murder tied to the Irons family. "And as I've already stated, regardless of Branson's intentions, or Dean's for that matter, trust me. I'm in no danger." He took a step forward and reached out as if to touch my face.

Leo sidestepped, moving in front of me just as I had with Watson. There was no need for words or even a snarl to sense the fangs my own park ranger possessed.

Angus was completely nonplussed, barely spared Leo a glance, though he dropped his hand. "I was merely going to thank you for your concern for my safety, Winifred. Believe me, it is well and intact."

"You got rid of the head of the Irons family so you could take her place." Maybe I should have felt in danger by saying what I suddenly knew without a shadow of a doubt to be true, but I didn't.

Clearly not on the same page as me, Leo tensed and readied in preparation. Behind me, Watson issued a little growl, feeding off Leo's reaction.

Again Angus merely smiled, but that time a confused expression crossed his face. "Winifred, my dear... as I have said countless times, you are smart and clever—honestly, borderline brilliant in some areas—but that's a rather outlandish accusation, don't you think? Ask Simone, read *The Chipmunk Chronicles*, look at any news website worldwide. How could I lead what doesn't exist? The Irons family has fallen." He took a couple of steps back and glanced at the door. "Now... I'm more than willing to give you as much time as you'd like, but... do you mind if I reopen for business? This much wool doesn't sell itself."

Despite the amazing sleep the night before, as Leo, Watson, and I drove home, exhaustion settled over me. We'd stayed late chatting with Katie at the Cozy Corgi, and the massive plate of cookies she sent with us felt like a tray of bricks on my lap. Even as my body began to shut down, my mind continued to whirl. There would be no sleep that night, either.

"Gotta turn off your brain, love." Without taking his eyes off the road, Leo placed a hand on mine as we turned into the relatively new development of mini-McMansions that preceded the little trail into the woods leading to my cabin. "I can feel it doing marathons over here."

From the back seat, Watson whimpered, though whether in agreement or anticipation of seeing Barry, who knew?

"I know you're right. I'm spinning in complete

circles." The answer hit me suddenly—I hadn't sat down and read a book by the fire in days. But it almost always worked, getting lost in a story while my brain was distracted enough to snap a few puzzle pieces together on its own. Relaxation washed over me, and I grinned at Leo. "After dinner I think I'll read a bit."

"Chances are you'll have a couple of new answers before bed." He squeezed my hand before letting it go. "Barry is making dinner, remember?"

"Oh right... So vegetarian it is." I glanced at the plateful of cookies. "That's good. We'll need some extremely healthy food to make up for eating every crumb of these piles of chocolate."

All plans of a quick and easy dinner followed by getting lost in a book by the fire fled as we exited the surrounding forest to see that Mom and Barry's van wasn't the only vehicle parked in front of my little cabin.

Leo chuckled. "You think they told Percival and Gary that *Barry* was cooking when they invited them over?"

I couldn't answer for a few seconds, physically feeling the loss of my reading-time retreat. "I love my family. Deeply." With a sigh I looked over at Leo.

"Do you think I can ask them all to just leave. We have no idea when or if Dean will get arrested. They can't stay forever."

"Have you met your mother?" Leo cocked his eyebrow at me as he shifted into Park. "She's just as stubborn as you."

Watson seemed to be experiencing his own inner turmoil as we walked toward the front door, frolicking one moment in clear anticipation of seeing Barry, then offering his classic corgi disapproval glare toward Percival's car. He didn't dislike my uncle, necessarily. I think it was more a case of there only being so much of the spotlight the two divas were willing to share.

"Surprise, we decided to have an extra spades night." Mom greeted us at the door. "We thought the distraction would be helpful."

Hoping to distract from my probably less-than-convincing smile, Watson decided to go with unfettered joy as he burst through the front door, rocketing toward Barry so quickly he yanked his leash completely out of my hand. Though I was ready to have my simple, quiet evenings return to normal, Watson would be a little devastated when his nights didn't contain both Leo and Barry.

"And surprise!" Percival called out from the kitchen where he was attempting to arrange my little seafoam-green table with six place settings. "Not a single dead animal to be found, save for yet *another* steak wasted on the Royal Highness, Queen Sheds-a-Lot." Though his words were embedded with scorn, there was a touch less vitriol in Percival's tone than he usually displayed at Barry's creations. If I had to wager a guess, I'd bet he was secretly starting to enjoy the meals. Barry was a good enough cook that even the most voracious omnivore left his vegetarian offering feeling satiated.

"Barry..." I offered a tired smile to where my ever tie-dye-clad stepfather greeted who might very well be his favorite grandchild. "You can't keep giving Watson steaks. One, it's expensive, and two, he's going to absolutely refuse to eat once you leave."

Percival snorted from the kitchen. "Right, like that fat thing has ever refused to eat."

"Oh, hush." Mom swatted the air toward her brother as she joined him in the kitchen. "So rude."

I paused, inspecting the three of them. Though their words were light, I sensed a heaviness, a tension. Even Barry's fuchsia and lime tie-dye couldn't quite mask the gray pallor over his features.

"What's going on?" Though I addressed all three of them, I walked toward the kitchen door and settled on Mom as she turned around from her spot at the stove. "Did something happen?"

"No, dear." Confusion flitted over her face but smoothed quickly enough. "Nothing's wrong." She shrugged and turned back toward the stovetop. "Other than we're all concerned, of course. No news about Dean. I'm ready for this to be done. Finally."

"Where's Gary?" Leo joined me, and I could tell he picked up on the same vibe as me.

"Oh, he's doing a quick appraisal of an estate. He should be here any moment." Before I could ask why Percival hadn't taken part in it, he looked around me and yelled into the living room, "Barry, get in here. This tofurkey bananalana dingdong fake roast thing looks like it's separating. Come fix it."

"Bananalana..." Barry muttered, but he squeezed past me into the kitchen.

Watson stayed right on his heels, though he shot a quick adoring glance up toward Leo on his way.

On cue, the sound of another car approached, and everyone stiffened, save Watson, who'd already abandoned Barry to travel toward Mom when she opened the oven to check on the steak.

I laughed out a sort of sigh. "Good grief. We've

all got to quit being so tense. That's obviously Gary. If Dean was going to attack, or Branson, they'd hardly drive up."

"Branson!" Mom yipped and released the door of my mint-green 1960s-style oven so it slammed, making us all jump. "What do you mean Branson?"

"I think it's good that he's here." Gary's deep voice was calm and seemed more at ease than the other members of my family, though with his large ex-football-player build, he was easily the most crammed at my small kitchen table. "If we're worried about Fred's safety, even though Branson's one of the bad guys, he'll be more protection for Fred."

Mom chewed her lip, which was the only thing she'd chewed since sitting down to dinner a few minutes before, while listening as Leo and I explained about Branson. "In theory, yes. But at some point, the kind of love, or obsession, really, that Branson has for Fred will turn. That's the nature of it. Maybe that's already happened, maybe it hasn't. But either way, he's just as dangerous as Dean."

"Exactly." Leo nodded definitively at Mom and glanced at me. For a second, it looked like he was trying to hold back but then allowed himself. "You see that, right?"

"Yes. I do." I could hear the truth of it in the sound of my voice, and both Leo and Mom looked reassured. And I *did* feel that way. Although, while I would never classify Branson as safe again, for some reason I didn't feel like we'd crossed that line—not yet.

"Well..." Gary shrugged and looked at me, though he addressed the table. "If he's here, why? No way that's a coincidence with the Irons family falling."

"We think he's the one who killed all the Irons family members the night before Beulah's arrest," Leo answered for me. "And no, definitely not a coincidence."

Gary took the next leap almost instantly. "And he must've had something to do with it, with the Irons family arrests. Maybe he turned informant."

"He did." I had played around on the edges of that theory, driven close to it and then evaded, but as Gary spoke, just as it had earlier in the afternoon with Angus, everything clarified. Despite Gary being the one who made the assertion, I looked at Leo. "Branson and Angus teamed up, bedfellows, like I suggested to Angus. *They* sold out the Irons family to Simone."

"Fred!" Mom gasped in shock. "Angus! Think what you're saying. That he's been part of the Irons family this whole time. Not only that, but he helped Branson murder all those people?"

Percival paused in his cutting of the meatless roast, which he'd not offered a solitary complaint over. "No way. Angus isn't..." He shrugged. "That's so outrageous I can't even finish the thought. Just... No."

Barry scrunched up his nose as if considering, but stayed quiet, lost in thought.

Gary looked between the three of them. "What are you talking about? *Beulah* was just arrested for being the founder of the Irons family. *Beulah!* I find that a lot harder to believe than Angus being involved. Granted, I can't see him as a killer, but neither could I with Beulah."

Percival was dismissive. "That's because you haven't known Angus as long as us."

"They've both been part of the Irons family for years, this *whole* time. Beulah *and* Angus." I reached across the table and took Mom's hand, hurting for her, with all that it implied. The people she'd known her whole life were directly responsible for her husband's murder, even if they didn't pull the trigger themselves. "I'm sorry, Mom. Beulah and Angus *are* Irons family. Whatever deal he struck with Simone is getting Angus off the hook."

"Fred..." Tears brimmed in her eyes, and Barry slipped an arm over her shoulders, pulling her close. After a shaky breath, she tried again. "The Irons family is gone. Finally. You told me the other night you'd let this go. That you'd live! And that was *before* the Irons family was even gone, but they are now. It's over." She lifted a hand in the air and let it fall back to the table weakly. "The things you're saying right now. Not only that Angus is involved, but that he's somehow corrupted an FBI agent, so he stayed free?" Her gaze flitted around the table, searching for help, searching for agreement. "Maybe it was Dean. Maybe he turned on his grandmother." A tear finally rolled down her cheek and she wiped it away.

Guilt cut through me. She'd been through so much, so, so much. Over the past several days it'd been nonstop. Not only was she worried about me, but I was certain she was reliving the horrible, dark time after Dad's murder. I didn't need to drag her through all of it again. She was right, though. I had promised I'd let it go. And while I was going to break that promise, and would figure it out, I didn't have to rub it in her face as I did so.

Watson popped up, shoving himself between Mom and Barry, looking at him expectantly.

Barry chuckled and ruffled the fur between Watson's foxlike ears. "Finished your steak, huh?"

"Here." Percival made a show of lifting his plate in the air and then sliding out from the table. "Have this. Although you won't find an ounce of meat in it."

Despite the heaviness in the room, I laughed as Watson's eyes went utterly saucer-wide, and he gaped at Percival with a nearly human expression of shock.

"Oh, calm down." Percival glowered at him. "I'm not nearly as horrible as you think I am."

Without commentary on that, Watson disappeared under the table and got lost in making a long series of extremely unappetizing sounds. And from the frequent belches that accompanied, he didn't notice the absence of meat.

The distraction helped, and I was able to find a pleasant bunny trail to help change the subject. "Did you hear the news about Simone's goodbye party?"

"I did!" Percival latched on to the topic, as well as my hand as he reached out and grabbed it. It might've been his desire to have a distraction, but more likely just his love of gossip. "The Pink Panthers have teamed up with Carla to have a goodbye party for Simone tomorrow night." He cackled. "I plan on showing up early. Ethel Beaker is going to die deaths that her daughter-in-law and Delilah Johnson are taking over the Koffee Kiln for a party. I only wish I had a Pink Panthers jacket to wear for the occasion."

I only had a moment to be impressed that Carla would take part in the party when she was so clearly hurt by Simone before Gary snorted. "Just wear your pink silk bathrobe, that should suffice."

"Don't think I won't!" The smile that spread over Percival's face was equivalent to the joy of a thousand children on Christmas morning. "Oh... don't think I won't!"

Gary beamed affectionately at his husband and gave a little shake of his head. "Now... Ethel Beaker. If there was anyone in town I had money on being a secret member of the Irons family, she was it."

"I was having that same thought when I was in the Koffee Kiln the other day." I couldn't help but laugh. "Maybe she was too obvious."

. . .

A few hours later, after a couple of crowded rounds of spades, my uncles left, and Mom and Barry retreated to the guest room. Though I wasn't curled up by the fire with a book, I had something just as good. Leo and I were nestled together on the old driftwood bench on the front porch, a plate of chocolate chip cookies at my side, a blanket wrapped around us, and sharing a massive mug of hot chocolate as Watson snored underneath.

The cool night was crisp and cloudless, skies so clear that not only did innumerable stars twinkle, but the depths of the Milky Way radiated through, at once making me feel limitless and so very small.

We'd been silent for a long time, just enjoying the stars, the swaying of the trees, and the comforting power of the towering mountains. However, when Leo spoke, it was clear his attention wasn't lifted heavenward as mine had been but lost in the dark forest. "You think he's out there right now? Watching us?"

From the lack of worry in his tone and the hint of gravel, I didn't have to ask if he meant Dean or Branson. "Maybe."

Leo wrapped me tighter in his embrace and didn't speak again for several minutes. "Katie and Joe are making the right decision. Even if they are moving fast, life is short, uncertain."

I hesitated, started to twist so I could look into his face, but didn't want to break the contact so continued to stare out at the night. "Well, Joe hasn't asked her *yet*." A little warmth trickled in at the mental image of my next thought. "Nor has Katie asked *him* yet, for that matter."

Leo laughed, relaxing somewhat. "I can see her doing that. I can see Joe loving it."

"Me too."

Several more minutes passed before Leo spoke again, and though his tone was still warm and soft, there was a hint of trepidation. "Would it bother you if I said I want to be the one to propose?" He rushed on suddenly. "It's not like I think it's wrong or insulting or anything for a woman to ask a man. But..."

I swiveled then, knocking the mug so some of the hot chocolate spilled on the floor and the corner of the blanket slid over my shoulder and down my back. I barely noticed, and I kissed him. There was no thought of Dean or Branson in the woods. No thoughts of the Irons family—only love, right then, right there, and that moment. Only the hopes and dreams of a gentle and beautiful future with him as we built our life together. Finally I pulled back, meeting his gaze, barely visible to the shadows. "I don't think it would be wrong or insulting either, but personally, I'd rather be asked."

A smile curved his lips, and he gave a little nod before reaching around me to adjust the blanket before pulling me back into a long, long kiss.

SIXTEEN

If there was ever a time to not go off half-cocked and without a plan, I was in the middle of it. As a result, I opted to use the day to let things simmer and percolate. With the exception of Dean, to my knowledge, there was no immediate danger, so there was time.

I started with another morning stroll through the woods with Leo and Watson, where we stumbled upon a small herd of elk, which wasn't uncommon in the slightest. There was no hide nor hair, nor footprint, of Branson or Dean or any other big bad bogeyman. And with the promise to Leo that I wouldn't go traipsing around downtown searching for clues—at least not without letting him know in advance—I convinced him to not call off work for the second day in a row. I had to dampen my tendency to resist being told what to do. All it took was to put myself in his shoes and know that I'd be making similar demands. Probably more.

After a dirty chai... okay... *two* dirty chais... and a spinach-and-feta croissant, which since it had spinach I figured counted as a salad, I left the bakery when the locals began their breakfast rush. Sometimes listening to gossip or tossing around theories helped to figure things out. But it wasn't what I needed, so I wandered down to the bookshop and into the mystery room. We had no customers, and Ben occupied himself on the computer near the cash register as I got to work pondering how to arrange the new shipment of mystery novels.

To my surprise, barely five minutes passed before I heard a familiar little plop onto the fabric behind me, and I turned to see Watson doing his typical spin on his fancy ottoman in front of the fire, preparing for naptime.

With a leatherbound edition of *Sherlock Holmes* in my hand—I'd splurged for an expensive collector's edition set, complete with artfully frayed edges of the pages; even if they never sold, I'd get a thrill with them just sitting in their glory in the mystery room—I walked around the portobello lamp and the antique sofa to perch on the edge of Watson's ottoman.

He'd already curled up into a ball, so he shot me a glare as my weight shifted his position slightly.

I chuckled and stroked his fur, further annoying

him. "Thank you for joining me. I figured you'd spend the day in your apartment."

He grunted, nuzzled my hand with his nose for all of one and a half seconds, then grunted again—that time a very clear, *buzz off, Mom, sleep to be had.*

Being the obnoxious mother I was, I leaned down, pressed a kiss to his forehead, and ruffled his fur for good measure before standing.

He chuffed after me as I returned to the shelves.

For the next couple of hours I got completely lost in the new arrangement of books. I knew it was simpler just to put them all up in alphabetical order, but I didn't. I broke them into so many sections that most people would think I was crazy. There were so many types of mysteries to be read, I figured I might as well celebrate it. And the fact that I'd picked out so many that I had yet to read sent a comforting thrill through me. With the long nights of fall and winter coming on, I was well-stocked and prepared for a lot of happy moments by the fireplaces in the mystery room and my cabin.

And sure enough, as I pondered the cozy mystery section and wondered if simply dividing up contemporary and magical cozy mysteries was enough, or if I wanted to break them down into further subgenres where the witch section was separated from the vampire, and the ghost-themed separated from enchanted cats, things began to click. While there weren't new revelations, nor based in any real facts that I'd uncovered, a story began to solidify in my mind of how things had gone down.

Judging from the last several conversations I'd had with Angus, things had soured between him and Beulah. Actually, I'd gotten that sense from Beulah herself. I'd forgotten, but she'd referred to Angus as recently going senile. Though I wasn't certain, I had a feeling it had to do with Ebony, or maybe Dean. Maybe Angus hadn't approved. Or perhaps he'd insulted her grandchildren and Beulah had cut him off. Whatever reason, the result was the same—a seismic rift between two life-long friends.

I wasn't sure about Branson. When he confessed to me about being part of the Irons family, he made it very clear he wasn't certain of all involved, a claim that was backed up with everything we found out over and over again about the Irons family—how their methods of secrecy protected them for decades. Had he known about Beulah? Branson hadn't been aware that Angus was part of the Irons family. At least he claimed to not be sure when I asked him when I'd first begun to suspect the elegant old knitter. But clearly Branson had decided that Angus was, and that he was a threat, given that Branson had left Raul's body in Knit Witt to taunt him. Whatever the case, it looked like they had joined forces to bring Beulah down. If not, Branson would've taken Angus out at the same time he'd killed the rest of the Irons family members in town.

I paused at that thought. *Had* Branson killed the rest of the local Irons family members? Or just certain ones? And if he only selected those six households, then why? What was the criteria that led to their executions?

The bigger question was... what were they planning next?

And Dean... where was he? How big of a threat was he to me really, to those I loved? Whatever plan Branson and Angus had concocted, if I was correct, Dean wasn't part of it. I didn't think Angus was faking how much he detested Beulah's grandson. That thought led to another one. While I couldn't judge Dean's intelligence, surely he was aware of the coup that had transpired. He would know I wasn't the one who did that, so maybe he wasn't after me at all? There were much bigger fish to fry. As Simone had said, the world didn't revolve around me. Neither did the Irons family, even if I had let it consume me so much in recent years.

Someone cleared their throat behind me at the exact same moment Watson growled.

I turned, my heart giving a leap.

Simone Pryce stood in the doorway, the light streaming through the windows at her back and the fire burning in front of her illuminating her in radiant glow. She lifted both hands toward Watson. "I come in peace, pup." She looked over at me, voice unusually soft. "May I come in?"

"Of course." I gestured to the antique sofa. "Care to sit... do you need—" I nearly asked if she wanted a pastry from the bakery, then remembered her health-conscious lifestyle and her Barbie-doll figure. "—um, a coffee?"

"No, I'm fine, thank you." She took me up on the offer to sit, however, perching casually on the edge of the sofa and giving a wary glance toward Watson.

I joined her and patted Watson's fluffy behind. "It's okay. We're okay."

"He has every reason to treat me like that after the way I left things yesterday." Simone cleared her throat, glanced at him again, then focused on me. "I didn't want to leave town like that, to have our final interaction be so... ugly."

I hadn't expected that. "Well, to be fair, things are a little tense and life-and-death at the moment."

"Isn't it always with you?" She chuckled, easing back a little into the sofa. "And with me, for that matter."

"Touché." I grinned, and with a final pat on Watson's rump as he finished his growl and his eyes turned sleepy, I also settled back into a more relaxed position. I wasn't sure where to go. Was I allowed to ask questions, should I push things again?

Simone, as was usual, guided the conversation. "I also wanted to make sure you know that you're invited to the going-away party tonight." Again she lifted a hand. "Although there's no pressure to either. But I wanted to extend the invitation. You're more than welcome."

"I'd love to be there. Of course." Some of the warm feelings I'd had for Simone returned.

She leaned forward, lowering her voice to a mock whisper. "I will ask that you don't bring any of Katie's baking. I don't think Carla can handle anything else."

I burst out a laugh at that, a real one. "Deal." Only then did I notice that not only was Simone *not* in her FBI uniform—she was wearing her silk Pink Panthers jacket. For some reason, the pink sheen sparked a little pain in the center of my chest. "You actually like it here in Estes, don't you? You like the people."

"I do." She nodded and surprised me when her voice caught. "I've been friends with Carla for a while, but we've grown closer. Just because she never knew all of me, doesn't mean our friendship wasn't... isn't real." She sounded as if she'd either had that conversation with Carla or was preparing. "And I do truly love Delilah and the rest of the Pink Panthers." Her smile grew wry. "I didn't think I would at first. I thought Delilah was nothing more than... well..."

"We all made that mistake with Delilah." I couldn't help but reach out and pat Simone's knee. "Luckily, I think Delilah likes it that way."

Another laugh. "She really does."

"You could stay. Couldn't you? Or..." I debated for a heartbeat. I could just let this be simple, end things pleasantly between us. But I was still Winifred Wendy Page, for better or worse. "Or are Angus and Branson demanding you have to leave?"

Though she flinched a little, Simone didn't seem angry or even flustered. "No. It would be nice to stay, but I want to go. I meant what I said yesterday, even if I said it to you when I was upset. Helping bring down the Irons family, being the one to bring down

Beulah, is a huge boon for my career. I'm not letting that go."

And still I pushed. "If Angus has something on you, or Branson, then you'll forever be in their pocket. You'll have no choice but to be a dirty FBI agent. Sooner or later."

Though her lips tightened, her tone remained relatively calm. "I won't be in *anyone's* pocket. *Ever*." She shook her head, her trademark coils chiming in her braids, and as ever, making Watson growl from his place on the ottoman. "That brings me to the other thing I want to say. I admire you. I've researched enough and been involved with the Irons family history to have researched your father. He was a good cop, a great detective. And he'd be proud of you."

Of all the things I hadn't expected, that hit me out of left field, and my throat clenched so I could barely whisper a raspy, "Thank you."

She waved it off. "In that vein, especially with how I was the other day, I feel like I owe you something." She sighed. "Don't get your hopes up, because I failed. But I wanted to let you know I tried." Before I could ask what she meant, Simone marched on. "Beulah is out of my hands, obviously. She's already in Denver, she won't stay there for very long either. But I requested the higher-ups to ask a particular question during one of her rounds of interrogation."

I felt my eyes grow wide, and though she already said she'd failed, I was desperate for the answer as I thought I knew what she was going to say.

"With the minutiae around Beulah starting the Irons family, how it was named, her children's involvement, all of that, I already knew before she was taken in. Those details had been"—she winced—"procured by other means."

I was willing to bet that meant shared by Angus when he'd turned traitor on Beulah, but I kept my mouth shut.

"I know you've been asking about that photo Ebony sent you, the one with your great-grandmother, your parents, Beulah, and her husband. I had them ask about her, about Evelyn Oswald, to see if she had any connection at all to what Beulah built."

"And...?" I couldn't help myself, breathing out the word before Simone had a chance to finish a thought.

Again she shook her head. "Like I said, I don't have anything to offer you. Beulah refused to answer. From what I understand, she's refusing to answer *anything* during interrogation. Even refusing to eat. Apparently hunger and speaking strike in one." She offered another smile. "But I wanted you to know that I tried."

"Thank you." I meant it with every fiber of my being. Ultimately, it didn't matter. My great-grandmother was long gone, before I'd been born. The past was in the past. Simone was sitting right in front of me—my concern should be for her. "Simone, if... if I can help. You know, with whatever... *whoever*"—might as well try to ease into it— "has something on you and is keeping you from looking into who really killed all those people the other night, instead of pinning it on Dean, I will. You're a good cop. I want you to stay that way. Please don't—"

"That's not why I came to see you. Don't worry, I'll *always* be a good cop." She stood, but instead of the sharp sting of anger I had expected, there was a hint of sadness. "Will I see you tonight?"

I sighed, getting up, but smiled. "Definitely."

"Good." She grinned at Watson. "I know Carla doesn't like dogs in the Koffee Kiln, but... bring your sidekick, okay?"

Percival, in fact, did *not* wear his pink dressing gown to Simone's going-away party, though I doubted that indicated he didn't have one. Instead he lifted his scarecrow-long arm, covered in his trademark boysenberry faux-fur coat sleeve, and waved as Leo, Watson, and I entered the Koffee Kiln after our walk from the Cozy Corgi. Not that he could see Watson through the sardine-packed crowd. I thought I could make out Barry beside him, which probably meant Mom was there as well, though there was no way I could see her through all the much taller heads and shoulders between us. Another scan of the room and I found Gary chatting with Joe and Katie. They didn't notice us.

"Why in the world did they have this here?" Leo gaped around the crowded room, but before I had a chance to reply, he glanced down as Watson lifted to his hind legs and pawed Leo's thigh. Leo reached down with a chuckle and scooped him up. "You know it's crowded when he's actually *asking* to be held."

"I know the feeling." It wasn't a sensation I had typically, unless I was in a really tight space like a cave or trapped under those heavy restraints of a roller coaster, but a wave of claustrophobia whispered in my ear. "And... Carla is why. No matter what she's feeling, Simone is her friend, her business partner. I'm sure she wouldn't consider having the going-away party anywhere else. No matter that the whole town would've showed up anyway, let alone when it's publicly revealed that the resident potter is actually an undercover FBI agent sent to help take down the Irons family."

The Koffee Kiln was a fraction of the size of the Cozy Corgi, if that, considering it was only one floor and probably a third of its space was taken up with the kiln and pottery storage in the back. As a result, people were crammed into the little coffee shop shoulder to shoulder, not even able to pass one another easily, but having to swivel this way and that. It looked like some of the tables had been set up for pottery painting, but that idea was laughable, and several of the pottery pieces had already been knocked off and broken. I couldn't even see the pastry case or the espresso machine through the horde. It was crowded enough that even though Leo and I had just arrived, people were beginning to gather on the sidewalk and on the street.

"Speaking of..." Leo tilted his chin upward, attempting to scan the space as he readjusted Watson in his arms. "Where is Carla, or Simone, for that matter?"

That question was answered almost immediately as Susan shifted her position a few yards away from us, clearing up the view just in time to see a line of pink jackets emerge from the back hallway. All six members of the Pink Panthers entered, and not surprisingly, the crowd parted around them. Also unsurprisingly, though it was Simone's night, it was auburn-haired Delilah Johnson—the leader, newly elected town council member, and all-around throwback to the pinup-girl days—who led the pack, though Simone was right behind her. To my surprise, I realized that Carla was there as well, though not in a pink jacket.

"A bunch of hussies, if you ask me." From out of nowhere, Anna Hanson spoke over my shoulder. She waited to continue until she had Leo's and my attention, then wagged her finger between us. "But I *knew* there was something up with that Simone woman. I knew."

She glanced around to face her husband, Carl, elbowing him lightly with her other arm. "Didn't I, Carl? I told you there was something up with that Simone woman."

"Yep." He nodded, a little smile playing on his lips as his eyes twinkled away. "That's what you said. Carl, you said, there's something up with that Simone woman."

Anna nodded in satisfaction and scowled. "Of course I thought she was probably operating a secret brothel somewhere in the park. I wouldn't have guessed FBI."

Leo barked out a laugh. "Is *that* what you think goes on in the national park?"

She sniffed. "Well, I assure you I *don't* know. A lady such as myself wouldn't dare speculate about such unseemliness." Anna shifted her attention from Leo to Watson, her scowl transitioning to a beaming grin as she cupped Watson's face. "And hello, my sweet love. I never expected to see you here." She shot a reproachful glance my way. "Too crowded for such sweet puppies. I left my little Winston at home. But I wish I'd brought you a treat."

Watson went stiff in Leo's arms, chocolate eyes widening at his favorite word.

"No, dear," Anna cooed at him. "I'm sorry. I'll

bring you one tomorrow. I promise." She leaned in and gave him a kiss on the nose, which, for once, Watson wasn't quick enough to avoid.

Looked like Anna Hanson was in rare form, although when *wasn't* she?

Anna opened her mouth, but stopped with her jaw open as the Pink Panthers headed our way.

"Hello, handsome." Delilah addressed Watson first, though she gave Leo a quick kiss on the cheek before offering me a raised-eyebrow expression. "Simone tells me that you've known for a while about her double life." That perfectly sculpted eyebrow dipped to furrow with its twin as she turned back to Leo. "Which probably means you did as well." She crossed her arms in a playful pout. "I should probably be hurt I wasn't trusted enough to be let in on the secret after all this time, but I'm too pleased with the results to care." She turned to Simone. "And proud." Her smile flashed toward Anna. "Hopefully it proves once and for all that the Pink Panthers have only the most stellar caliber of women as members."

Anna sniffed but didn't offer comment.

"I'm glad you could come." Simone reached around to squeeze my arm as the rest of the Pink

Panthers offered their greetings to Leo and Watson. "Thank you."

"Though I did tell you that dogs are no longer allowed in the Koffee Kiln." Carla broke in before I could respond. There wasn't anger in her tone, just the typical Carla bite, and while her eyes were no longer bloodshot and swollen, sadness cloaked her.

"I invited Watson personally." Simone smiled toward her friend. "He's been a big part of a couple of events I've experienced here. It only seemed right."

"I suppose." Carla acquiesced and actually started to reach out to pet Watson. She caught the movement, jerking her hand back the very same moment Watson flinched away from her touch, before she shook her head in apparent amazement at herself. Then her green gaze returned to me, softening, as well as her tone. "Simone tells me that you saved her life, in this very building last year... when that horrible Branson Wexler broke in." She sighed and refocused on me again. "Thank you."

I'd forgotten. How funny, or... maybe not funny at all that so much had happened that watching Branson nearly kill Simone while I demanded he stop was just another blip on the radar. "You don't need to thank me for that."

"Yes. I do." Carla's smile was sincere, and she turned it on Simone, a tear escaping again. She wiped it away and cleared her throat.

"We should make the rounds." I couldn't tell if Simone was giving her friend an out, or herself. Maybe both. Then she addressed Delilah. "Catch up with you in a bit?"

"Of course," Delilah responded while shaking out her long fall of hair, before offering a wink at Carl. "Our very first town council meeting together is next week. I'm looking forward to it." She finished with another wink before turning away. Behind her, Nadiya, a fellow park ranger, rolled her eyes toward Leo, and shrugged her pink jacketed shoulders as if saying, *what are you going to do?*

I'd learned to deeply respect Delilah and counted her as a friend, but she was still herself. She enjoyed being the center of attention, causing a scandal, and had no problem flaunting her affairs in people's faces. However, those particular winks were doubtlessly to get under Anna's skin and had no intention of raising Carl's blood pressure.

Expecting an outburst, or slap at Carl, I looked to Anna, who was bright red. Instead of either of her typical reactions, she took a deep breath, let it out slowly, and gave a dignified nod before addressing

Leo, Watson, and me. "I'm so excited for that town council meeting. Finally having Carl Hanson on there!" She swatted at me, smacking my arm in a gossipy yet stinging manner—apparently needing to take it out somewhere. "He's going to do *marvelous* things for this town. You just wait and see." Not requiring a response, she took Carl's hand in hers and yanked him away. "Come on, Carl. Let's go see Percival."

Utterly beaming like he'd just hung the moon, Carl waved goodbye toward us and practically floated on cloud nine as he was dragged away.

"Do you think when we're married for that many years, we'll act like that?" Leo laughed as he looked after them.

"Maybe." I chuckled with him. "And while I'm very confident in you and in us, I'm not too proud to admit that I'm thankful Delilah is our friend and doesn't flirt with *you* like that."

Readjusting Watson yet again as he turned, Leo lovingly pressed his shoulder against me, as his arms were occupied. "Even if she did, I've already got my own redheaded bombshell."

A couple of minutes passed before I realized, yet again, that things were a foregone conclusion at that point. How easily we'd spoken of being married for decades like the Hansons. At the thought, I glanced over at Katie and Joe. For the first time in our friendship, I felt a twinge of jealousy that she was probably soon going to receive a proposal. The feeling both surprised and pleased me. And... kind of made my heart speed up, at knowing I'd get one too, sometime.

Maybe feeling my gaze, Katie looked my way and waved us over to where they were talking with the Pacheco twins and Nick's girlfriend, Lavender.

"How much longer? Bakers aren't supposed to stay up this late. Nick already went home and he's, like, a decade younger than me." Katie glanced at her cell phone. "I don't want to be rude and miss Simone's speech, but... early morning pastries don't bake themselves." She stiffened, eyes narrowing as her brown spirals danced around her face. "Maybe that's Carla's ploy. That way she can have the majority of the breakfast rush when Nick and I run out."

Joe snorted affectionately and shifted so he could wrap his large arms around her. We were taking shelter in the narrow hallway outside the restrooms to give Watson space to move around and offer Leo a break. "I don't think you have to worry about the Koffee Kiln. With this many people tonight, I'm sure they'll be out of product for the morning. It's not like they had much time to prepare for the party in advance."

"It's a whole different ball game when you get them shipped and you simply have to pull your scones from plastic." Still, Katie scowled. "Did you know that a huge portion of premade cakes contain propylene glycol? The very same thing that's found in acrylic paint, shoe polish, antifreeze, brake fluid, and—"

"And..." Joe squeezed her tighter. "We've shifted into Google mode."

Katie wasn't to be dissuaded. "You want to know what's in mine? Flour, sugar, butter, vanilla—from real vanilla beans, mind you—"

"And..." Joe had to stoop so he could continue to hold her and pressed a kiss to the side of her face. "I love you, you little baking, random-factoid freak."

The clatter of shattering ceramic from behind us cut off whatever Katie was about to say.

Leo grunted. "Hopefully Carla is planning on doing something else along with her coffee, other than pottery, with Simone gone. I don't know how many things have been broken tonight, but she's got to be running low."

Over the past hour, the crowd had only

increased, and along with it, the breaking of the Koffee Kiln's supplies as people were jumbled together. Although it wasn't just Simone's pottery pieces waiting to be painted that were being sacrificed. I'd seen more than one of Carla's coffee mugs, plates, or serving trays lost to the night's events as well.

As Katie launched into another diatribe about the benefits of freshly made pastries with a fervor that bordered on religious fanaticism, I stared out into the writhing mass of locals. Not only did Watson have a place to stretch his little legs from our spot in the hallway, but it was easier for me to observe, only having to look around the steady pass of people going back and forth to the restrooms. That preferred vantage point, however, so far had proved a waste. Nothing suspicious had occurred. Angus, at least as far as I'd noticed, hadn't made an appearance. I wasn't certain if that meant something or not. Neither Branson nor Dean had shown up either, not that I'd expected them to. While trickles of claustrophobia came and went, the benefit the cacophony of the goodbye party provided was that it offered a much needed mental break. Other than observing the townspeople, no new theories, puzzle pieces, or answers had made themselves known.

Before Katie had finished her listed dangers of prepackaged foods, Carla cleared a space in front of the espresso machine. From our angle in the hallway, we could barely see, but there was no room to shift over, so I strained to see around those in front. Delilah joined her, and the two of them made a strange pairing as they stood together to address the attendees.

As the crowd slowly quieted when it gradually realized the moment had arrived, Delilah straightened, lifting her chin in preparation to speak.

"Thank you all for coming tonight." Carla spoke first, earning herself a glare from the leader of the Pink Panthers. "As we recently discovered, we've had a hero living among us, a genuine crimefighter and a defender of justice, cloaked as a mere potter."

I'd never heard Carla so effusive before. At another crash of dishes somewhere, she paused and sent a glare out into the void.

Taking advantage of the distraction, Delilah jumped in. "We Pink Panthers have always prided ourselves with having women strong of character, iron will, and the ability to cut their own path through life." With a presidential smile over her gorgeous face, Delilah lifted a hand. "Simone Pryce is the epitome of that. We're so grateful we have the privilege to know her, and for her service not only to this great country, but to our beloved Estes, specifically."

The crowds cheered and clapped at that. But as we joined in, Watson quickly darting underneath my skirts, I wondered how Simone felt about the accolades. There was a price she paid to bring down Beulah, I was certain of it. A price that if it didn't smudge her soul, probably did her badge. This moment had to be bittersweet. Not to mention that it was clear she had some regrets about leaving.

"Simone!" Carla called out again, taking a step in front of Delilah. "Come up. You're the star this evening."

The crowd hushed further, and the silence quickly shifted to awkward when Simone didn't approach Carla and Delilah.

The two women scanned the coffee shop and shared a questioning glance.

Turning around, Carla noticed me in the entrance to the hallway. "Fred... she might've gone to the back room. Will you check, please?"

Both surprised at being called out in front of everyone and Carla's pleasant demeanor toward me, it took just a heartbeat to register. Probably just long enough so I looked awkward. "Of course. Be right back." Turning, I stepped over Watson, taking away his hiding place, and headed down the hallway and past the restrooms.

He followed along at the end of his leash, Leo at his side, even there refusing to let an opening for harm to come my way.

I pushed open the door to the back room. "Simone?" A sense of déjà vu washed over me from a couple of days before. Again the space was empty, and again there was no fire in the kiln. That much seemed normal, until I realized I'd expected to find an overflow of people back here as well, judging from the crashing pottery.

That thought told me what I'd find before I walked all the way in.

From the lowering of Watson's ears and the beginning rumblings of a growl, he realized it the same moment I did.

Motioning Leo to follow—a pointless gesture, considering he was glued to my side at the moment—I walked farther toward the far kiln.

There'd been another murder in the back of the pottery studio over a year before, just a few feet away from where I'd stopped Branson from killing Simone.

That's where we found her body.

Simone lay in a pile of ceramic shards, blood pooling underneath her back. Though it looked like she'd been stabbed a couple of times, judging from where the large knitting needle protruded, the killing blow had been directly to her heart.

Beside her, in danger of getting overtaken by the growing pool of blood—crafted in a similar position to the bagel-sized sleeping Watson I had on my mantle—was a knitted mountain lion... or... a panther, in this case. Even in its miniature form it was lifelike. Or at least would've been, save for its pink hue.

In my years of knowing Detective Susan Green, I lost count of how many times I'd seen her angry, how many times I'd seen her furious. I'd thought I'd come close to seeing the limit of her rage. I'd been wrong, so very, very wrong.

I also thought that the steam coming off the top of an angry person's head in a cartoon was hyperbole. I'd been wrong on that as well—almost.

Susan glared from the corner of our little round table in the corner of the Koffee Kiln, the streetlamps glowing through the window behind her back as she stared murderous eyes at the FBI agents walking back and forth from the coffee shop, bakery portion, and the back room. And though actual steam didn't rise from the top of her head, at some point she'd raked her fingers through her typically slicked-back hair, and as a result her nub of a ponytail had come loose and her brown hair shot out with a mixture of curly poofs and awkward angles. She looked like a deranged, homicidal Albert Einstein, but it softened her somewhat.

We'd been sequestered at the little table for less than a minute, and she already looked on the verge of an aneurysm. "That's nothing more than an insult." Susan gestured to the yellow caution tape one of the FBI agents had secured around the table, as they'd threatened if any of us stepped even so much as a centimeter outside its boundaries we'd be arrested, Susan and Campbell included. "Nothing more than a gross abuse of power."

"I'm surprised they let us stay at all. I figured—" Officer Cabot quelled as Susan's glare shot his way.

"I might press charges." Carla clenched and unclenched her fists over the table, looking nearly as furious as Susan. "Trying to kick me out of my own shop while my best friend is lying—" Her voice broke before she slammed her eyes shut, tears rolling down her face again.

Campbell attempted to put a reassuring hand on her shoulder, but she shrugged him off.

Though we'd not known it, there'd been another FBI agent present during the party, which, in hindsight, made sense. As a result, they'd swarmed the place within three minutes of me discovering

Simone's body, and had the Koffee Kiln cleared of all people nearly as fast, having enough agents to interrogate the guests in record speed before sending them on their way. The showdown between Susan and one of those FBI agents—judging from their interactions, it wasn't their first two-step—had almost been terrifying to watch. As offended as Susan was, I was along Campbell's way of thinking. It only spoke to Susan's fierceness that we were allowed this much space. I'd been doubly shocked that she fought so hard to keep me and Leo, and Watson, as well.

Someone called out from the back room, and the agent, the one who'd just finished fastening the yellow tape, pointed a warning finger at us wordlessly before disappearing down the hallway.

"She couldn't have been back there more than... I don't know..." Carla managed to choke out some words but didn't open her eyes. "Less than three or four minutes. I'd *just* been talking to her. Delilah, too. I don't know why Simone would... She knew we were about to—"

At the next break in her voice, there was a rustling under the table; a moment later, Watson's head poked up and he rested his head on her knee.

I expected her to shove him away, possibly yell. But instead, after a second or two, one of her fists unclenched and she lowered her hand under the table and rested it on Watson's head, before she sighed again with a little tremor.

"It's not Angus, right?" Leo spoke, glancing toward the back room and returning to us when none of the FBI agents emerged. "A *knitting needle*, and Simone's body beside one of his creations? It's too obvious, a clear setup."

"Unless *that's* the point." Campbell darted a glance toward Susan but continued when she didn't shoot any daggers in his direction. "Perhaps he made it look so obvious to throw us off, so we'd think it was too... obvious."

"I can't see Angus stabbing Simone. For one, the strength it would take—" I stopped talking as Carla shuddered. I turned toward her, lowering my tone. "I'm sorry, I wasn't thinking. We don't have to—"

"No." She looked up then, green eyes blazing, one hand still clenched in a fist and the other remaining on Watson's head. "We discuss it. We do whatever it takes to catch whoever did this to her. I don't care who it is."

"Okay." I offered a sympathetic smile with a nod and pushed on. "I don't think Angus would have the strength to stab anyone with a knitting needle, of all things. Especially Simone. She was in phenomenal shape, strong, and trained."

"Unless he had help." Leo's whisper was dark, and his gaze met and held mine.

"Branson..." Susan hissed from across the table.

"No." My answer was too immediate, so I took a second to judge why my gut responded so instantly to that. It was clear enough. "That's not Branson's style. Multiple stabbings and making that production with a knitting needle and the panther. No way."

Leo still hadn't looked away from me. "Branson did a production with Raul's body when he hung it in Knit Witt."

"True." I considered again. I supposed he had. "But that was personal for him, a message to Angus. Would Simone have felt personal? Either way, even then he didn't actually hang Raul, he shot him first. Once, clean and simple."

"So... Dean." Campbell nodded definitively.

Susan sent him an approving nod. "Agreed. And killing Simone was *definitely* personal for him. *She* was the main one who took down his grandmother. Right in front of his eyes. And Dean might've gotten away, but he had to abandon his grandmother to do so, and then watch as his entire family empire fell worldwide."

"That makes sense." Leo let out a long breath, clearly thinking those things as well. "But then why the panther? That's Angus's work, I'd know it anywhere. And clearly for Simone or one of the Pink Panthers. Does that imply Dean is somehow working with Angus? I suppose it's more likely that Dean stole it from—"

"No." Carla spoke up again. "Angus came by before the party. He was so sweet, bragging on Simone, all the work she's done to make the town safer, the risk she took on herself. He apologized for not being able to attend, as he had..." She scrunched up her nose. "I don't remember... something he had to do. Anyway, he gave her that panther as a token of his appreciation and respect. Simone was thoroughly touched. I don't think I've ever seen her so..." Carla blinked and absentmindedly continued to stroke Watson's head. "Oh... I thought..." She looked back and forth between Susan and me, completely leaving out Campbell and Leo. "I thought Simone was touched, overwhelmed by the kindness. She got so quiet, kind of... I'm not sure now. If you all think Angus is somehow involved, maybe she was... afraid?"

Susan sat up straighter, some of that anger at being roped in evaporating in her quest for clues.

"Was Angus ever alone with Simone? Did they go to the back room together?"

"I..." Carla hesitated, still petting Watson. "I don't know. I was busy with preparing for the party, and Jonathan came by about that time so I could tell Maverick good night, since he'd be in bed long before I got home... I just..."

"It's okay," Campbell soothed and again reached out to stroke her back.

That time she let him, and between the officer and the corgi, Carla seemed to ease under their comfort.

Susan and I exchanged glances. "Why would he give her that? A taunt?"

From the sound, Susan's question had been rhetorical, but I answered anyway. "I'm telling you, Angus has something... *had* something on Simone. That's why she is... *was* pinning every murder of that massacre on Beulah and the Irons family, even though it makes no sense."

Carla flinched so hard that Watson scurried back with a yelp. She didn't notice as she snarled at me. "Don't you dare, Winifred Page. *Don't you dare*. Simone has been gone for two seconds, and you're going to besmirch her name, her reputation? She wasn't a dirty cop. She wasn't!"

"I'm sorry, Carla, but you don't know for certain." Somehow, Susan managed to line some sympathy in her bark, then refocused on me. "I've been thinking about that. You're right. Nowhere else, other than Estes Park, was there a mass late-night killing in the areas where members of the Irons family were captured. Only here."

"Which means the people murdered here weren't Irons family." Leo shook his head the moment the words left his mouth, realizing his mistake. "No... it means they weren't a threat to the Irons family. They were only a threat to whoever betrayed the Irons family."

And it clicked, finally. "I didn't need any more proof that Angus and Branson were working together, but if I did, that's it. Angus didn't kill those people, Branson did, like we've said previously. And if what Branson told me before is true, if what Paulie says is true, and what we found from every source— even the questionably reliable ones like Jake's books —when Beulah set up the Irons family organization, her little net of secrets, only letting a few members be aware of each other is what helped keep it all going. So..." Again, I considered just for a second, though I didn't even need that. "Angus cut a deal with Simone and turned on Beulah, turned on the

Irons family, but he needed to get rid of all the Irons family members who personally knew *he* was connected as well."

"Cleaning up in advance." Susan sat back, her muscular arms bulging the sleeves of her uniform as they crossed over her chest. "That's it. Now to prove it."

One of the FBI agents emerged from the back room, and Campbell's whisper was barely audible. "So... does that mean Angus might've killed Simone after all for that very reason. Cleaning up his tracks?" As Leo had done, he answered his own question. "That would seem a little quick, with things having not had time to go to trial yet. I would think he would need Simone alive to help keep his cover."

"Unless she managed to already get an immunity so strong for him that Angus believed she was expendable. Maybe another higher-up in the FBI got on board." Susan threw it out more like a theory than a disagreement.

"Stop it!" Carla smacked the table, making Watson yelp and dart under my skirt, not that she noticed. "Quit acting like Simone was one of the bad guys. She *wasn't*. She would never."

"What do you mean Simone was one of the bad guys?" The agent came over, towering over all of us at the table from the other side of the yellow tape. "What do you know?"

"I said she *wasn't* one of the bad guys, you idiot!" Carla shot upward and slapped the man across his face. "And get out of my shop!"

Half an hour later, Leo, Watson, and I walked back down Elkhorn Avenue toward the Cozy Corgi to get my purse and things we'd left at closing. It was nearly midnight, and the night was clear and beautiful, if more than chilly.

Leo slipped his hand into mine, and there was just a touch of humor in his voice. "You know Susan has to have mixed feelings about making sure Carla doesn't get smacked with assault charges."

"*Especially* since she now has to share every last detail with all those FBI agents in there." I shook my head at my own words. "Although Susan's pretty by-the-book. I'm willing to bet she would've shared it all anyway."

"Yeah, but now she's *forced*. That's a very different thing. Susan will resist that." He squeezed my hand. "One of the ways you two are alike."

"What!" I pulled a fake gasp. "Are you insinuating that *I'm* obstinate and stubborn?"

He chuckled. "Oh no. Wouldn't dream of it."

Chuckling along, I paused just enough to reach down and scratch Watson. "Neither one of *us* are obstinate or stubborn, are we?"

He peered up, his sweet face washed out in the lamplight, but the flash of hope that stated he thought my tone indicated a treat might come his way was crystal clear. When the treat didn't instantly materialize, he grunted and looked back down the street, dismissing me.

"Nope. Not a bit." Leo hummed.

We finished the short walk to the bookshop. Maybe it was the tranquil night, both of us replaying the events, or the utter lack of calm that had come before, or simply working through clues, which allowed neither of us to notice the glow of the mystery room fireplace until I unlocked the door and we stepped inside—until Watson went rigid, then growled.

Out of the darkness, with the light of the fireplace illuminating half of his face while leaving the other in shadow, Branson spoke from his place on my sofa directly under the unlit portobello lamp. "Come on in, you two lovebirds. I brought a tray of cookies down from the bakery, and I made some hot chocolate again, though not as good as yours, Fred.

Although by this point, I'm afraid it's gone cold. You two aren't nearly as quick after a murder as you used to be."

Leo and I both stood, utterly frozen.

Watson continued his growl.

"Calm down, Watson. How many times do I have to tell you that I'll never hurt your mama?" Though I couldn't see it, as we weren't very far from the entrance, I could hear the humor in Branson's tone. "Don't get mad, Fred. I never promised I wouldn't break into the Cozy Corgi and surprise you, just your house." He reached for a cookie and took a bite. "Actually, I don't quite recall the parameters of that promise. Either way, come have some. Katie's skills have improved, which I didn't think possible. These little things are delicious."

"We're not doing this." My voice returned before my body was able to make itself move. Somehow, in some weird loop, hearing the iron in my tone, my lack of fear, actually made me feel that way. "We're not sitting down and having a chat, Branson."

"Fred..." Leo hissed a warning, quiet enough I didn't think Branson could hear.

I ignored him. "What we're going to do is, I'm calling the police, and you're going to run away. Or... stay here and finish the cookies and go to jail for a late-night massacre, among countless other things. I actually like that option better."

"Oh really?" There was amusement in his tone and a strange husky caliber that made my skin crawl. Still holding the cookie elegantly in one hand, he shifted the other in his lap, the firelight glinted off the barrel of a gun aimed toward Leo. "Fred, I offered an invitation because I know you hate being told what to do..."

Leo sidestepped in front of me.

It took all my willpower to remain where I was, to not walk around and stand in front of Leo. "You promised Leo would be safe, remember?"

"Safe is relative." Branson leaned slightly so he could see my face around Leo's shoulder. "I won't *kill* him. But I'll hurt him." He shifted back, addressing Leo. "I have before. How many of your teeth did I knock out with the butt of the rifle?"

Leo straightened, shoulders broadening and chin lifting in defiance.

"How many?" Branson barked as he shot to his feet, the cookie falling and exploding on the floor as the gun swung upward and halted in line with Leo's chest.

Watson went wild, and I barely managed to hold onto his leash as I moved to get in front of Leo. But Leo stuck out an arm, holding me back.

"Stop it." Fear and anger shot through me, and I hit Leo's arm, trying to bat it away. "He's not going to shoot me. He won't even hurt me."

Branson smiled and took several slow steps forward. "But Fred, Leo's not so sure of that, and he fancies himself a hero. So..." A few more steps. "How many teeth was it, Leo?"

Leo's jaw twitched, and I could feel his body tremble.

"You're not sure if I'll hurt her or not, are you?" Branson shifted the gun, lifting it so it was pointed over Leo's shoulder at me.

"Three." Leo hissed the word through those clenched teeth.

The gun stayed where it was. "Did you get them fixed? You're a pretty boy, I'm assuming you did."

"Yes."

"Show me." Branson's smile grew, revealing his own movie-star gleam. When Leo didn't respond, Branson rushed forward several steps, bringing him into the doorway of the mystery room, leaving him completely silhouetted in the firelight at his back. "Show me!"

Leo shifted, and though I couldn't see, I assumed he smiled or grimaced, as a moment later Branson's gun dipped back down toward Leo's chest.

"Exceptional work, from what I can tell." Branson's tone was back to his easy, casual grace. "I wonder if they'd do as good a job the second—"

"Stop it!" That time, I moved far enough to the side that I bypassed Leo's outstretched arm, at the same time wrapping Watson's leash tighter so he didn't move forward at the unexpected slack. "What are you doing? What are you trying to prove? We're not doing this. We're not your puppets." At that point I wasn't certain Branson wouldn't hurt me, or if it was just my temper taking control.

Leo grabbed me, though that time he pulled me to his side instead of behind him, probably aware at this point that I'd fight him as well. Because no matter what, I was certain at the bare minimum I was safer than Leo in Branson's presence.

Nonplussed, Branson sighed. Though I couldn't make out his backlit expression, the disappointment was clear in his tone. "Oh, Fred. Why do you make me tell you what to do? You always did that. If you would just listen. But you always push and push and push." The tone changed again, some of that husky quality returning, making me queasy. "Although they say the very thing you love most about a person is what ends up driving you crazy. I've always loved your strength and determination. Even when it's exasperatingly stupid."

Despite everything, that word made me flinch. Being called stupid would do that to me every time. Branson had never come close to saying anything like that before. Maybe my reaction to it was just that, stupid. But still...

"I'm sorry." Branson lowered the gun the rest of the way instantly, took another step forward, and then stopped, genuine remorse written all over him. "I'm sorry, Fred. I didn't mean to say that. I would never hurt you. Never insult you. I'm sorry."

He was crazy. And while I'd started to realize it during our last interactions, I had to admit that Leo had been right the whole time. I'd never been safe with Branson, not ever. Even if Branson believed he would never hurt me, he would. And... at some point he'd try, though it might destroy him after.

When I didn't respond, Branson sighed again, then moved backward, somehow retaining control and grace even in that movement. He barely had to spare the briefest of glances at the sofa to return to the position he was in before. He gestured toward the tray of cookies. "Come on. Have some. Join me."

So we were back to where we'd started, except more on edge. More refusal would be pointless, and to one degree or another, bloody.

Leo's hand slipped into mine, and he squeezed as he whispered, "It's okay."

Knowing we were powerless, we did as Branson asked, as he commanded. Going so far as to even sit where he told us—me at the end of the antique sofa, opposite him, Leo on Watson's ottoman. I started to pull Watson onto my lap, then pushed him toward Leo. "Here, hold Watson. He'll need you."

Leo started to protest, and even Watson tried to get back to me, but I released him and sat in the same motion, trusting Leo to grab onto him.

He did, and with a glance that held a touch of betrayal, Leo folded Watson to himself, safe and tight.

"Always one step ahead, aren't you, Fred?" Branson was once again half lit by the fire, and he smiled a look of genuine appreciation. "You're right. Leo is a little safer with Watson there. I am less likely to risk hurting Watson than your... boyfriend." The smile faded, and his words hardened. "Show me your hand, Fred. Your left one."

"My—" The flash of confusion vanished instantly, but it took a few more moments to quell my desire to refuse. Then I held out my left hand, palm down.

Branson visibly relaxed. "I knew you weren't married, I would've found proof of that, But I thought maybe..." He glanced at Leo. "What is wrong with you? Slower than frozen molasses." He shook his head. "That's why I'm still in this godforsaken town. I can't trust you to do what needs to be done."

From the expressions colliding over Leo's face, he and I were having similar emotions. However, my confusion turned to a truly wild, irrational fear that I was about to find out Leo was on the same side as Branson and Angus and not following protocol quickly enough. The notion barely had a chance to flit across my mind before I dismissed it. There was no chance of that. None.

"What are you talking about?"

Branson ignored Leo's question and looked back at me. "How are you?"

I dropped my hand and laughed. I couldn't help it. "Seriously? How am I? You're holding us at gunpoint and you ask how I am? Why are you even here? You're—" I started to say insane and barely caught myself.

"I'm still in town because of what I just told Leo." He shot a glare of scorn at Leo before returning to me, softening again. "I'm here tonight to see you. I'd like to find time without him, but clearly that's not going to be possible."

"So it *was* you the other night in the woods?"

"I was certain you'd know it was me. That you'd feel me." His sigh that time reminded me of myself after taking the first long draft of my morning dirty chai. It changed quickly, with another glare, this time filled with utter hate at Leo. "Couldn't even get you alone then."

For a flash I wanted to admit I thought he'd been Dean. Rub it in his face that I did not *feel* his presence, that his heart did not call to mine, as he seemed to be indicating. Instead I got onto things that mattered. "Why would you be outside my cabin right before going to slaughter all those people?"

He brightened, and he made such a picture there by the fire. The last time I'd seen Branson he'd looked older, a little disheveled, like he was on the run, which he had been. But now? Even with a crazed look in his bright green eyes, he was the epitome of tall, dark, and handsome—his black hair classically swept back over his broad brow, just the hint of five-o'clock shadow darkening his chiseled jaw, the classic cable-knit plum sweater over olive-green pants that were probably directly off the rack of some Italian designer. If the devil was beautiful, he'd embody Branson Wexler. "I love how you don't even have to ask if I was the one responsible. You just knew, didn't you?"

I didn't answer.

"How?" Branson wasn't put off by my silence.

"How did you know it was me? Because you felt me in the woods?"

"No." I didn't mean to let the word slip, it just did. But then... really, what did it matter? "It was your style. Clean, efficient. Like you did to Eddie at the Green Munchies right after I moved to town. Like you have to so many people."

He beamed, so thrilled I'd held onto his style of murder.

My stomach turned at how close I'd been to him for that brief while.

"You are truly sick." Leo's quiet voice sounded between us, and from the little twitch of his arms around Watson, I thought he might've experienced the same thing I had, his thoughts rising unbidden to his lips. And like me, he doubled down. "You sit there and practically gloat about the lives you've taken, like it's nothing more than eating a tray of cookies."

Branson glanced his way, not at all insulted. "No. That's just proof you don't understand me or know me. Killing is nothing at all like eating cookies." When he refocused on me, his gaze was quizzical. "Do you know why not? Can you explain to Leo?"

I might not have answered, but I saw the gun tremble in Branson's grip in his lap. He might not even have known he'd had that reaction, which was all the more reason to do whatever we had to do to get out of this. "You kill because it's a job, a means to an end, something you're good at. Not because you love it or even enjoy it all that much."

That time, his sigh held the tinge of ecstasy. "Exactly."

I could feel Leo glance my way, but I didn't look at him, instead remaining focused on Branson. "But you do enjoy the power, and you're proud of your skill."

"True." Branson shrugged one shoulder, retrieved another cookie and took a bite.

If we were going to do this, if we were stuck doing this, then we'd do it by my rules, at least somewhat. I leaned closer, uncomfortably near to Branson, considering the sofa wasn't all that long. "The last time you were in town, you left me with the impression that Angus was on your hit list."

He grinned then closed his mouth as he finished chewing, but apparently didn't mind the turn of questioning. Finally, after swallowing, he responded with a question of his own. "Raul?" With a chuckle, he didn't wait for confirmation. "You read that gift correctly. But..." Branson shrugged again. "Circumstances change. Strangely, it's surprising how often a mortal enemy suddenly becomes an ally."

"What made Angus turn on Beulah?" Might as well go for the gold if he was in the mood to answer questions.

Branson laughed and rolled his eyes. "You know, I have to admit, I've come to admire that old knitting grandma over the last few months. The man's got class, exquisite taste, and a quite devious, devious mind." Another eye roll. "But it's embarrassing that he didn't predict things ending up this way decades ago. Blood always wins out. Always. Any fool knows that."

Part of me was surprised Branson was willing to even pretend an answer, and it was enough of a clue that the leap was easy. One I'd pretty much made already. "Ebony and Dean."

He nodded. "Ebony and Dean."

At Branson's laughter that time, Watson growled, earning himself a glance. Leo cooed into his ear.

I pulled the attention back to me. "My guess is that Beulah was giving her grandchildren something she'd promised to Angus?"

It worked. "That's the other thing that's embarrassing about the old codger. He *only* asked for

Colorado. That's it. After decades of working with her, of being an equal in many ways to her, outside of actually being family, *all* he asked for was one measly state in which to rule." Branson flicked a hand, terrifyingly the one holding the gun. "And she couldn't even give him that. It makes no sense, on either side. Angus should've seen it coming. And Beulah… should've seen the inevitable betrayal—all she had to give up was *one* state. And in truth, I bet she could've talked Angus down to just Estes Park." He laughed again. "But the minute she brought in that airhead Ebony, Angus knew it was over. He reached out to me within a week. Then when Dean arrived… well…"

I thought he was done, and I'd thought my distraction worked, but then he glared over at Leo.

"*That's* why I'm still here, little Boy Scout." He cast an intentionally slow, dismissive glance over Leo's body and returned it to his eyes. "That's why I'm still in Estes. Because you wouldn't be able to do your job. When it comes down to it, you aren't capable of doing what needs to be done. No matter your thuggish past." Branson actually shot a glare at me then. "I didn't really think giving you that information about Leo's secrets would change things, but I had hoped. You do have your weaknesses, clearly."

Leo provided the distraction for me that time, and proved quicker than me as well, as I hadn't understood Branson's meaning. "I won't let Dean touch Fred."

The grit in Leo's voice only highlighted the unhinged quality of Branson's laughter that time. "Oh please." He gestured wildly with the gun again, that time toward me. "You can't even keep her safe from *me*. Granted, Dean's a lot less of a threat than I would ever be if I chose. He's a killer, a good one, but not very adept at improvising a plan."

"You're staying in town to protect me?" I gaped at Branson, and though I almost felt humor in his claim, it did nothing more than chill my blood. "You're staying here to guard me from Dean Gerber?"

He merely cocked a thick, perfectly formed eyebrow. "You saw what he did to Simone. From what I hear, Dean got a little carried away..." Branson pulled a dramatic face, then glowered. "I was looking forward to her, sooner or later, but he got the job done." Another laugh. "With a knitting needle, no less! Cute." He tapped the gun to his temple. "See what I mean, the boy can't think on his own, if he really believed that would set up Angus."

"He'll betray you, you know." I needed to get back on my turf. "Angus."

"Of course he will." Branson lowered the gun, letting it rest casually in his lap once more, and finished the cookie with another bite. He took his time chewing and swallowing, then picked up a napkin, which he must've brought down with the cookies, and wiped his crumb-free lips. "And *Angus* has no problem thinking on his own. He knows I'll betray him as well, if agreements aren't kept. Which..." Branson seemed to consider. "He *might* actually follow through with his end of the bargain. I can't quite tell. But I think... maybe."

Leo beat me to the punch but was on the same page as me. "The two of you are going to replace the Irons family."

The distasteful glare suggested Branson had forgotten Leo was present, or at least capable of fancying himself an equal. He studied Leo for a minute. "You are handsome. Younger than me by a decade or so. But I don't think that's it." He looked toward me. "Is it *really* because he's *good*? You're a smart woman, Fred. Surely you realize that's just a construct. Just a set of rules society puts on you to control. That even those, the rules of what makes someone good, changes over time."

I opened my mouth to respond but stopped, remembering Branson was more off-balance than I'd believed and knowing I could never pretend to be safe in his presence from that point on. If I told him again that I hadn't left him for Leo, but I'd merely left Branson because of who he was—even before I knew all of his secrets, that he still wasn't the man I wanted to be with—I wasn't sure what his reaction would be. One, two, or three bullets might get fired. Or... he might just shrug it off. The fact that I wasn't certain and didn't understand him quite that well scared me to death. I stayed silent.

It was the right move.

Branson stood, dusting off his pants, though there wasn't a crumb on them either, and glanced at Watson, who never stopped his undercurrent rumbling growl. "Always good to see you, handsome chap. Glad you're taking such good care of your mama. Clean up the crumbs of that cookie I dropped, please." Then he looked back at me. "I'll be here until you're safe. I'd like to see you again, but in case I don't..." He stood there just looking at me. Maybe he thought he was memorizing the picture, maybe he was imagining slitting my throat. I didn't know anymore. "It was good to see you. I've missed you."

He backed out of the mystery room, gun on Leo. When he turned, he surprised me yet again by his footsteps—though they didn't speed up into a run, they didn't stroll, either, revealing that Branson wasn't under the delusion that he was uncapturable.

Those footsteps hadn't reached the back door before I called Susan.

Despite falling into bed at a ridiculously late hour, after Susan's arrival at the Cozy Corgi, and then explaining everything to Mom and Barry when we reached the cabin, Leo and I were both wide-awake at the crack of dawn.

Watson? Not so much. He didn't even attempt a grunt while I went through the morning routine of brushing my teeth and getting dressed. Proving just how tired he was, the grinding of coffee beans didn't lure him out of his bed either, even though they indicated time for breakfast.

Mom and Barry were apparently of the same mind, as they remained tucked away in the guest bedroom. For our part, Leo and I went through the morning ritual in a strange silence. There was a touch of comfort in picking out a cream-colored peasant blouse and a soft mossy-hued broomstick skirt, while Leo rejected his park ranger uniform for dark jeans and a pale blue hoodie; in putting exactly eights scoops of coffee beans into the grinder while Leo slid whole-wheat slices into the toaster; in getting the mugs and creamer while the coffee brewed as Leo retrieved the butter and chokecherry jelly. Occasionally we glanced each other's way, held the gaze, then continued with our given tasks, just a touch soothing, a constant awareness of mutual safety.

The morning routine stopped there, however. As I peered out to the vibrant pink sunrise ushering in the birth of a new day, the postcard-perfect scenery that surrounded my cabin seemed to hold hidden, dark secrets.

Was he out there? Had Branson passed by the cabin just as many times as the police cruisers while we'd all slept? Or were we currently surrounded—Branson on one side, Dean on the other, the two of them pacing in a macabre dance as they closed in, neither aware the other was only a few yards away? I didn't think so... Since Dean went for Simone, surely his next target would be Angus, not me... but... I wasn't sure.

Watson finally managed the energy to issue a

grunt as Leo scooped him into his arms when my exhausted furball refused to leave his bed, then carried him to the door. I did notice his little nub of a tail wagging furiously as we crossed Mom and Barry's paths as they woke when we left, but that was it. He fell instantly asleep in the back seat of the Mini Cooper before I'd even started the engine.

By the time we got to the Cozy Corgi, it wasn't clear if Watson was genuinely filled with such exhaustion that he couldn't manage to exit the car, or if he was simply enjoying being treated like royalty. Either way, he entered the bookshop in Leo's embrace once more. We were early enough that Ben hadn't even arrived to light the fires or begin to prepare for customers, so Watson was saved the expenditure of energy of a joyous greeting as well.

When we reached the top of the staircase, things changed. Watson perked up, his foxlike ears somehow seeming to go even more pointed than normal, his chocolate eyes widening to alert, and he finally gave his trademark impression of a beached seal as he thrashed in Leo's arms. His change was so abrupt, Leo nearly dropped him, but managed to get Watson on the floor with four feet instead of on his head.

For a second I thought maybe Ben had arrived and was helping Nick and Katie in the bakery, but a quick glance toward the art deco-inspired bakery made it the quickest solved mystery ever.

Athena Rose stood on one side of the thick slab of Velluto marble, scribbling notes on a pad of paper. Despite that the rest of the town was probably just getting ready to wake up, the older woman looked runway ready as always. The pale rose bell-shaped wool hat perched on her perfectly coiffed hair matched the hue of the formfitting tweed jacket that rested over the soft gray dress hitting just below her knees. Despite the early hour, her high heels—*high heels*—were of the same rosy hue. As she turned our way, with a blink of thick false eyelashes, a smile broke across her face, radiating her beautiful dark skin that looked decades younger than the seventy-some years it truly was. Her smile wasn't really for us. Setting down her pen and paper, she bent, and with French-tipped nails unhooked her purse, offering a coo as she pulled it open. "I think you'll want to wake up for this, sweetheart."

A tiny white face popped out of the purse, its mouth opening into a petite yawn revealing impressive fangs that belied the toy poodle she was.

Watson pranced like a puppy all the way over, the need for sleep thoroughly forgotten, and continued with a jig around the purse.

Proving the feeling was mutual, Pearl hopped out, gave a shake of her tiny body, and frolicked along with Watson, only pausing here and there for an assortment of sniffs and licks.

"Ah... puppy love." Athena smiled down at them and gave a throaty laugh. "Looks almost fun enough to make me want a man again. *Almost.*" Athena offered an exaggerated shudder.

"Oh, come now." With a giggle, Katie swatted at her playfully. "They're not all that bad."

Athena gave her a skeptical glare, narrowing those false eyelashes. "Not all of us can be as lucky as you and Fred. Leo and Joe are the cream of the crop." She barely caught herself and leaned over to point toward the mixer where Nick had flour up to his elbows. "And you as well, dear. I was just telling Lavender yesterday how she lucked out."

Nick only responded with a deep blush.

As Watson and Pearl's greeting slowed and grew less frantic, Leo and I entered the rest of the way and gave quick hugs of greeting to Athena.

"You're up early." I pulled back from her, eyeing

her ensemble one more time. In truth I had absolutely no desire to go through whatever it was Athena had to do every morning to look like a fashion icon. But I definitely admired the artwork. "And from the looks of things, I'd say you were up way before us."

She cocked an eyebrow playfully. "Careful, Fred. One *might* assume you're insinuating that I don't wake up as the epitome of perfection." She winked again. "I assure you, I do." Without waiting for a response, she gestured to the ingredients spread out in front of Katie. "I'm working on the blog that accompanies the chocolate espresso torte episode of Katie's documentary—I needed a refresher."

"And you know how I'll take any excuse to make chocolate!" Katie's tone was just a touch too bright. "And I bet you need some. *After* a dirty chai... with a few extra shots."

Quick as ever, Athena darted her a skeptical glance, then turned toward Leo and me. "What am I missing?"

As Athena was another frequent member of the Scooby Gang, I didn't hold back. For the next several minutes, Leo and I filled them in on our late-night mystery-room rendezvous with Branson.

Though I'd called Katie the night before, despite the hour—just so she and Joe would take more precautions—Katie shuddered. "The thought of that man being right below our feet only just a few hours ago gives me the willies." She shot a glance toward Nick, who nodded his agreement. "I barely convinced Joe to leave Nick and me alone this morning. But I doubt Branson is a threat to either of us."

"I don't think there's any predicting Branson at all at the moment." Leo's tone was dark, just a touch scratchy from exhaustion and disuse that morning. "I've always said he was off the rails and more dangerous than we thought. But... he's *enjoying* himself. That's worrisome."

Athena let out a long sigh and turned toward the wall of windows, glancing across the street toward the pet shop. "I hope Paulie's safe. Branson really did torment him all that time." Her perfectly painted lips thinned, and she let out a sigh of relief. "Although he's got all of us now, and Officer Cabot. It's nice the two of them are so close."

"I like Campbell. I do." Leo didn't sound like he had any of the relief Athena felt. "But he's no match for Branson. Not even close."

I agreed, though really it wasn't a fair comparison. "I think Paulie's safe. And while I agree Branson is worrisome, I can't imagine Paulie is on his radar anymore."

Katie growled where she stood at the espresso machine. "That's just rude. Men like Branson always dismiss men like Paulie. Just because he's not tall, strong, and handsome, just because Paulie is good and kind. Why... Paulie is worth a *thousand* Branson Wexlers."

"In this case, Katie"—Nick spoke up from where he continued working with dough of some sort—"I'd say that's a good thing for Paulie. If Branson really has dismissed him, then he's not in any danger."

"Well, that's true." Katie sounded partially placated, and after handing me an extra dirty chai and Leo a pumpkin spice latte, she returned to working on the chocolate torte as she spoke. "The question is, then, who else *is* on Branson's radar? And Dean's, for that matter. Now that Simone is..." She finished with a shudder.

"Fred." Leo held his latte mug so tightly I feared it might crack. "As ever, she's the main thing on his radar."

Athena exhaled a nervous breath.

"I don't think I am." I'd tried my best to lose

myself in the routine of the morning, and as a result, the back of my mind had done its casual gymnastics, as it often did when I read a book, or rearranged the mystery room, for that matter. And a new theory had started to form. One that I was willing to bet Susan would come up with sooner or later, after the night sleeping on it as well. I rushed to clarify as all four of them gave me matching skeptical expressions. "I mean, I am. He's in lo—" That time, I stopped myself with a shudder, before I corrected, "Branson is obsessed with me, yes. I'm sure that played a part in last night's visit, but I think there was a little more strategy to it. It was too easy to get him to answer questions. He didn't even pretend to hold back on confirming that Angus was part of the Irons family, that Angus was the one who betrayed Beulah. That he and *Angus* are in cahoots, possibly trying to replace the Irons family." I narrowed in on Leo. "Like you suggested."

Leo didn't attempt to argue that Branson's actions weren't all about me, as I expected him to do, but instead considered and finished with a slow nod. "Okay then... he wants you to know about Angus. Wants Susan to know that. So either he's setting Angus up as a scapegoat who has no involvement or —" He grinned, cutting off my protest. "Which we know Angus *is* involved. So that leaves that Branson is betraying Angus, already."

"But why?" Katie didn't sound convinced.

"Because he's Branson." Leo shrugged. "That's what he does. It's worse than the whole 'no honor among thieves' sort of thing with him. He's evil, he can't help himself. He's like a rabid dog, biting whoever gets close to him."

While I didn't fully agree with that assessment, I didn't argue against it.

Katie did, however. "That may be true, but I *also* think he has a plan, always."

Leo nodded his agreement, but I took over. "Which means whatever Branson has plotted, he's got it set up so it works best in his favor if Angus is out of the way quickly."

"Then why not kill him?" Nick sounded as if he'd been speaking to himself and flinched a little in embarrassment when we all looked his way. Though his blush reemerged, he continued. "Branson already killed all those people in one night. Why not kill Angus? What's one more dead body?"

"I think it has to do with Simone." I wasn't sure, I hadn't been heading that direction, but Nick triggered the notion. "Maybe not. But Angus clearly had leverage on Simone, which he was using to escape all consequences associated with the Irons family. Maybe Branson was using that as well. I don't know. But I don't think Branson or Angus planned on killing Simone, at least not yet."

"Ah..." Leo nodded, a smile of understanding curving his lips. "So last night, here with us... with you, really... was a pivot. A change of plans."

"Maybe." I nodded, considering. Without pausing I retrieved my cell. "Let me run it by Susan. The sooner we figure this out, the better. The more chance we have of bringing in both Angus and Branson. The question is, how vital is it to know what dirt they had on Simone? Or is it simply a matter of Branson setting Angus up for the entire fall?"

Before I could touch her name on the screen, a snore reverberated through the bakery.

Pausing, I moved toward the end of the bar, felt my heart melt, and then waved Athena over. "Come look."

Athena followed, resting her hand on my arm as she peered around me and sighed. "Like I said, puppy love *almost* makes me want a man. But not a one of them would be as chivalrous as Watson."

In his little apartment under the shelves of Cozy Corgi merchandise, Watson had given Pearl the entire use of his miniature sofa, where she lay sleeping. Watson had taken sentinel on the floor beside her, but had propped his head up over the side, resting against her hip, where he snored in a very unromantic fashion.

I allowed myself a few moments to enjoy the innocence, to find peace in the sweetness of creatures who didn't plot murder, betrayal, or revenge. But only a few, before I tapped Susan's speed dial.

As ever, she answered with no greeting. "Let me make this perfectly clear to you, Winifred Page. You are not my type. Yours is *not* a voice I want to hear at the end of the night, and then again at the beginning of the day."

Her voice sounded scratchier than Leo's. And... apparently I'd been wrong to think she'd already be up and at 'em. "Oh, sorry. I didn't think you'd still be in bed."

"Bed!" Genuine offense filled Susan's tone. "I've been up for hours. I was merely saying..." She sighed, and I could practically see her combo of headshake and eye roll. "Never mind. Besides, I was going to call you in the next hour anyway."

"Oh great, glad I could help." I nearly snorted a laugh at all her offense, but figured she'd hang up the phone. "I've had some thoughts about Branson and

Angus I wanted to run by you. What was on your agenda?"

"Dean Gerber." With the figurative snap of the fingers, she was all detective again. "Just got word barely fifteen minutes ago. Dean was almost apprehended just east of Salina, Kansas."

A shot of excitement coursed through me before I narrowed in on the most important detail. "Dean was *almost* apprehended?" I spoke louder and turned toward the others, including them in the information.

"Yeah, *almost*." Susan waited a beat, and when she spoke again, irritation dripped like honey, as if I'd let her down. "*That's* the only thing you notice there, Fred? Any other details important?"

I replayed her statement, once again getting caught on the *almost*. I nearly said no, there wasn't another detail, then gasped. "East of *Salina*! Dean was on his way to Kansas City. To his dad."

"Yep." Though not impressed, Susan sounded a little relieved I had just proven myself not to be a complete dunce. "Probably still is, considering he evaded capture, *again*. Funny how those FBI agents just aren't all they're cracked up to be." She gave a dark chuckle, though it faded quickly—probably thinking of Simone's fate.

Some relief entered at that, one less threat. But...

I launched in, telling Susan of the new theories and possibilities. If we were right, Branson had plans to betray Angus, and if he'd been honest about hanging around Estes to protect me, then how did Dean no longer being in the vicinity change the equation?

"Now that's a nice surprise in the middle of the morning." The smile Angus shot our way when we entered Knit Witt was so genuine, it could almost convince me I was completely off track. Even the warmth radiating from his green eyes couldn't be faked. Could it? His gaze dipped to the tray in Leo's hand. "You come bearing gifts from the talented Ms. Pizzolato. Even more of a pleasure."

"We figured it was best to share the wealth." Leo walked ahead of Watson and me, taking the platter with assorted danishes and cookies to the counter.

Angus glanced at the tray, then reached a hand out to finger the sleeve of Leo's hoodie. "This is a good color on you. I should knit you a sweater in this hue. Although, maybe just a touch more green in it. I think that would suit you better."

I faltered in my step, just the tiniest of things, but it was noticeable, and Angus's sharp gaze didn't miss it. His comment didn't mean anything. It couldn't, but Angus's words made me picture the plum sweater Branson had worn the night before... Had it been an Angus creation? Like that even mattered. "Maybe a cable knit. Those are always handsome."

"A classic choice." Angus gave a nod of approval, and if I'd been hoping for some sort of telltale sign, there was none, as he refocused on Leo again. "Taking another day off from the park? From what I hear, you're really turning Chipmunk Mountain into something spectacular."

"Thanks. I've got my fingers crossed it will live up to the hype." Leo kept it casual. "I'm heading up there at noon." I didn't hear any of the strain in Leo's tone that I knew he was experiencing. He'd wanted to take the entire day off, but at my insistence, he was making a half-day appearance. There was no reason for Leo to hang out at the Cozy Corgi all day. Dean was in Kansas, or possibly Missouri by that point, and if Branson ever went off the deep end and decided to kill me, it wouldn't be in the middle of the day. Leo accompanying me to visit Angus, striking while the iron was hot, was the compromise.

As ever, Angus offered his hand to Watson.

Watson ignored him entirely.

"Sorry. Watson had a long night and is a bit

sleepy. He woke up for a little bit when he saw his girlfriend, but I'm afraid when Athena and Pearl left, his bad mood returned." I reached down and scratched his head and then went in for the kill. "In truth, I'm not in the best mood myself. Branson paid a visit to us in the Cozy Corgi last night after Simone's murder."

Not a flinch. No twitch, nothing. Only a small intake of breath, and the hand that had touched Leo's sweatshirt, and had been offered to Watson, lifted to squeeze my shoulder. "Are you okay?"

Even his grip was kind. And if there was any threat in there, judging from Watson's lack of a growl, it wasn't evident.

"It sounds like you think Branson would hurt me." Might as well try, even if it was obvious. "Why? Has he said anything?"

Maybe there was a slight tightening of his fingertips... maybe. "Oh, Fred. I'm afraid your implication is a little obvious." He dropped his hand as he issued a soft laugh. Then he glanced toward the knitted Samson. "He did hurt poor Raul, so..." He refocused on me. "Although I'm certain Branson is more taken with your charms than he was Raul's pasta, so... there's that."

"We do bring good news, other than Katie's

creations." Leo broke in, taking us a different direction. "Dean Gerber was nearly apprehended in the middle of Kansas."

"Yes." Another chuckle. "For not having enough creativity to knit a garter stitch scarf, that oaf has proven to be quite evasive. Beulah will be proud."

I nearly pointed out that he didn't even pretend to not be aware, then realized that might not mean anything. It had been a couple of hours. Though I hadn't heard, the announcement of Dean's escape could've made the news.

Angus didn't give me the chance as he turned to smile my way once more. "One less anvil hanging over your head, my dear. I'm glad of that." He sighed, and for the first time a touch of impatience entered his tone. "Let's quit dancing around it, shall we? We all know you're here to either try to get clues or trick me in some way or make accusations." He gave a little wince. "I must admit, it's growing wearisome. And a little painful to have people I care for and respect continuously look at me with suspicion and accuse me of dark deeds."

"You've let me see on more than one occasion that you're not just a sweet, grandfatherly knitter, Angus." I felt a little relief at the turn, the direct confrontation helping me get my feet on solid footing. "When you were out for blood when Gerald was murdered. The threat I overheard you make toward Jake Jazz as he tried to buy your shop, how—"

"I think that might be the most offensive thing you've ever said to me, Winifred Page." Even as his gaze hardened, there was a touch of humor in the sharpness of his words. "*Grandfatherly*. I have no children, thankfully, and no grandchildren, even more thankfully. I am *not* a grandfather. Nor do I pretend to be. Nor have I *ever* pretended to be a doormat. I am loyal to my friends and would have strung up Gerald's killer without a moment's hesitation if you hadn't helped the police apprehend her. And in truth, I do wish I'd been the one to take down Jake Jazz."

"See? How easily you speak of murder?" This is what confused me the most about Angus. How he so adamantly denied any involvement and yet seemed to gloat about it at the same time. "In a way, you remind me of how Branson talks about it. As if killing is nothing more than another day at work." I gestured toward the elk. "Or maybe no more complicated than knitting."

He laughed loudly at that, genuine amusement crystal clear. "I can promise you, murder is much simpler than knitting. Don't let my talent fool you.

My mastery of the skill has taken a lifetime to perfect. Any brute can stick a knitting needle into someone, or screw on a silencer before pulling the trigger as their prey sleeps. No talent involved."

"So, which is it, Angus?" Some impatience slipped into Leo's tone. "Are we supposed to believe you're not capable of murder, or that you're more talented at it than Dean and Branson, or am I reading your implication incorrectly?"

"No, you're reading it spot-on." Angus spared a glance toward Leo but refocused on me. "Lackeys like Dean and Branson are a dime a dozen, no matter their talent. I have never said I wasn't capable of murder. Though I've never committed it..."

Was there an unspoken *yet* at the end of that statement?

I didn't always use Watson's reactions to people as the true north of a compass. There had been times that he'd liked a killer, and there were people he couldn't stand who would never hurt a fly, so the fact that he merely sat there staring back and forth between the three bickering humans didn't necessarily mean anything. Or... it could imply that Angus was so skilled with threats they were nearly imperceptible.

I locked my gaze on Angus. "Do you think it

makes you any less of a murderer to have Branson shoot all those people in their sleep, than if you'd done it yourself?"

Still no reaction, other than a slight quirk to the corner of his lip. "I do understand, unfortunately, how Beulah became less enamored of you as time went on. She was quite the fan when you first moved to town, then found you utterly tiresome, and I defended you heartily. But now... I'm not there yet, but I'm getting close."

"What happens then?" I refused to let the icy tingle of fear that whispered take hold. "You command Branson to shoot me in my sleep when your patience with me is exhausted? Or are you going to have other lackeys for that sort of thing?"

He glowered. "There you go. More accusations. I swear, you would see the Irons family in the middle of Disney World. You could be on a deserted island in the middle of the Caribbean and think they were responsible for coconuts dropping from the trees."

At the change in Angus's tone, Leo shifted, tensing slightly to a more defensive stance.

Proving that he was indeed reading the room as much as he could, Watson followed suit, a little growl sounding.

Angus didn't seem to notice either of them.

Feeling like we were finally getting somewhere, I pressed on. "You say that, yet I knew Beulah was part of the Irons family."

"Fred, come on. That was practically spoon-fed to you." He sighed, relaxing a bit. "You said so yourself, Beulah was spelling it out for you letter by letter. So forgive me if I'm not overly concerned you're—*yet again*—accusing me of being a member of the Irons family as well. Everyone within a half-mile radius of you gets accused of that at one time or another. You even thought Ethel Beaker was part of it." He laughed. "As if that self-centered cow could ever be more than a Real Housewife of Estes Park."

"Angus—" Leo's voice sounded a bit of a growl as he took a step forward.

I laid a hand on his arm, not wanting my view of Angus blocked, needing to see his reaction, though I was already completely certain, if I hadn't been before. "I don't blame you for being upset. While I liked Ebony at the beginning, she proved to be a truly lackluster person, both in terms of decency and subtlety."

There it was. He flinched, hardly anything more than a tightening at the corner of his eyes.

I pressed on. "Then when she was finally out of the way, and you not even having to lift a finger to get rid of her, Beulah replaces Ebony with Dean. Promising her *grandson* control of the area that she promised to *you*. As you said, you are a loyal friend, to Gerald, to Mark and Rocky and board-game-night boys... to Beulah. And then she takes away what she'd promised you for... how long... decades?" I took a step closer. "Would you have settled for control of just Estes Park? Did you even ask, or were you afraid that you knew the answer?"

Another tightening at the corner of his eyes followed by two swift blinks was the most of a confession I'd ever gotten, or probably ever would from Angus Witt. And in that flash, I could see the confusion of how I knew the specifics and then the realization that he'd been betrayed, yet again.

At one point I would've had enough sense of loyalty, due to Branson's and my past to not even consider what I did next. Those days were long, long gone. "One of my favorite books when I was little, that my dad would read to me at bedtime, was *The King, the Mice, and the Cheese*. You see, there was this King who had a problem with mice overrunning his kingdom because of all the wonderful cheeses they made in the land, so he pulled his wise men together, and they recommended bringing in cats to take care of the mouse problem. Then the cats overran the kingdom, so they tried again, with dogs. And it happened again and again, where the solution was so much worse than the problem. I think you fancy yourself the King of Estes Park, Angus, but you're *that* king. The king who tried to fix your problem by bringing in a wild animal so much more dangerous than the one who had been threatening you to begin with."

Angus seemed befuddled at first, but by the end looked thoroughly offended. "Branson isn't more of a thre—" He stopped himself and took a step toward me, bringing us only inches apart.

Leo's hand shot up, pressing against Angus's chest as Watson's growl took on a slight wolfish quality from below.

Angus paused in his glare at me and scowled down at Leo's hand, then lifted his gaze to Leo's face. He didn't need words for his threat to be clear. Even so, when Leo kept his hand where it was, Angus refocused on me once more. To my utter shock, when he spoke, his voice was calm, completely. "Like I've told you before, if you keep digging, you may not like what you find. You're so concerned about what your great-grandmother may have done, but what if she's not the only... Well, be careful what stone you turn. I've learned blood is thicker than water, but even it can betray you, and I'd hate for your delusions of your perfect little family to shatter. Your Pollyanna view of your past and legacy really is charming." His tone shifted, growing warmer and laced with care and concern I'd heard from him since our first meeting. "Fred, my dear, as I'm certain you've been told many times, the Irons family has fallen, and you need to stop searching for it. Immediately. The attention you give it might cause it to rise from the ashes." He swallowed, then let out a heavy sigh. "Please, Winfred. *Please.* Let this go. Live your life. I know you're determined to have vengeance for your father's murder, but Charles wouldn't want this. Your whole family suffered enough. Don't continue to look for trouble where there is none."

"You really think threatening Fred and her family is going to—"

Angus stepped back, cutting off Leo's words and making it where his hand was no longer on Angus's chest. After smoothing out his sweater, Angus took a couple of steps toward the counter and lifted one of the cookies. "Now, I don't want to leave things like that between us. These look splendid, like little pots of chocolate gold. Let's partake together, shall we? I have some milk in the back room. Let me get it." He paused and looked at Watson, smile widening and his affection warming. "In fact, I recently got some dog treats, breaking my own rule." His voice went up in a lilt. "What do you say, Watson? Want a *treat*?"

For the first time in his entire life, Watson didn't shudder in utter joy at his favorite word. Didn't bunny hop, didn't prance, didn't look up at me with hopeful chocolate eyes. Instead he bared his fangs and growled.

"Come on, sweetheart." I pulled his leash tighter as I took a step back. "Let's go."

Watson didn't budge, even after another couple of pulls. He went so far as to snap at Leo when he bent down to pick him up. That broke the spell, as Watson instantly looked remorseful and whimpered.

"It's okay, buddy," Leo managed to whisper softly as he nuzzled Watson's head, never letting his gaze leave Angus. "You're a good boy. A very good boy."

I couldn't help but look back as we left Knit Witt. "You sealed your fate when you aligned yourself with Branson. You were better off with Dean. Like you said, he only bit when he was told to."

"I can stay. The things I need to get done at the mountain can happen tomorrow, or any day." Leo grabbed my hand as we sat on the mystery room sofa. "Even if they couldn't, it doesn't matter. I can—"

"No." I tried to make my voice sound cheerful but didn't even come close. I altered track and infused iron instead. That one I achieved. "Go to work. I'm at the Cozy Corgi. I'm safe. And it will drive me batty knowing you're just hanging out here when you have a million other things to do." At the refusal in his eyes, I adjusted one more time. "Please."

Leo sighed. "I don't want to leave you like this. You seem..." He winced, then pressed on. "You seem afraid. More than I've ever seen you before."

"I am." Why lie? Doing so would only make him dig in his heels deeper. "And that's only normal. Everything with the Irons family is coming to a head.

But again, I need some normalcy. It will help. I'll work on books in here, have dirty chais, eat too many pastries with Katie. I'll see if Ben will let me help him with query letters to publishers for his book." I forced a smile at Watson who, though curled up on his ottoman, was glancing back-and-forth between Leo and me. "I'll drive this one crazy with too much affection, and he'll be over the moon to see you at closing time, even more than normal."

Another sigh, and I could see him begin to acquiesce. "Fine. I'll go. Just promise me that you'll stay—"

"I promise." I cut him off before he could finish that sentence, and I squeezed his hand. "I'll make safe choices. I promise." A sudden thought hit me, and I wasn't sure if Leo would do the same or not, which probably said more about my state of mind when I knew him so thoroughly. "And don't you dare hang around out back like some secret security guard. Go to work." Guilt bit at me as I knew I was being manipulative. "Promise me. I won't have a moment's rest if I think you're just out there pacing and that I'm driving you crazy."

For a moment I thought he was going to refuse, then he leaned forward and kissed me. Long and hard. It wasn't romantic or warm, just a touch defiant and claiming. Then he pulled back and met my gaze.

"Fine. But swear to me, if there's even a second that you think something might—"

"I'll call." My smile was easy that time. That was a promise I could keep. "If I feel the slightest bit in danger, I'll call. I'll call you, Susan, Joe, the cavalry."

"I'm serious." He scowled.

"So am I." I couldn't help but laugh, as I meant it. "Like I said, this is all coming to a head. Even if Angus and Branson are the only members of the Irons family left in town, I'm not about to pretend I can handle both of them on my own."

After searching my eyes, Leo finally gave a nod, seemingly satisfied. He kissed me again, softer that time, then ruffled Watson's fur before departing for Chipmunk Mountain.

For my part, I went up to the bakery, filled Katie in on what had happened with Angus—at least mostly—got another dirty chai, and headed back to the mystery room.

Despite expecting Watson to leave me for his apartment, he'd trotted right past it. Though there would soon be plenty of locals for the lunch rush, both levels of the Cozy Corgi were empty—save for me, Katie, and the Pacheco twins—so Watson followed me back down. Proving that it wasn't just the absence of people and that he was picking up on my state of mind, as Leo had done, Watson abandoned his ottoman and jumped up onto the dusty golden tapestry-like fabric of the antique sofa and curled up, his side pressed against my thigh. Within moments, with my hand stroking his fur absentmindedly, he drifted back to sleep.

I stared into the Cozy Corgi mug, watching little ripples across the surface of the dirty chai caused by my hands trembling. The light from the purple portobello lampshade above me altered the color of the divine liquid, changing it slightly red—not quite bloodred, but close enough. Before it ruined my favorite drink forever, I shifted, tilting upward to fit a hand in my pocket and pulled out Dad's black pendant with the little silver star. Feeling slightly more grounded, I lifted my gaze to the river rock fireplace and allowed myself to be captured. The flames flickered and danced, the bright blue of their center flaring out to orange and yellow-red, flecks of glowing white.

Finally, I sighed. Not in relief, not even close. But with Leo gone, I could let myself think, let myself go where I knew I needed to. Where I feared I needed to go.

Leo might've caught the implications of Angus's words—he hadn't veiled them very much—if Leo hadn't been so focused on the actual implied threats to my safety. But... I'd caught them. And looking back, I realized Angus had hinted at them several times. Maybe I just hadn't wanted to see? And as far as me not wanting to peruse them with Leo... Well, I wasn't sure, outside of simply pondering the possibilities in my own mind, it felt like a betrayal to speak them out loud? Not a chance.

So as the mystery books lining the shelves around me remained closed, as flames danced, as the dirty chai slowly cooled in my one hand, as Dad's amulet warmed in the other, and as Watson's soft snores provided a modicum of comfort, I allowed myself to wander down trails more horrible than any I'd ever considered.

I'd been right, though I'd second-guessed and doubted myself countless times since meeting him. Angus had been part of the Irons family, and outside of being a blood relative, seemingly second-in-command to Beulah. I'd suspected *him* long before I'd ever wondered about Beulah. Maybe Angus had been a part of the Irons family nearly since the beginning, so he would have all the facts... he would have access to details going back decades. And he was making it pretty clear about the things he knew.

"You're so concerned about what your great-

grandmother may have done, but what if she's not the only..."

Not the only what? Not the only member of my family involved with the Irons family? That was the obvious implication.

Maybe it was just that. An implication, a taunt, a threat, nothing more than a scare tactic to make me quit looking, because I'd rather not know. But if that was Angus's goal, he didn't understand me. I'd always choose the painful truth over pleasant fiction, at least outside a book's pages.

And if the Irons family had found its way into my own family somehow, then with whom, how, and when?

Maybe the twins... Zelda and Verona? Or their husbands, Noah and Jonah? Barry's daughters hadn't shown up until they were adults. Barry hadn't even known of their existence. Maybe that had all been a fairy tale, perhaps they were plants from the Irons family? With that possibility percolating, I could practically *feel* Zelda and Verona on one side of the Cozy Corgi as they worked away in Chakras, and Noah and Jonah on the other at Arc & Whale. Though horrible, I eased a little bit at that. They made the most sense. Outsiders who'd been grafted into our family. Or, even if the girls truly were

Barry's daughters, they'd had their whole upbringing to be indoctrinated into the Irons family system, so...

My own response to that notion told me I was wrong. That I'd felt an easing, a relief. More guilt cascaded through me, the obvious implication of my response. I loved them. I did. I counted them sisters and brothers. Counted their children as nieces and nephews. No... not only counted, they were *family*, in every sense of the word, period. All of them. But... while hard and devastating, their betrayals would be the easiest.

Easy wasn't the kind of threat Angus had presented. In reality, if I'd been in the mood to laugh, the notion of Zelda and Verona or Noah and Jonah being members of the Irons family might've been the funniest thing I'd ever heard. While I loved them, all four of them were a little left of center as far as how they functioned in the world. Even if they were play-acting, that wasn't how the Irons family did things.

I didn't want to go on. I felt horrible enough at considering the twins, horrible enough wishing they were the ones who'd betrayed us.

I could stop. I really should.

Right...

I took another drink of the lukewarm dirty chai, not letting myself look into its depths, staying focused on the fire while worrying my thumb over the metal star.

"You may want to reconsider. I've discovered that gold, at least—or wool, actually—will not betray you. But even those you count as family, not only can, but will. It's just a matter of time."

Count as family... maybe that. Similar to the twins. Someone grafted in. By marriage. Maybe my ex-husband, Garrett. But he was even a more laughable notion, if Angus thought that would hurt me. So... Barry.

He was an option, and in a way, made the most sense. He'd been born and raised in Estes Park. He'd never left. He'd been friends with everyone in town his entire life. Some of those who he loved and trusted had already proven to not be so innocent. Gerald Jackson, who'd been one small leap away from Angus. Barry had a relationship with Angus himself, and Beulah. But *Barry*? Really? He was just as left of center as Zelda and Verona and their husbands. And yet... not really. He was quirky, individualistic, and marched to his own drum, but he had a wide net of influence. Though people would never guess by looking at him, he had wealth. He owned several properties in town. Wealth and that kind of power could be used, could manipulate, could shield.

He'd known Mom and the rest of my family his entire life as well. They'd been childhood sweethearts. Barry could have...

I gasped and gave a little jerk at the thought.

Watson peered up at me questioningly, startled awake. Then grunted and turned his head to the sofa.

Mom had moved to Estes, married Barry barely a year after Dad died. For a while it had hurt, felt like a betrayal of Dad, his memory. But I understood. She'd returned home after devastation and found comfort, found a new life. Found a man who was so different from my dad yet was able to love her just as much.

What if that hadn't been fate simply being kind, hadn't been Providence or the power of love? What if it had been orchestrated? I wasn't a church type of woman, but I knew the Bible, and recalled the story of King David falling in love with a woman he saw bathing on a rooftop. He'd ordered that woman's husband to the front of line in battle. When he'd been slain, King David took the man's wife as his own. With Barry's history and his connections and ties to these powerful people, if he was a member of the Irons family, how easily that could have been managed.

I didn't know if I could handle that.

And Mom.

Mom would never recover. To know that she'd married the man who'd ordered her husband killed and...

Watson's snore startled me again, pulling my attention away from the fire.

I watched him breathe, not a care in the world. My lips twitched as he let out a little burp in his sleep, and I felt my soul ease a bit.

Watson wasn't a true north of the compass, just as I thought with Angus. He didn't have some preternatural insight into every person. But... Barry was one of the three people who held deity-like status in his little heart. Hardly proof...

Letting Dad's amulet rest in the lap of my skirt, I stroked Watson's side. He sighed in contentment, shuffling closer to me in his sleep.

No, his adoration of Barry was hardly proof, at least if we were in a courtroom in a trial. But... for me? It was enough. I sat with that for just a moment, judging if that were true. And it was. Barry was no King David, nor was he an Angus in disguise. He was a man so pure in heart that he captured both my mother and my beloved Watson. That was all there was to it.

The lunch crowd was beginning to pass by the

mystery room door and head up the steps to the bakery, but I barely noticed. With a final stroke to Watson's fur, I took another sip of the dirty chai, not tasting it in the slightest and once again turned toward the flames.

"If you go down this path you believe this photo is leading you, it's not just your murdered father in the photo alongside Beulah. You have other members of your family here."

Percival or Gary. Maybe Percival *and* Gary.

It could go one of three ways. Just like Barry, Percival had grown up in Estes. Though he'd left for a time, he had just as many connections. He also had wealth and would've profited from smuggling and trafficking with his antiques-and-collectibles business.

Or Gary. Maybe the Irons family had approached him after he retired from playing pro-football. Maybe he'd wooed Percival and been the one to talk him into returning to Estes. He had his own wealth from his career and would profit just as much from the antiques.

They both would profit. So maybe they were in it together. I couldn't picture sweet Gary having a deceitful or cruel bone in his body. Not even a little. And Percival... well... he was more complicated in that regard, possibly. Like Delilah Johnson, he proudly lived his life however he chose, not giving the slightest care to anyone else's judgment. If he believed the Irons family was worth—

I didn't even finish the thought as I recalled his feelings about my great-grandmother, his grandmother. Though I wasn't certain what role Evelyn Oswald had played in Beulah setting up the Irons family, I was certain she had. That picture Ebony sent of them together was proof enough. And I was crystal clear on Percival's feelings about Evelyn, how cruelly his grandmother treated him when he'd not been the typical little boy, like all the others in town. When he'd been more interested in jewelry and sparkly things than baseballs or playing in the dirt. His emotions around the past hadn't been faked. He would never have aligned himself with Evelyn or anything she'd started.

So who did that leave?

Like I didn't know.

"I've learned blood is thicker than water, but even it can betray you, and I'd hate for your delusions of your perfect little family to shatter. Your Pollyanna view of your past and legacy really is charming."

Delusions of my perfect little family.

A tear rolled down my cheek as my throat

constricted. And the pain that arched through me confirmed the truth of it while more of Angus's words echoed in my mind as he'd told me to stop my search into the Irons family. I moved my hand from Watson and snagged up Dad's black stone.

"Please, Winfred. Please. Let this go. Live your life. I know you're determined to have vengeance for your father's murder, but Charles wouldn't want this. Your whole family suffered enough. Don't continue to look for trouble where there is none."

The sentiment could've been said by anyone. It was sound advice, and I knew it. But it was nearly word for word those spoken by another's lips. Pleaded by another's lips.

After setting the dirty chai on the side table and grabbing my purse, I stood and slid Dad's stone back into my pocket. Feeling as if I was in a trance, I didn't bother with Watson's leash, just scooped him up in my arms and walked out the back door without a word to anyone, got into my volcanic-orange Mini Cooper, and drove off.

"Well, hi, dear." Mom's eyes widened in surprise when she found Watson and me on her doorstep. She'd clearly just gotten out of the shower as her long hair hung mostly damp over the shoulders of her bathrobe—its typically silver hue a dark gray as it dried. Even the lock of auburn that matched my own was a deeper red. "Barry went down to the magic shop. Mark has been complaining about the front door lock, and you know how the Greens can be about slow maintenance. But we'll head back to your place as soon..." She blinked a couple of times, then peered behind me and blinked again, then to Watson in my arms, before finally putting the picture together, as if remembering all the latest events happening. "Why are you here? Where's Leo? Something wrong with Watson?"

I opened my mouth, ready to be blunt. Ready to rip off the Band-Aid just like I'd planned. It's what I did, I rarely beat around the bush. But instead, my throat constricted, making a weird croaking sound, and tears began to flow unfettered down my cheeks.

Watson whimpered and licked the underside of my chin.

"Baby!" I hadn't noticed Mom had been holding a towel, but she dropped it. Though I was so much taller and larger than her, she wrapped her birdlike arms around me, pulling me into an embrace that encompassed every bit of the last forty-one years, as if I was a child once more.

Watson grunted at being squished between us but didn't thrash.

I shuddered and another half cry, half croak sound broke from me.

She tightened her grip, her own voice trembling. "Leo? Is it Leo?"

I managed to shake my head, tried to tell her no. Tell her that Leo was fine, that Watson was fine. "How long have you known about Angus?"

Oh... there it was. A few moments later than intended, but there, nonetheless.

Mom went utterly rigid, and when she pulled back, she glanced over her shoulder as if expecting him behind her, then refocused on me with terror in her eyes. She began to shake her head, water droplets falling from her hair.

No, *that* I couldn't handle. I couldn't have Mom lie to me, not anymore. I pushed on, not giving her the chance. "Are you part of it because of your grandma? Did Dad know?"

She took a step back, bumping into the partially open door and nearly stumbling. "Did your dad...? Did Charles...?" A flash of anger ignited in her eyes, and I saw some of my own quick temper in a place so rarely found, but it was replaced once more by horror, or fear. She shook her head again.

"Mom, don't lie to me. Not you. I can't take it. How are you involved in—"

Her hand moved so quickly that I flinched, thinking she was going to slap my face, though she had never done anything remotely close before. I didn't move fast enough, but when her hand made contact, it was only to cover my mouth, though she gripped my chin tightly and shook her head.

Watson whimpered in my arms, confused as he glanced between us, but didn't offer a growl.

Mom stepped forward again, closing the space between us as she stepped out onto the porch and shut the door behind her. As it clicked shut, she finally spoke. "It's not safe to talk in there." She glanced around the porch. "I don't know if it's safe to talk out here, either."

I puzzled over that for a moment but jumped to the most obvious conclusion in a couple of heartbeats. "Angus is listening?"

Mom seemed to consider the front porch furniture, then with a shake of her head, motioned to a little outdoor log table and chairs that she'd bought from Cabin and Hearth a few years ago. Halfway to them, she began to speak again. "I don't know if these are safe either, but since they're fully in the elements, probably."

The fact that she didn't feel safe in her own home, on her own property, caused my world to shift. Only then did I realize she was trembling, probably not just from fear. The August air was cool, and she was wet. "We can sit in my car. I can turn on the heat."

"No." Her answer was instant, and she didn't stop her trajectory. "I doubt your car is safe."

I halted, looking back at my beloved Mini Cooper as if it had betrayed me. "You think Angus has my car... bugged?"

"I don't know." She sounded utterly exhausted. "Angus, someone else in the Irons family, I have no idea."

Deciding to worry about the car later, I followed Mom the rest of the way and took the seat across from her. I started to put Watson on the ground, then remembered I hadn't taken the time to grab his leash, and while he would stay near, it wasn't all that unheard of for a mountain lion to snag a small housepet. "Sorry, buddy. You're staying on my lap. Or I can put you in the car."

He grunted, clearly not pleased, but again he didn't thrash.

In truth I was glad. Having his warm weight against me was a comfort.

Mom pulled us back on track. "What happened? Did Branson visit you again? Did he say something?"

"No. I went to confront Angus with Leo." It seemed like years ago. "He hinted that if I kept searching, I wouldn't like what I found. That there'd be betrayal. He's hinted at that for a while. I was just a little slow to catch on." I'd been looking at Watson as I spoke but forced my gaze up to meet Mom's. "He told me to quit looking, to live my life. Said that Dad wouldn't want me to..." My throat threatened to restrict again, so I cleared it and pressed on. "He almost said the same words as you, verbatim. When I realized he was suggesting somebody in the family—"

"You decided it was me." She took a shuddering breath, and her eyes flashed again. "You think I betrayed your *dad*? You think I would have anything to do with Charles's—"

"No!" It burst from me, loud enough that both she and Watson flinched, and I shot out a hand, reaching across the table to grab her. "No. I don't." I hadn't been so sure until that very moment. Hadn't really let myself go there, to think that Mom had anything to do with Dad's murder. But that wasn't feasible. Not at all. "Never, Mom. Never."

She studied me, judging my sincerity, then gave a nod. "Good." She covered where my hand gripped her arm, her thin skin soft and cold against mine. "No matter what Angus or anyone else might hint or suggest, I swear to you on everything, on your father, on your life, I am *not* part of the Irons family. It wasn't until you started questioning after Ebony sent that picture that I even considered that my grandmother might've been. I have no idea."

I believed her. Without a doubt, I believed her. Whatever Angus wanted me to think was another manipulation. Pure and simple. "But you knew Angus was part of it?"

She nodded.

"Beulah?"

She shook her head.

Another thought that would be too much to handle crashed into me, and I had to steady myself as I pleaded through my eyes into hers. "Branson? Did you know about Branson?" It wouldn't have been as bad as her having anything to do with Dad's death, but the notion that she would've known that Branson was a dirty cop while he and I—

"No." Her grip tightened, and revulsion filled her tone. "Darling, no. I swear. If I had, there wouldn't be any threat Angus could make that would've kept me silent. I didn't know about him until after what he did to you and Leo." She glanced to my lap. "And to Watson."

Relief floated through me. Though I'd already felt certain of it, maybe I hadn't been completely. Anything else I could handle. Anything. And with that relief came the other message, and what she'd said. "Angus has been threatening you?"

She nodded.

"Mom, just tell me everything, okay?" I wanted answers, no matter what they were, and I wanted to get her into the warmth so she'd quit shivering. "Don't make me ask questions or try to protect me. Just... just tell me all of it, whatever there is, no matter how ugly it might be."

Mom started to shake her head again, glanced to the car, then to her house, her worry clear.

"Mom." I waited until she looked back at me. "It's time. I don't know how this will end, but it's time for it to. *Everything* gets put on the table. No matter how it changes things."

Watson licked the underside of my chin again, maybe there'd been more tears and I hadn't realized.

Mom's gaze dipped to Watson. She leaned forward, taking the hand that had covered mine and stroked his face. "You're such a good boy, Watson Charles Page. Such a good boy."

He grinned his corgi smile at her and licked the back of her fingers as she returned her hand to cover mine once more. It was like that, Watson in my arms, and my other clasped in my mother's embrace, that she told me of the nightmare she'd been living during the past decade.

"When Charles was killed, a couple of weeks after the funeral, actually, I found a box of his things he'd hidden in the attic. Things about the Irons family that he'd uncovered and hadn't turned in to the police yet. File folders after file folders full."

"That he hadn't..." I didn't mean to interrupt, and I answered my own question before she could.

"He was worried about a leak in his department? Maybe the Irons family had someone there."

Mom nodded and continued, "I wasn't sure what to do with it. Wasn't sure who to trust. My first inclination was to go to Marcus, but if your dad hadn't shared it with his best friend, I wasn't certain I should, and it would put Marcus in danger. I couldn't do that. So... I left it where it was. I put the amulet I'd made for Charles in the box and closed it."

That was the box. I remembered when Mom gave me the amulet on my fortieth birthday, she'd said she'd found it in a box of Dad's old things. I'd started to ask, but then... I wasn't sure... maybe I'd gotten carried away with someone else at the party and never returned to it.

She kept going, not lingering on the stone she'd made to protect Dad, which he'd left behind on the day of his murder. "I'd go through it from time to time, trying to find answers. Trying to..." She shrugged a narrow shoulder. "I don't know what I thought I would do. How I could solve this when Charles was unable to."

"But Angus knew you had it?" True to form, I couldn't help myself, asking questions, hurrying on, even with my own mom. "He started threatening you?"

"Not then, no." She took a steadying breath and told the next part quickly, with a glance toward the house. "It was there, a couple of months after Barry and I got married. You know Barry, he's always been wonderful about Charles, not an ounce of jealousy, and never hesitated to grieve with me. I showed him the box, we went through it, he was going to help me try to put together the pieces. And then... a couple of days later I got..." She hesitated, obviously debating, then released me and stood. "I'll show you. I need you to understand why I didn't tell you. I don't think words will capture it. I'll be right back."

I watched her go, her pretty pink bathrobe dragging on the ground behind her, picking up leaves then dropping them a few feet later.

She wasn't part of the Irons family, *of course* she wasn't. Fury washed through me that I had allowed Angus Witt to make me consider such a thing for even a moment. It wasn't until Watson grunted and shifted that I realized I'd pulled tighter, clutching him too close. I let out a little chuckle and pressed a kiss to his nose. "Sorry, sweetheart. You're being very patient with all the holding."

He licked my nose, eliciting another chuckle.

"And being very sweet with all the kisses. *Very* unlike you."

If he was offended, he didn't let on.

Before I could offer any more commentary, the door to Mom and Barry's house opened, and she emerged. She'd changed into a winter jacket and pulled the hood over her hair, and it bounced as she hurried with a thick envelope in her hands. Wordlessly she handed it to me, and then surprising both of us, took Watson and placed him in her lap as she sat down. "Goodness, you are a heavy, fat little thing, aren't you?"

Though Watson looked thoroughly ill at ease, he didn't struggle, just stared at me with his wide chocolate eyes.

"You'll need both of your hands." Mom nodded toward the envelope.

With a sense of dread, I opened it and pulled out a massive stack of photos.

My jaw fell open at the first one, and as Mom's hug had done, the years fell away.

Though grainy, it was easy enough to recognize Garrett and me coming out of Houston's.

I just gaped, pulled back to that moment.

He and I had gone to the Plaza. Garrett had a steak. I'd had what had been probably the best chicken strips I've ever tasted, and cheese bread to die for. What a strange thing to remember. As I stared, I could taste them again, remember the way the cheese melded with the seasoning on the buttery breadsticks. Could hear the crunch of the crust on the chicken strips. Hear Garrett's voice as clear in that moment as it had been so many years before, as he told me he'd been having an affair, that he wanted a divorce. I hadn't remembered he'd held the door open for me as we'd left, but that's what the picture showed.

The next one was me alone, again in the Plaza. I didn't remember the occasion. I was staring into the fountain as water spilled out of dolphins' mouths with Poseidon riding on their backs. That would've been after the divorce.

The third one was Charlotte and me, in front of the building we purchased for our publishing company, right after I'd left teaching at the college.

There were many shots of Charlotte and me at the publishing house. Enough that I nearly stopped until I came across a picture of the cemetery—me kneeling at Dad's grave, with Watson sitting in front of me. I gasped and felt tears burning anew. I gaped at Mom. "This is the day, maybe the moment, that Watson showed up. Just wandered up to me in the graveyard as if sent from Dad and..." I stared back at the picture.

"That part's probably coincidence, dear. I'm sure it is." Mom's voice was husky. "With all the pictures they've taken of you, they were bound to get a couple of memorable ones."

I wasn't even a tenth of the way through the stack. "These are all of me?"

"Mostly." Mom attempted a smile as she stroked Watson but didn't quite succeed. "There's a few of the twins, the grandkids, but mostly you. They became more frequent when you moved to Estes." She met my gaze. "I received another one yesterday. You were arranging books in the mystery room."

I nearly dropped the stack of photos again. Mom had been right, seeing them made it much more real than if she'd simply told me I was being observed. Angus, or someone—maybe Branson—had been in the Cozy Corgi Bookshop that very week, taking a picture of me, and I'd not known. And I understood. Completely. "Mom." I set them on the table, and not knowing what to do, left my seat and knelt in front of her, once again squishing Watson between us in an awkward embrace. "I'm so sorry. He's been threatening you for... years... since... Dad died."

"Almost. A couple of months after Barry and I got married, but... Yes." Still holding Watson with one hand, she stroked my hair as I pulled back from the embrace. "There's nothing for you to be sorry about. Nothing."

"But all of my digging into the Irons family, all of my interrogating." It was more than I could handle. "I thought you were just afraid in general, not that... not that I was heightening some specific threat that was—"

"It's okay. It's okay." She leaned nearer, pressing her forehead to mine for a moment. "I knew you wouldn't stop. I have always said, you are your father's daughter, but I did hope you would."

We both jumped as a car approached.

Watson finally thrashed and let out a howl. It was his leap of joy from Mom's lap that caused my flare of panic to ease, even before I saw the Volkswagen van.

Barry hopped out and went into a graceful kneel as Watson leaped into his arms. "Hey there, buddy! What a wonderful gift in the middle of the day."

He reached his hand round Watson's collar for the leash, but finding none, scooped Watson up yet again. There was absolutely no thrashing at that, and Barry's face was lathered with twice as many kisses as I'd received.

Though he wore nothing warmer than his trademark tie-dyed tank top, Barry beamed at us as he walked our way. "A wonderful gift to see you too, Fred. What brings—" His smile fell as he looked between us, then met Mom's gaze. "Phyllis?"

"She knows." Mom had been so strong the entire time, but with those words she began to cry again and shake. "Barry, she knows."

He was beside us in a heartbeat, giving Watson to me and wrapping Mom in his thin bare arms. "It's okay. It's good. It's good, baby." He held the back of her head, his thumb stroking over the hood's material. "Fred is strong. It's time. Whatever happens, it's time. Past time."

Though I was moved and grateful for his care and love of my mother, I stared at Barry. *He* knew? Maybe that was obvious, but still. They'd both known of Angus this whole time.

It wasn't a betrayal, it really wasn't, and yet... "Mom?"

She pulled back from Barry, meeting my gaze again.

"Who else in the family knows?" Surely it didn't matter. It couldn't. But... "Does everyone know?"

"Just us and Percival." Mom said it quickly, clearly realizing how I felt. "I went to him when I got the first picture, to see what he thought I should do. My first inclination was to ask Marcus, nearly called him. Well, I did. His number rang twice before I remembered he'd passed. Maybe a blessing that I didn't have the chance to burden him at the end. Percival, Barry, and I decided we'd do whatever it took to keep you safe." Her hand found Barry's and their fingers locked as she spoke. "To keep our kids safe."

Selfish. I had been so selfish. I hadn't looked at all the photos, hadn't seen the ones of Zelda and Verona's families, of Barry's grandchildren. "Oh, Barry. I'm sorry. I wasn't thinking. You have just as much reason to fear as—"

"None of that." It was the first time Barry had ever used a harsh tone with me, and he repeated it the second time. "*None* of that, Winifred." He didn't let go of Mom's hand, but he embraced me with his eyes as he spoke, his tone softening then. "You have nothing to apologize for. Don't ever take other people's evil deeds on yourself. The target was always you, even when they tried to widen the net, it was really always you." He smiled, a loving thing. A *fatherly* thing. "But yes, I did have just as much to fear. So did your uncle. We love you every bit as much as your mom." He chuckled a little. "Well... that may not be humanly possible, but as close as we can manage."

Several more moments ticked by before I was able to find my voice, probably wouldn't have been able to if not for continuing to hold Watson. "Gary? He doesn't know?" I wasn't certain if his omission had been intentional or not.

"No." Mom was the one who answered. "Percival made the call. You know Gary, he's a little too pure. Percival feared he might try to be heroic, or tell you, and only end up putting himself in danger."

"Yeah." I felt myself nod. "I could see that." I glanced back at the pile of pictures, and whether because it was habitual, or because it was a comfort, my brain did what it always did and looked for puzzle pieces. "Wait... how did Angus hear you talking to Barry about Dad's box of Irons family stuff? Why do you think your house is bugged?"

"Fred." Mom smiled reproachfully. "I was a detective's wife. A good one. It didn't take a genius." She actually laughed. "Little things. Side comments from Angus, little details about my... our life that he'd drop into casual conversation. They could've been conscious, but..." She shrugged. "And just a feeling that grew over time. A sense from him. Like he knew that I knew."

As he'd done with me, exactly. Only Mom had been quicker. I glanced back at the cabin. "But... that was years ago. Surely whatever bug was planted wouldn't still be functional."

"I doubt it." Again Mom glared at the house. "But it's the Irons family. Angus has said a few things over the years and let me know he's still listening. Whether they invented some never-ending bug, which is doubtful, or they somehow planted more here and there, who can say? The result is the same. What good would it do to go hunting. I... we had no way to fight him. While I didn't know about Branson, there'd been dirty cops in Kansas City. Why not here?"

She had a point, but my brain sought for another puzzle piece, found one that didn't quite fit. "But Mom, you said when you gave me the pendant..." I could feel it at that moment in my pocket, the weight of Watson on my thigh pressing it into me. "You said you found it in a box of Dad's things. You still have all his records and whatnot of the Irons family? Angus didn't make you give them to him?"

"Why would he? He's no fool. I could make a zillion copies of them, photograph them, do a million things, then give him the box." She huffed out a breath that was almost corgi-worthy. "I've learned Angus doesn't waste words or effort on pointless things. He knew what would work to keep me silent. That was enough."

"And now that's over." I was glad to hear the steel in my voice, as I felt it down to my very bones. "This ends. You're not living like this any longer."

Mom didn't look relieved at all. "What are you going to do?"

"I don't know. I think we should call Susan and —" I glanced back to their house, where Mom was even afraid to speak. Then I nearly suggested the police station, but... who knew? "I'll call Susan, she can meet us at my house. And I'll call Leo, Katie, gather the troops. Make sure we're together, that we're safe. And we end this."

"Okay, see you in half an hour." I started to hit End, then yanked the phone back to my ear as I emerged through the trees into the clearing in front of my house. "And I love you."

"I love you too." A soft sound escaped Leo from the other side of the line, and I could practically see him pause at the top of Chipmunk Mountain on his way to the tram. "You really think we can end this?"

"I do." After shifting the Mini Cooper into Park, I glanced toward Watson and considered for a heartbeat. "Yeah. I do."

"Okay, I'll be right there."

From the passenger seat, Watson cocked his head, then gave a disapproving glower as if he could hear Leo end the call.

I ruffled the fur of his muzzle. "Okay, little man. One more time of being carried, and that will do, for a while." There were spare leashes in the house, and though it was a short distance from the car to the front porch of the cabin, with being completely surrounded by forest, I wasn't taking any chances. Branson and Dean were hardly the only dangerous things lurking in the shadows, even in the daytime.

He squirmed all the way to the front door, clearly over this new form of transportation, and grunted out in pure annoyance as I sat him down to slide my key in the lock. As the door opened, he trotted inside before it was wide enough, and he bumped his fuzzy hip on the way in, shooting an even more offended glare as he trotted over to the hearth of the unlit fireplace.

Pausing in the doorway watching Watson curl up, a strange sensation washed over me. Though I'd not been thinking of it, or even considered, some part of me had expected the fireplace to be ignited and Branson to be sitting in my overstuffed armchair, ready to offer me hot chocolate.

He wasn't, of course.

But was it *of course*? That didn't seem all that unreasonable of possibilities.

Shivering from another sensation, this one of eyes watching me from the trees at my back, I stepped inside and locked the door. I'd texted Susan and Katie, telling them to meet at my house before I called Leo. In the next little bit, all of us would be together, Mom and Barry promising they'd be over as soon as she was dressed properly, and they were going to call Percival.

For a tremulous moment, I wanted to rush across the room and collapse in a heap beside Watson. It was all too much to take in. For the past decade, Mom had been living with that shadow hanging over her. Hanging over Barry and Percival too. She'd never felt completely safe in her own home.

That wave of weakness burnt away and I might as well have plunged into Lake Estes in the middle of Christmas morning, for all the ice that seemed to pour over me as the obvious became just that—obvious. *Of course* Mom and Barry's wasn't the only place bugged. They hadn't mentioned Percival and Gary's, so maybe there'd not been any concern there, but Mom had been worried about my car. If Mom's house was under surveillance, then without a doubt, my cabin...

My gaze lifted of its own accord from Watson—who was already falling asleep—up the river rock and settled onto the mantle. I forced myself to take step after step across the hardwood floor in the living room, the little creaks and groans here and there seeming like screams.

With trembling fingers, I stretched out my hand and picked up the bagel-sized knitted Watson, looking exactly like a miniature version of the real McCoy at my feet.

There was no doubt. None. But if there had been, it was swept away by another comment Angus had made when Leo and I visited him only a few hours before. I hadn't caught it at the time. He'd mocked me for thinking Ethel Beaker could be part of the Irons family. In a way, that wasn't exactly far-fetched, but was it a theory I'd ever spoken to him? I didn't think so. He'd heard it the other night as we'd discussed the possibility over dinner in the kitchen.

In the kitchen...

I looked over my shoulder, seeing the seafoam-green table, the mint-green 1960s fridge and oven, the tie-dyed flamingo curtains framing the window over the porcelain sink. None of those retro finishes held the charm they normally did. Then I refocused on the knitted Watson. It had been on my mantle for a long time. Would whatever bug sewn inside it still work, be powerful enough to pick up our voices in the kitchen? Or were they everywhere?

Other things came back—Angus commenting about Katie and Joe soon getting married. I'd assumed it was just an obvious assumption.

I sucked in a breath at another memory. Simone. Simone had been in my living room when we talked about her being an FBI agent. Angus had let slip that he knew of her real identity as if it was nothing more than common knowledge, forever ago. He pointed out, rightly, that nothing stayed secret in Estes, and that he wasn't exactly the dimmest bulb in the box. But that hadn't really been true, at least about the rest of the town. I'd never heard anyone else mention Simone being undercover. People had been shocked and amazed when she was the one to arrest Beulah. I stared in horror at the beautiful rendering of Watson in my hand. Had it given Angus the keys to Simone's undoing, allowed him to search for whatever weakness he had uncovered to manipulate her? Had it cost Simone her life?

I shoved the little Watson back on the mantle as if it would wake up and lunge for my throat when its treachery was discovered. Then I spun, looking at every spot of my house, my sanctuary, where I curled up by the fire to read, where the Christmas tree would stand glistening by the window in a couple of months. Where my family had gathered, where I'd fallen more and more in love with Leo every day.

All of it on display. All of it overheard. All of it used to hurt, manipulate, and control.

Angus.

I began to tremble again. It was wonderful, the rage devoured every bit of fear and dread that had been creeping in. How he'd laughed to himself as he'd stolen private moments, used them to terrorize my family, to manipulate the town. He and Branson probably had a good laugh at how stupid they thought I...

Branson.

So many emotions crashed through me, I nearly collapsed at the thought of his name.

Him listening. Branson in the room with me as I was reading by myself.

Branson in the room while Leo held me close.

I reached out once more, steadying myself by gripping the mantle, and my fingertips brushed against the knitted Watson, pulling my attention back to it.

How could the man still hurt me? After all this time? When I was *crystal* clear on the type of monster he was? It should have been expected, it shouldn't feel like a betrayal. But it did. The man betrayed me again and again and again.

I wanted to shower. Wanted to rip my clothes off, shower, and run from this house to be clean, to be free, to...

While the mental image that painted might be laughable, I realized it wouldn't work, either. I could be standing in the middle of my clearing and still not be alone, eyes could still be on me.

I was at the front door before I'd even been aware of moving. It wasn't until Watson bumped against my leg as he trotted along with me that I looked down and realized what I was doing. I hadn't allowed myself a moment to consider, just let the rage take over.

I opened the door wide enough to squeeze through and closed it again before Watson could get out with me. "Sorry." Even my own mumbled apology wasn't enough to break the spell. And though I hadn't stripped off my clothes or showered, I rushed out into the clearing, past my car, until I stood a few yards away from a line of trees, then lifted my voice and screamed, "*Branson!*"

A few birds took flight from the treetops to my left, pulling my attention, but there was no other movement.

"Branson!" My bellow seemed to echo around. I spun, searching, looking at the edges of my cabin, expecting him to be peering around, then stupidly glancing up at the towering mountains.

I screamed toward them as well. "Branson!" Already my voice hurt.

Some other little voice, a quiet one in the back of my head whispered that I was being ridiculous. That for a woman who didn't believe in coincidence, I was sure expecting a lot for him to just be languishing in the forest and waiting for my beck and call.

"Branson!" Tears burned then began to fall, hot with anger, heavy with powerlessness.

"Branson." It was barely a whimper that time.

He emerged from the trees. Nothing more than a shadow stepping from behind the branches of a pine, and then growing into the man with every step he took. He paused at the edge of the clearing, partially illuminated by the soft afternoon sun. He wore boots, dark pants, and a deep red sweater. At the sight of him, I recalled my thoughts of the night before. He really was a devil. Possibly Satan himself.

And the demon smiled, though there was concern in his bright green eyes. "How did you know I was here? Could you feel me? I wasn't even planning on being here today, but *you* changed that."

Now he was in front of me, I was rendered speechless. For the first time in my life, I considered murder, genuinely saw it as a viable option. My hands were empty. But there was a stone at his feet. I could grab it...

"You love to throw a kink into things, Winifred Page. It's one of the things I love about you." Though his gaze still seemed wary, he let out a warm laugh. "I knew you'd tell Angus about our conversation last night, let him know I wasn't going to keep our agreement a secret, but I thought it might take a day or two for you to flesh some things out. But you moved up the timeline."

Why was he talking? Like any of this mattered.

"So *I* needed to speed up my timeline as well, thanks to you." Branson gestured from where he stood toward the cabin. "I was coming to leave you a goodbye gift when you pulled up. I didn't want to startle you." He smiled again. "I'll be back soon, though. Now that Angus knows... well..." He shrugged. "There are games afoot. Games, but I'll have to be in town to win."

Games.

Games!

Once more my feet did for me what I couldn't do for myself, and without any thought I raced across the clearing—in the distance Watson's barking was a thousand miles away. As I crashed into Branson, nearly stumbling as I reached him, I slapped him as hard as I could across the face.

He stumbled to the side, his foot catching on the rock I'd noticed.

I used his rare moment of clumsiness to my advantage, and on the next swing, curled my fingers into a fist and punched him with every bit of strength in my body—let every ounce of fear and rage that had built up over the years fly in one swift arc.

The crack of impact was the most beautiful thing I'd ever heard, and the blood that sprayed from his broken nose only prompted me to pull my fist back again.

His bright green eyes that I'd found so beautiful at one point flashed in pure demon's light as his rage attempted to match my own. Regaining his balance quicker than I could move, he shot out both hands, grabbed me by the shoulders, and squeezed hard enough that I'd have bruises for weeks.

He shook me, causing my hair to fly and making me lose my footing. I would've fallen if his grip hadn't been digging into my skin.

"I hate you." I twisted, trying to lurch free from him, but not to run—to reach down and grab that rock and finish what my fist had started. "I'm going to end you."

The fury that had ignited in him faded, giving way to hurt. Hurt and confusion, which only proved the man was truly insane.

"*I* am not a game. My *family* is not a game." I twisted again, for all the good it would do, but I couldn't hold back. "You want to laugh at what you've done to my mom? Do you enjoy making promises that you'd never hurt me or my family, and all the while you're spying on her, spying on me? Taunting her with pictures. Threatening my life, the lives of her grandchildren?"

His grip lessened a bit as his brows furrowed.

It was enough that I twisted free, and I punched him again, that time barely glancing off his chin. "I never dreamed you'd be pathetic enough to do Angus's bidding. Or that you'd stoop to taking pictures of me in the Cozy Corgi the other day. Was it you? Do you snap pictures as you stand in these woods and stare like some sleazy psychopath?"

"Fred!" Branson's grip was on me again, stone-tight, and he shook me again harder, before jerking me still. He snarled—his lips pulled over his teeth erasing every bit of beauty the man possessed. And his eyes. I'd seen Branson kill, pulling the trigger and murdering two of the people who trusted him without any more than a flinch, but the bloodlust had never flared as it did then. "What are you talking about? What pictures? What do you think I did to your mom?"

I stared, following the blood running from his nose over his lips and traveling down his chin and neck and into the collar of that red sweater. And while he had fooled me for a long time, there was no deceit in him now. "You didn't know about the pictures Angus has been sending Mom for the past ten years? Pictures of me, indicating he'd take care of her daughter if she shared what she knew of the Irons family?"

He flinched. "Your mom knew about—"

When his grip loosened again, I didn't bother trying to escape, only leaned closer, giving a snarl of my own. "You didn't know he's been listening to me in my house? You're going to claim you haven't laughed together that I've been stupid enough to think I'm safe in my own home, even though *you've* helped yourself to entering on more than one occasion?"

He blinked in confusion and dropped his hands. "I swear to you, I did not. I... would never." Once more proving his insanity, he lifted a hand toward my face as if to cup my cheek.

I twisted out of his reach and stepped back.

"Don't you touch me. Never, *ever* touch me. You're a monster. Evil. And I will bring you down, I swear." Maybe I was the one who was insane. Threatening him when the most I could ever really do to him was a bloody, broken nose.

"Fred, my love. I would never—"

My stomach roiled. "Your love?"

I must've made some horrible expression, as pain slashed across his face before *he* took a step back. "Don't, Fred. Please don't. You've got to believe me. I would never—" Branson didn't finish the thought as the sound of a car approaching once more interrupted things. He looked over my shoulder, hate flashing again, then looked back at me. "Never. I would *never* hurt you. I never will." He turned and ran into the trees.

I watched him go, standing dumbfounded as he disappeared like a mist.

My shoulders ached from where he'd grabbed me. The knuckles of my fist hurt, having never been used as a weapon like that before, though the feeling of my pulse in them acted as a sort of balm, recalling the feeling of his nose breaking under their impact.

Susan appeared beside me, weapon drawn. "That was Branson?"

I only nodded.

She rushed after him, gun in one hand and raising a walkie-talkie with her other to call for backup.

I stared after her as she too disappeared into the trees.

It didn't matter. He was gone. She wasn't in danger from Branson, nor would she catch him.

For a few more moments I continued to stare, not sure what to think or feel, until gradually Watson's barks broke through once more.

Turning, I moved zombielike across the clearing, onto my porch, and opened the door. Gathering him in my arms yet again, I held Watson in my lap on the front steps until the others began to arrive.

Two hours might've passed, or it could've been two minutes, as I sat on the porch steps. With every beat of my heart, my entire countenance altered. One moment I tried to put together the puzzle pieces of what Branson meant about the timeline. The next, rage flared. Then the next, an unsettling numbness that let me catch my breath. And then the following ushered in a crushing ache for what my mother had endured. And the next...

Through it all, Watson didn't struggle, just pressed against me, whimpering. I didn't know if I stroked him, clutched him too tight, or if my hands were at my side.

It must've been a matter of minutes instead of hours, because everyone began to arrive at once. Mom and Barry first, with Officer Jackson and Officer Lin right behind them.

Watson wriggled in my lap, his excitement at

Barry's appearance attempting to bring me back to the moment. And it did so, partly. Though everything had transitioned to slow-motion as a weird haze settled in that I couldn't seem to blink away.

As Katie, shortly followed by Percival and Gary, joined the small growing crowd, Susan emerged from the far side of the clearing, closely followed by Campbell. I hadn't even noticed he'd been with her. With a grimace, she shook her head, and stormed our way. "Fred, what in the world were you doing chatting it up with Branson in the middle of the—"

"No." I shot upwards, and it seemed I did have a grip on Watson, as he remained in my arms. "No." Adjusting him, I lifted a finger to my lips as I took several steps away from the porch to whisper, "They could be listening."

The momentary flash of confusion on Susan's face disappeared instantly, and she glanced toward the cabin. "Of course." I'd very briefly explained in the group text to her and Katie, letting them know we needed to meet immediately.

I kept my voice low. "He knitted me a little Watson. Angus has been listening through it, though probably through other locations as well."

"Here too?" Gary spoke, and for once his low, soft baritone wasn't its typically quiet timbre. He shot a glare at Percival. "How about our house? Did you even think of that?"

Percival winced and reached out a hand toward his husband, but Gary sidestepped and sent me a sorrowful glance.

Apparently, Percival hadn't been able to get away from Gary without explaining, or maybe he'd just decided it was time.

Mom, still in her winter coat, but now with actual clothes underneath, moved toward the couple. "Gary, please don't be—"

"Save it." Even in a whisper, Susan's bite held authority. Then she looked at me. "So where? The police station is probably not an option, either."

I searched, discarding every place that came up in a mental Rolodex. The Cozy Corgi, Leo's apartment, Katie's, none felt safe. The Irons family had probably infiltrated every location in town. *Branson* had probably infiltrated every location in town. I glanced over to where he'd emerged, not really expecting to see him staring back, although I wouldn't have been all that surprised. My gaze flicked a little to the right, to the trail I walked with Watson nearly every morning. Of course. "The clearing." I returned to Susan. "Remember that little clearing in the woods? Where you told me about your promotion to detective?"

"Perfect." She gave a sharp nod and lifted her hand in the air, her finger pointing skyward as she spun it, as if lassoing us all together. "No talking until we arrive. Let's move."

Leo arrived then, pulling his Jeep around the growing caravan of cars; he'd had the farthest to drive.

Watson wriggled so much at Leo's appearance that I had no choice but to set him on the ground, and he took off like a rocket.

Leo started to greet him but froze when he looked up and saw my face. Straightening, he strode directly to me, Watson prancing at his feet, begging for his attention. "Fred... what else happened? You look—"

"Save it." Susan barked again, and earned a glare from Leo. She gestured toward the cabin and softened her tone a little. "We're going to the clearing."

Leo understood, and though he didn't argue, he shot me a worried look.

I tried to smile encouragingly. I doubted I achieved it. Watson continuing to bound around Leo, hitting his thighs with his forepaws, pulled my attention. "His leash. Let me—" I turned back toward the cabin and halted. I couldn't go in there.

"Here. Let me." Leo squeezed my shoulder, started to head that way, but flinched when I gasped in pain, his honey-brown gaze darting to where his hand touched my arm. "You're hurt?"

I guess I was. I'd forgotten. "Not bad. I'll explain. Later." At the reminder, the knuckles that had smashed into Branson's nose throbbed, as if wanting sympathy as well.

He hesitated for a moment, staring between my eyes and my shoulder, and from the darkening in his expression, he'd guessed correctly.

Once Watson had his leash affixed and had been patted by Leo, the eleven of us tromped through the woods in heavy silence, save for a cacophony of breaking twigs and scattering pebbles. Though my morning strolls were leisurely, with a large group, the small distance seemed to take forever, before we paused on the outcropping looking over the picturesque meadow framed by forests of pine and aspen and sheltered by purple mountains. As so often was the case, a herd of elk grazed. They froze and lifted their heads to attention as one when we emerged from the other side of the forest.

It wasn't enough.

I knew Branson wasn't there. As arrogant about his own skills as he was—rightly so or not—he hadn't hung around. The line of trees was too close to my back, maybe it was just birds and chipmunks, but I could feel eyes crawling over my skin. The analogy didn't make sense, but that was exactly what it felt like. I pointed to the meadow. "Let's go there."

Unsurprisingly, considering it wasn't uncommon for elk to travel down the middle of Elkhorn Avenue right between the shops, they didn't scatter as we invaded their meadow, though a couple of them focused on Watson with wary concern. One of the bulls pulled my attention with the ridges on his gorgeous crown of antlers catching the light of the sinking sun. He brought to mind Samson, both the real animal and the wool one in Knit Witt. For some reason, he provided comfort, the whole herd of massive animals did, and for the first time since I'd gotten home and held the knitted Watson in my hands, I eased a bit.

Despite there being no chance—at least, I supposed there was no chance—of the meadow being bugged, Susan kept her voice low as she looked at me. "Was Branson bleeding, or was I seeing things?"

"I punched him, broke his nose," I answered before I turned my attention away from the elk.

"Nice." Susan grinned and gave an impressed chin-thrust.

"You broke..." Leo turned horror-stricken eyes on me and started to reach for my shoulder.

"Yeah. I realized the knitted Watson I have on the mantle was bugged. Realized Angus and Branson had been listening to us this whole time. I got so furious. For some reason I had a feeling Branson would be watching from the woods. So I—"

"You..." Leo took a step back, and his jaw fell open as he shook his head in disbelief. "You... *went* to him? Alone? When you—"

"No." Susan broke in again, her whisper gone. "We don't have time for dramatics." She included Gary into her reproachful gaze. "Save all the drama for later. Everyone can be mad about secrets that were kept or pretend they're surprised Fred stumbled into danger without thinking, but right now we've got to figure out our next move and do it quickly."

Guilt had already been coursing through me at the look on Leo's face, remembering my promise as I'd coerced him to go to work. Then with Susan's flippant insult, shame was piled on top. But she was right. None of that mattered.

"That's a little harsh, don't you think?" Katie had

already been near but stepped up to my side. "Let's not—"

"I said *no*," Susan snarled. "Focus on what matters." She looked at me. "Are you able to break it down for us?"

I nodded, took a deep breath, and caught everyone up to speed. Going over what Mom had endured—her interjecting a detail here and there, what I suspected about the knitted Watson, and how Angus had known about Simone. About what Branson had said in the clearing with needing to move up the timeline because I'd alerted Angus about Branson's upcoming betrayal sooner than he'd anticipated.

Susan began to pace. "Well, that answers a ton. It helps a lot of things make sense all of a sudden. What I don't understand is Branson's end game. Why did he want you to let Angus know he was going to double-cross him? And what exactly does it mean that he's got to move up his timeline?"

"I don't know." I shrugged, then went to my knees in the grass, needing to pet Watson, needing the centeredness he provided to think through things. "But like we've guessed, I think the two of them replacing the Irons family, making a crime dynasty of their own."

"Branson planned to use Angus to get that started, then take him out of the picture." Leo shrugged as if it was obvious. "He'd kill him when the time was right. He'll do it now instead of later."

Mom muttered at that, and though a couple of others in the group started to speak, it was Officer Cabot raising his hand like an elementary school student that captured the attention. "Um... maybe... but..." He cleared his throat and lifted his hand even higher. "If Branson was planning to kill Angus, why would he want Fred to alert him of that fact." When Leo started to argue, Campbell shook his head and sounded devastatingly apologetic. "I'm sorry, Leo, but I think your very appropriate dislike of Branson is tainting your ability to think of him clearly."

"That's my boy!" Susan slapped her partner's back so hard, Campbell stumbled forward a few steps, nearly falling. "Although you need to be *forceful* when you actually use that brain of yours. Nice work." She cast an eyebrow-raising her glance toward Leo. "He's right."

Leo grimaced and let out a long, hot breath, his anger palpable. But he gave a tight nod of agreement. From my kneeling position, I saw his fingers clench and unclench into fists, revealing the powerless rage he was experiencing. A feeling I understood so well.

"What does it matter?" It was Gary who spoke then, anger in his quiet tone as well, but perhaps since he'd just been brought in on the decade-old secrets, he had the most clarity. "Maybe we can get Branson, maybe we can't. But we have all the proof we need for Angus. Phyllis and Percival have *finally* let the authorities know about what's been happening." He gave Susan a challenging look. "What more do you need? Arrest him. Pure and simple."

Susan blanched—she wasn't used to being spoken to in such a manner, but instead of growling in offense like I expected, her blue eyes widened slightly, and a little smile played at the corner of her lips. "You're right. You're absolutely right. Well, almost." Literally snapping her fingers on both hands, she went into overdrive. "It doesn't matter that he and Branson... or probably that he ordered Branson to murder his connections to the Irons family who could cut deals and rat him out. *You all* are alive. And you all are witnesses. It's all the proof we need to bring him in."

Mom sucked in a little breath, and I expected her to argue, but instead she smiled. "That's true. This is finally the moment to do it. Before he and Branson... or just Branson... replace the Irons family. Even if there are still members in town, even if there are dirty cops on the force." Her gaze flicked to Officers Jackson and Lin, and she gave an apologetic wince. "Not you two, obviously." She refocused on the group at large. As she spoke, she sounded more and more like a detective's wife. "There won't ever be a safer time. At least for us. With Beulah and so many of the other main Irons family in custody, things will be in complete disarray. Only Angus would be focused on us. And Dean, if he came back, he's not going to try to get vengeance because we arrested Angus. Just the opposite. They might've cast a net of fear over our lives for the past ten years, but in reality, we're small potatoes, now more than ever."

"Great." It was Barry, and he slipped his hand into Mom's. "So we call the FBI and let them—"

"You've had one too many edibles if you think I'm giving this to the FBI, old man." Susan rolled her eyes so hard it looked like it hurt. "He's *mine*. Pure and simple. Today, right now. I'm walking into that pretentious knitting shop, and not letting him go until I have enough to put him away forever."

"You don't think we need the FBI?" Officer Lin spoke up, a tremor of fear in her voice that I'd not heard before. Although considering we were talking about the Irons family, who could blame her? "With everything happening, there's no way Angus won't be prepared. He's not going to go down without a fight. He might have an armory hidden in—"

"No, he doesn't." I gave a final pat to Watson and brushed off my skirt as I stood. "He may have fooled me in a lot of ways, but I think I understand Angus. He told us that he's never killed anyone, and I believe him. Who knows how many deaths he's ordered, but I don't think one of them came from his own hand. Just like with Beulah. When she was arrested, she didn't pull out a bunch of guns and start shooting. Angus might own one, I don't know, but he's not sitting in Knit Witt preparing to be taken down." As I spoke, I judged the validity of my words and found them spot-on. "He thinks he's untouchable. He's not the least bit worried about any of us."

"I don't know, dear." Mom's tone was hesitant. "We can't be certain what he's overheard, maybe he got some of what we said in the doorway of my house a little while ago. Or maybe he was able to listen as we sat outside. Or maybe he heard when—"

"It doesn't matter." Susan addressed Mom with a gentleness I appreciated. "I think Fred is right. But even if she's not, it's like you said only moments before. There's not going to be a better time to take him down, and if Angus has overheard something, if he's been alerted, then every second that passes makes him finding a way of weaseling out of this more likely." She grinned and started to head back the way we'd come, walking right through the center of the group. "This ends now." She chuckled. "I can't wait to see his face when—"

"I'm coming." I followed her, right on her heels. When she paused and looked back at me, I closed the distance. "I'm serious, Susan. After all this, after everything, don't you even try to take this away from me. I'm going to—"

"—be right there rubbing it in his face as I slap on those irons..." Susan laughed and smacked her thigh. "Irons! Didn't even do that on purpose." She smiled at me. "Yeah, you're coming. Leave Officer Fleabag, though."

"Fred..." Mom hurried over, touching my hand. "You don't have to be there. Detective Green is capable, and—"

"I'll be with her." Leo joined us as well, leaving no room for argument in his voice. "She'll be safe." He looked to Barry. "Will you take care of Watson?"

Despite Susan's certainty, she paused when we left the woods. Wanting physical proof, she and the other officers went into the cabin. They emerged with Susan holding the knitted Watson in one hand, a small, clean slice though the wool and a tiny metal pill in the other.

After, she sent Jackson and Lin to Angus's house, just in case. She even had Leo and me ride with her and Officer Cabot. Showing her worry of the Irons family—or merely Angus—still having strings woven into the police department, Susan didn't call for backup, lest he be alerted, or actually use officers with guns to do what he would not.

So it was, with no flashing of lights or wailing of sirens, that Susan drove the cruiser from my cabin into downtown and parked directly in front of Knit Witt. With tourist season being over, the early setting sun, and the closing hour being merely minutes away, there were only a couple of shoppers meandering on the sidewalk, and they were safely across the street.

Though she'd allowed us to join, Susan and Campbell entered the knitting shop first, their weapons drawn.

"Angus Witt." Though I knew she was gleeful, Susan's voice was stone-cold professional. "You're under—"

She halted, and Officer Cabot made a weird sound.

I stepped around them, Leo by my side.

It only took a second to see. A glance toward the counter, which was empty, and I then found Angus.

I understood instantly—Branson's confusion and anger as I accused him of spying on Mom and taking pictures of me rushed back to my mind.

Branson broke his pattern when he killed Angus Witt. It wasn't a clean, solitary executioner's bullet that ended the life of the extraordinary knitter. Branson had been in a rage and had taken vengeance.

Though horrible, I couldn't pull my gaze away from the scene. There, in front of the beautiful wall of rainbow-hued spools of wool from floor to ceiling, stood the majestically knitted Samson. Angus's broken and bloodied body lay cradled in the elk's crown of antlers.

Susan and Campbell lowered their weapons, and the four of us just stared. Later I would wonder exactly how Branson had done it. If he'd walked through the door of the shop, then killed Angus in the back room and hastily arranged his body before leaving out the front again? I'd go over a million different possibilities, each of them terribly marvelous in Branson's murderous skill. But in that moment, no puzzle pieces clicked into place, no synapses fired. I was completely captured by the horror of it. Although the longer I stared, I had to admit there was a sort of terrible beauty in it, an artistry I almost thought Angus would appreciate. Branson had arranged his body so it truly was perfectly cradled in the antlers, like a dying king spread out over his deathbed, his hands and joints bent in a way to gently hang over the heavier spikes, as if resting.

A scarf hung around Angus's neck, long enough that it nearly touched the hardwood floor. For a moment, I assumed Angus had been wearing it when Branson had overtaken him. But it was only a mistake for a moment. There was no blood on the beautifully knitted scarf. Even more of a giveaway than that was its color—one of my favorites, a deep, rich mustard yellow. Branson had dressed him for me, a ribbon on a gift.

He really hadn't been aware of what Angus had done to me, to my family.

A flicker of gratitude whispered, but I pushed it away before it was more than a wisp. I would *not* be grateful for this. And while the vengeance put an end to things, it wasn't right. It wasn't justice. It wasn't what I would've chosen.

I started to turn away—disgusted at that flicker of

relieved gratitude, doubly compounded by my revulsion of the man who'd done it—when what remained of the sunlight outside glinted over something on the scarf.

I barely heard someone speaking my name in warning—Leo or Susan, I wasn't sure. But it wasn't needed. I wouldn't touch anything. I just needed to see.

Stopping a couple of feet away, I leaned a touch closer.

Nestled in the mustard-hued scarf was a small, glossy enameled pin. A corgi. The same coloring as Watson, a deep orange over his head, back, and flanks, white over his chest. Here and there, spread out like feathers, were little rhinestones. The only difference was that the jewelry had emerald green eyes, where Watson's were chocolate. The pin looked old, expensive.

Only then did I recall Branson saying he'd come to my cabin to leave me a gift.

Apparently, he'd delivered it after all.

"I'm offended. I should probably be ashamed to admit it, but... I am." Zelda tossed a long lock of brown hair over her shoulder as she glared at the rhubarb pie in front of her and stabbed her fork into it, hard enough the plate should've cracked. "Are we invisible? Are we not even part of the family?"

"You're..." Joe scrunched up his nose, causing his less-than-perfect features to go even more off-center. "*Offended* Chakras wasn't bugged?"

"Neither was Arc and Whale." Jonah sounded as thoroughly put out as his sister-in-law. "How are we *not* supposed to take that personally?"

"Again... You *want* your shops to have been bugged by the Irons family?" Joe looked back and forth between the married sets of twins, clearly flummoxed. "That's not a good thing. It's an invasion of space, of privacy. It shatters the illusion of safety."

"That's easy for you to say." Verona shared a nod

with Zelda though didn't attempt to break any china. "Rocky Mountain Imprints *was* bugged. *You* matter. And *you've* only been a part of things for a solitary hot minute."

"No offense meant!" Zelda piped in quickly, her mouth full. "We love you and think you're great."

"That's true. We do." Verona didn't quite match her twin's forcefully cheerful tone and ended with a mutter. "Apparently, so did the Irons family."

Joe looked like he was trying to find words and then gave up with an astonished gape at Katie, who sat beside him.

Chuckling, she patted his hand. "You'll get used to it."

Watching the exchange almost made me laugh, almost. After the last several days, after the last few *hours*, my emotions were so all over the place I was afraid if I so much as giggled, I'd end up in fits of hysterical laughter that might not ever end, even after I was carted off in a straitjacket.

After discovering Angus's body, Susan acquiesced and called in the FBI. And true to form, probably rightly so, they took over. And when they took over... *wow!* Reinforcements showed up so quickly it was like they'd been summoned on a Learjet. Possibly my perception of time was a little off, but whatever the case, they swarmed the downtown like angry fire ants. Those who didn't remain in Knit Witt spread out over the shops, searching for bugs and the like. They also let us know they'd search our homes next and we'd need to make other arrangements.

Thankfully, due to tourist season wrapping up, the whole host of us were able to make reservations at Baldpate Inn—the historic bed-and-breakfast nestled up in the mountains. In a way, it felt like a nice bookend, unintentional though it was. As we sat in the dining room, having gorged ourselves on the endless salad bar, and countless pieces of the inn's famous cornbread, I found myself staring out the log-framed windows that showcased a panoramic view over Estes Valley and the surrounding mountains. When we'd stayed here before, it had been a blizzard, which had trapped us in and stolen the electricity. Though no snow currently fell, I stared out into the night to the gravel parking lot below. The scene from murdered Lucas's cell phone superimposed itself, and I could see Alexandria, also murdered, trafficking something from the van in the middle of the flurries to a shadowy figure. I'd probably never have proof, but I could feel it in my bones—Dean Gerber had been that shadowy figure. What I didn't feel was his presence in that moment. He wasn't out in the trees staring at us; he was somewhere in the Midwest, probably with his father. We were safer than we'd ever been, and after the FBI sweep of all of our homes, that would be even truer.

"Can I get you anything?" Lisa Bloomberg, the owner of Baldpate Inn, touched my arm, pulling my attention away from the night. "More cornbread, chili? Pie?"

"No, thank you." It took a second for my manners to catch up with me and I smiled. "You've done more than enough, and we're so grateful you were able to bring all of us here."

She waved me off. "It's like tourist season started again. I appreciate you being patient with the slow service, since I'd already sent most of the staff home for the season. Although..." She scanned the crowded tables with a peaceful expression. "It's going to be kind of like a slumber party, and I'm so thankful all of you are safe."

Did I ever feel that! "Me too." As Leo squeezed my hand, I followed where she looked, that gratitude doubling with every face that came into view. The twins and their families were there, all four children safe. Zelda's oldest, Britney, who'd been struggling for a while, looked peaceful as she sat near Barry and Mom.

Percival and Gary were at a table next to them with Anna and Carl. The last time we were here was for their anniversary, and before the murders there'd been much glitter, glam, and excess, as was to be expected. The mood between them was much different in that moment. They looked older, tired, and Gary sat a little farther away from Percival than he normally would have. I knew they'd be okay, better than that, given time. I didn't blame Percival for trying to keep Gary safe all these years. But I understood Gary even more. It was one thing to find out your parents and your uncle had kept things from you in order to keep you safe. It was another from your spouse. If Leo had done so... well, I would've understood, but I would've been hurt, and angry.

Katie and Joe sat at the same long table as us, as did Athena and Paulie. Though there were other houses the FBI would search, they were starting with our immediate circle, both family and those who were, at times, part of the Scooby Gang.

My phone vibrated, and I glanced at the screen. It was from Susan. I scanned it, and then lifted my voice for the rest of the room to hear. "They've gotten all of the listening devices from my house, Mom and Barry's. They're still working through Katie's apartment, then they're going to Leo's apartment, and Joe's house."

"Can you ask them to do ours next?" Verona lifted her fork in the air, as if asking for permission, reminding me of Officer Cabot several hours before. "Surely they bugged our houses."

Zelda nodded as well, then looked concerned, but her expression cleared quickly. "If not, it's probably because we live in Glen Haven and don't have cell service. Maybe they don't have covert listening devices strong enough."

"*Right*, Mom," Britney groaned in full-fledged teenage disdain from her spot beside Barry. "The *Irons family* can't figure out how to bug Glen Haven. I'm *so* sure." She gave an eye roll that Susan would've been proud of and leveled her deadpan stare at Joe. "Run. While you can. Run. Like, really."

Katie threw back her head and laughed so hard tears begin to fall instantly. Several of the others joined in, and before too long the whole room was alight with laughter, even Britney.

I started to chuckle, maybe even tried to, but couldn't quite achieve it. Instead, I took the distraction and gave Leo a quick kiss on the cheek, before whispering in his ear, "I'm okay. I just need a few minutes."

He grabbed my hand, pulling my attention back to him as I turned, his gaze questioning.

"Really." I smiled and motioned through the doorway with my head. "I'm just going to be in the front room by the fire. I just need... I don't know... to breathe."

Though it looked like he wanted to argue, after a second he nodded and forced a smile of his own. I had to hand it to him, if we traded places, I might not have been able to keep myself from tacking on a *don't do something stupid* disclaimer.

As the entire group was gathered on the glassed-in front porch, I doubled back to the main dining room to not get pulled away by someone, padded past the salad bar displayed in an old cast-iron tub, then passed another couple of doorways into the large front room. As in many places in Estes Park and its surrounding area, Baldpate was fashioned after a log cabin, although in the bed-and-breakfast's case, more like a log cabin *castle*. The grand front room fit that description perfectly. Long and narrow, it had a massive stone fireplace and several couches spread over it. In the distance, through glass french doors, was another room filled with thousands upon thousands of keys hanging from the rafters and nailed to the walls. That curiosity didn't hold my attention, though.

I sighed, realizing this was exactly what my soul needed. Spread out around the fire was a small pack of dogs—three corgis, a toy poodle, and a tiny wiry, mangy mutt.

Paulie's corgis were themselves, even in sleep, both of them looked like they'd been midplay and then dropped dead. Flotsam lay half on the rock hearth and half on the hardwood floor, one foxlike ear smashed under his head, while his right rear leg stuck heavenward and twitched. Jetsam sprawled on his back in the middle of the floor, all legs up in the air, with his head twisted to one side and his tongue laying out on the ground like he'd fallen asleep midlick.

The other three were curled together on the hearth. Doubtlessly, Watson had chosen where he so frequently loved to nap. If I had to guess, little Pearl had joined him instantly, curling up against his side, while Anna's spasmodic little terror, Winston—who I'd recently grown to love—had more than likely yanked on Watson's ears and bounced on his back like he was a trampoline until he got a grandpa-like growl before he finally settled down beside

Watson and rested his head on Watson's neck as a pillow.

I watched him sleeping for several moments, maybe several minutes, and with the laughter just beginning to fade in the background, felt my brain ease—quiet, somewhat.

All was safe. *Everyone* was safe. More than we'd been since discovering Branson used his detective badge as a cover for the Irons family. Actually... safer than we'd been in well over a decade, though I'd not realized it.

Attempting to tiptoe across the room, I headed toward the overstuffed sofa facing the fire. A board creaked when I nearly reached the spot. I froze, expecting Flotsam and Jetsam to spring into hysterics. They didn't, though Jetsam's tongue made another pass over the floor in his sleep.

It wasn't until I settled into the sofa, stars filling the sky over the mountains through the window at my back, that I realized one of the dogs had woken.

Watson's chocolate gaze followed me as I sank deeper into the cushions. I thought I saw a question in their depths, and I smiled toward him reassuringly. Apparently, he didn't believe me, as a moment later he managed to free himself from being Winston's pillow. The little dog's head slid gently down Watson's neck to rest on the stone. Then he stood and padded over to me. In his absence, Pearl shifted slightly, and she and Winston made an adorable—though less so, in my opinion—bundle by the flames.

Proving that he knew better than me, the last remnants of stress vanished, truly, as Watson hopped on the couch, curled up by my leg, and rested his head over my thigh as Winston had been doing to his neck.

I sank my fingers into his fur, began to stroke, and breathed... *Really* breathed.

It was done. Sure there were loose ends—not all the Irons family would be captured, not ever. And crime, organized and other, would always exist. But that particular Hydra... the necks had been severed and the body destroyed. Whatever heads remained would never hold the power or venom they'd once possessed. As Mom noted in the meadow, in the grand scheme of things, we were small potatoes. With one exception: all the ones who would disagree with that were already captured or dead.

And that exception? Well... Branson was no longer Irons family, and I was certain we hadn't seen the last of him. But while I knew he was dangerous, it was a different variety. Less covert. If and when his obsession with me finally went careening off the edge, it would be from him, directly. There would be no more trying to guess who was living a double life and who wasn't.

Maybe there were *two* exceptions. At some point, Dean might decide to focus on us again as well. But...

Watson snored, already asleep, and as he snuggled more closely against my thigh, Dean Gerber and the remaining fractured pieces of the Irons family faded from focus. For the first time in a long, long time.

A few hours later found me still on the couch with Watson asleep beside me. The other dogs had gone up to their rooms with their masters, and there were no more friends and family members in the dining room—or snuggled in the surrounding couches as they'd gathered for a while.

Susan had texted a few more times with updates through the evening.

Much to their dismay, the twins' families were the only shops and homes that hadn't been bugged, of those present, at least with the exception of Athena. However, unlike Zelda and Verona and their husbands, Athena was grateful. A fact that Britney pointed out to her parents and aunt and uncle with much annoyance, was how a *normal* person would respond. Truthfully, while it was ludicrous to be jealous about *not* having your privacy invaded, I couldn't blame them for feeling a sting. Not when the FBI had uncovered that nearly every other shop downtown had been bugged. Some of them had listening devices that had stopped transmitting ages ago, but just as many were still live. There was no arguing that Angus and the Irons family—though it still wasn't clear what percentage of the listening devices came from the Irons family or were merely Angus specific—had found Zelda and Verona, and Jonah and Noah, to not be worth the effort. In a way, however, it also rather showed their innocence.

Maybe equally as strange, knowing that once the FBI was finished with my house it would be truly privately mine again, I did have a sense of loss about not having that knitted Watson on my mantle. Part of me was considering asking Susan... the FBI... someone... if I could have it once they were finished —*without* the bug. I wasn't sure, but I'd ponder that for a few days. Did I really want an Angus Witt creation in my home?

"You're thinking again, I can feel it." Leo's arms tightened around me and pulled me closer against his chest. "We're supposed to just be staring into the fire, remember?"

"Oh, right." I forced a laugh and did just that. It had been a while since I'd noticed, I'd been so captured in thought. What remained in the massive fireplace was little more than glowing embers—Lisa having stoked it into one final blaze more than an hour before. "Leo, I'm—" Hating to ruin the comfortable position we were in, I shifted, needing to see his eyes.

Though he grunted, Watson merely lifted his head as I swiveled to a different angle to face Leo, and lowered once more, let out a heavy sigh, and returned to sleep.

I started again and interlocked my fingers with Leo's. "I'm sorry about the choices I made today, some of them were intentional, and some just instinct, or... impulse." I couldn't say I regretted them, but... Instead of thinking that, I decided to share my truth out loud. "I don't know if I regret it, honestly, as the result brought all this to a close, but I do regret hurting you, worrying you." My eyes stung. "I'm sorry I broke my promise. I swear that part wasn't intentional. And I know if you'd put yourself in such danger, I'd be furious."

"I was." He shrugged one of his broad shoulders and gave a half smile. "Part of me still is, but... I understand. And I might've... *might've*," he repeated with a glare, "done the same thing in your shoes."

"Maybe you would've." I doubted it. Leo was less impulsive than me, although he surprised me from time to time. "Either way, I'm sorry."

He lifted the hand that was free of my grip and stroked his thumb gently over my cheek. I thought he was about to tell me he loved me, but he dropped his hand, his expression going serious. "I'm glad he's dead. Angus. I know I shouldn't be, but... I am." Before I could admit that I'd had that same sensation for a moment, Leo pressed on. "And I'm sure this says horrible things about me, but I hate that Branson was the one to do it. The one to make you safer. It should've been—"

"Don't you dare finish that sentence." Without thinking, I actually covered his mouth with my hand, and held it there until he truly met my gaze. "Don't envy Branson for that. Not with the toll it takes on his soul, not with the type of human it makes him." A chill crept over me as I remembered Leo had understood a particular truth much more quickly than myself. "And we both know that Branson's not safe. Even where I'm concerned. If anything, the way he took vengeance on Angus confirms that."

"He won't hurt you again." Leo didn't hesitate, nor did he leave room for misunderstanding. "I swear to you, Winifred Page, those bruises on your arms are the last mark he'll ever leave on your body. I'll make certain of it."

"Leo..." A different sort of chill arose." Don't do anything that's going to—"

He shook his head, cutting me off with a dark laugh. "Don't worry. I'm not hiring a hit man or anything like that." The laughter faded, though the steel in his eyes remained. "But I swear to you on my life, as long as I have breath, he will *never* hurt you again."

"Leo, I don't want promises like that." I realized I was squeezing his hand too tightly and relaxed my grip a bit. "I don't need it."

"*I* do." Leo didn't leave any room for argument. After another few heartbeats, his expression softened once more, a smile playing over his face as his hand returned my cheek. "Do you remember what happened on this very couch?"

"Yeah." With that, all thoughts and fears of Branson were swept away, and I felt myself smile, a real one, in what seemed like the first time in a long time. "Our first kiss."

"But not our last." His smile widened as his gaze heated, and he pulled me to him.

Help Fred and Watson solve their next murder surrounded by the glittering...

<u>Jaded Jewels</u>

Book Twenty-One of the Cozy Corgi Series

Read the complete Twister Sisters Mysteries series now!

Senior Citizens, Knitting, Casseroles, and Murder...

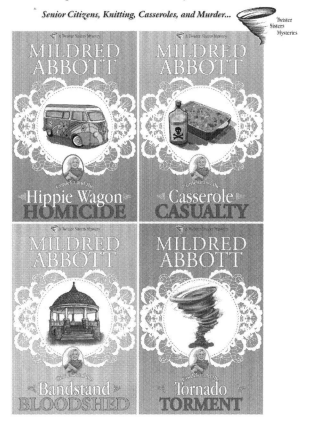

Link to Twister Sisters Mysteries

Katie's Perfectly Pooled Chocolate Chip Cookie recipe provided by:

Never miss a scrumptious recipe:
CloudyKitchen.com

Follow Cloudy Kitchen's creations on social media:

Cloudy Kitchen Facebook
Cloudy Kitchen Instagram

KATIE'S PERFECTLY POOLED CHOCOLATE CHIP COOKIES RECIPE

DETAILS

- Prep Time: 15 minutes
- Cook Time: 30 minutes
- Total Time: 45 minutes plus an hour chilling time
- Yield: 28 cookies 1x

DESCRIPTION

Lightly salted cookie dough surrounds puddles of dark chocolate, before being finished up with a heavy dose of flaky sea salt. These cookies utilise three different types of sugar - white, dark brown or muscovado, and turbinado sugar for a little crunch. They are easy to make and I show you how to get the best chocolate puddles in the recipe!

INGREDIENTS

- 225g Unsalted butter, at room temperature
- 170g Dark Brown or Muscovado Sugar
- 100g Granulated / White Sugar
- 50g Raw / Turbinado Sugar
- 1 egg
- 1 tsp vanilla bean paste or vanilla extract
- 300g All-purpose flour
- 1/2 tsp baking soda
- 1/2 tsp baking powder
- 1 tsp salt
- 350 g good quality dark chocolate, roughly chopped, plus a little extra for chocolate puddles
- Flaky Sea Salt such as Maldon for finishing

INSTRUCTIONS

1. In the bowl of a stand mixer fitted with the paddle attachment, or with an electric mixer, cream together the butter and sugars on high speed for 5 minutes, until pale, and light and fluffy. Add the egg and vanilla, and mix to combine, scraping down the bowl when necessary.
2. Sift together the flour, baking soda, baking powder, and salt. Add to the mixing bowl, and mix on low to just combine (you still want a few streaks of flour remaining that will get mixed in when you add the chocolate).
3. Add the chopped chocolate and mix until just incorporated. Remove the bowl from the mixer and give a few mixes by hand using a flexible spatula, to ensure even incorporation of the chocolate.
4. Using a 2 Tbsp Cookie scoop, scoop out balls of dough onto a baking sheet lined with parchment paper (you can place them close together). If you want big puddles on the top of your cookies, you flatten a ball of dough, press the chocolate onto the top side, then continue as usual and roll it into a ball,

which then gives you even chocolate distribution as the cookie bakes.
5. If you are not adding additional chocolate, there is no need to re-shape into a ball - you can bake right from the scooped shape. Cover the sheet pan with plastic wrap and chill the dough balls for an hour in the fridge.
6. Toward the end of the chilling process, preheat the oven to 350°f / 180°c. Line 2-3 baking sheets with parchment paper (you can bake these in batches)
7. Arrange 6 cookie dough balls on a baking sheet, leaving room for spreading. Leave the remainder of the dough balls in the fridge.
8. Bake for 13-14 minutes, or until lightly golden and beginning to set. Baking time depends on personal preference - if you like them quite soft, bake for 13 mins, if you like them a tiny bit crispy then bake for 14. Remove from the oven, and if desired, use a round cookie cutter slightly larger than the cookie to scoot them into a perfectly round shape.

9. Sprinkle liberally with flaky sea salt. Allow to cool on the pan - the cookies will deflate slightly as they cool. Repeat the baking process with the remaining cookies.
10. Store leftovers in an airtight container.

Merchandise

visit MildredAbbott.com

PATREON

Mildred Abbott's Patreon Page

Mildred Abbott is now on Patreon! By becoming a member, you gain access to exclusive Cozy Corgi merchandise, get a look behind the scenes of book creation, and receive real-life writing updates, plans, and puppy photos (becuase, of course there will be puppy photos!). You can also gain access to ebooks and recipes before publication, read future works *literally* as they are being written chapter by chapter, and can even choose to become a character in one of the novels!

Wether you choose to be a villager, busybody, police officer, super sleuth, or the fuzzy four-legged star of the show himself, please come check the

Mildred Abbott Patreon community and discover what fun awaits.

Personal Note: Being an indie writer means that some months bills are paid without much stress, while other months threaten the ability to continue the dream of writing. Becoming a member ensures that there will continue to be new Mildred Abbott books. Your support is unbelievably appreciated and invaluable.

*While there are many perks to becoming a patron, if you are a reader who can't afford to support (or simply don't feel led), rest assured you will *not* miss out on any writing. All books will continue to be published just as they always have been. None of the Mildred Abbott books will become exclusive to a select few. In fact, patrons help ensure that writing will continue to be published for everyone.

Mildred Abbott's Patreon Page

AUTHOR NOTE

Dear Reader:

Thank you so much for reading *Wretched Wool*. If you enjoyed Fred and Watson knitting the Irons family into their rightful ending, I would greatly appreciate a review on Amazon and Goodreads— reviews make a huge difference in helping the Cozy Corgi series continue. Feel free to drop me a note on Facebook or on my website (MildredAbbott.com) whenever you'd like. I'd love to hear from you. If you're interested in receiving advanced reader copies of upcoming installments, please join Mildred Abbott's Cozy Mystery Club on Facebook.

I also wanted to mention the elephant in the

room… or the over-sugared corgi, as it were. Watson's personality is based around one of my own corgis, Alastair. He's the sweetest little guy in the world, and like Watson, is a bit of a grump. Also, like Watson (and every other corgi to grace the world with their presence), he lives for food. In the Cozy Corgi series, I'm giving Alastair the life of his dreams through Watson. Just like I don't spend my weekends solving murders, neither does he spend his days snacking on scones and unending dog treats. But in the books? Well, we both get to live out our fantasies. If you are a corgi parent, you already know your little angel shouldn't truly have free rein of the pastry case, but you can read them snippets of Watson's life for a pleasant bedtime fantasy.

Book Twenty-One, Jaded Jewels, will arrive by March 2021, and is available for pre-order. In the meantime, again, please continue to share your love of the series with friends and write reviews for each installment. Spreading the word about the series will help it continue. Thank you!!!

Much love, Mildred

PS: I'd also love it if you signed up for my newsletter. That way you'll never miss a new release. You won't hear from me more than once a month, nobody needs that many newsletters!

Newsletter link: Mildred Abbott Newsletter Signup

ACKNOWLEDGMENTS

A special thanks to Agatha Frost, who gave her blessing and her wisdom. If you haven't already, you simply MUST read Agatha's Peridale Cafe Cozy Mystery series. They are absolute perfection.

The biggest and most heartfelt gratitude to Katie Pizzolato, for her belief in my writing career and being the inspiration for the character of the same name in this series. Thanks to you, Katie, our beloved baker, has completely stolen both mine and Fred's heart!

Desi, I couldn't imagine an adventure without you by my side. A.J. Corza, you have given me the corgi covers of my dreams.

To the members of Mildred Abbott's Cozy Mystery Club on Facebook, thank you for all your help and feedback.

A huge, huge thank you to all of the lovely souls who proofread the ARC versions and help me look somewhat literate (in completely random order): Melissa Brus, Cinnamon, Ron Perry, Anita Ford,

Bernadette Ould, Victoria Smiser, Lucy Campbell, and Sue Paulsen. Thank you all, so very, very much!

A further and special thanks to some of my dear readers and friends who support my passion: Andrea Johnson, Fiona Wilson, Katie Pizzolato, Maggie Johnson, Marcia Gleason, Rob Andresen-Tenace, Robert Winter, Jason R., Victoria Smiser, Kristi Browning, and those of you who wanted to remain anonymous. You make a huge, huge difference in my life and in my ability to continue to write. I'm humbled and grateful beyond belief! So much love to you all!

ALSO BY MILDRED ABBOTT

-the Cozy Corgi Cozy Mystery Series-

Cruel Candy

Traitorous Toys

Bickering Birds

Savage Sourdough

Scornful Scones

Chaotic Corgis

Quarrelsome Quartz

Wicked Wildlife

Malevolent Magic

Killer Keys

Perilous Pottery

Ghastly Gadgets

Meddlesome Money

Precarious Pasta

Evil Elves

Phony Photos

Despicable Desserts

Chattering Chipmunks

Vengeful Vellum

Wretched Wool

Jaded Jewels

Yowling Yetis

Lethal Lace

Pesky Puppies

Deceptive Designs

Antagonizing Antiques

Malicious Malts

Salacious Socialites

Dastardly Ducks

Stormy Stars

Baffling Bachelorettes

Bamboozled Brides-Coming Soon

(Books 1-13 are also available in audiobook format, read to perfection by Angie Hickman.)

-the Twister Sisters Mystery Series-

(*4-Book Series*)

Hippie Wagon Homicide

Casserole Casualty

Bandstand Bloodshed

Tornado Torment